El Rancho Rio

El Rancho Rio

Mignon G. Eberhart

Thorndike Press • Chivers Press
Thorndike, Maine USA   Bath, England

This Large Print edition is published by Thorndike Press, USA and by Chivers Press, England.

Published in 1999 in the U.S. by arrangement with Brandt & Brandt Literary Agents, Inc.

Published in 1999 in the U.K. by arrangement with The Estate of Mignon G. Eberhart.

U.S. Hardcover 0-7862-2070-8 (Mystery Series Edition)
U.K. Hardcover 0-7540-3899-8 (Chivers Large Print)
U.K. Softcover 0-7540-3900-5 (Camden Large Print)

The text of this Large Print edition is unabridged.
Other aspects of the book may vary from the original edition.

Set in 16 pt. Plantin.

Printed in the United States on permanent paper.

British Library Cataloguing in Publication Data available

Library of Congress Cataloging-in-Publication Data

Eberhart, Mignon Good, 1899–
    El Rancho Rio / Mignon G. Eberhart.
        p. cm.
    ISBN 0-7862-2070-8 (lg. print : hc. : alk. paper)
    1. Large type books. I. Title.
[PS3509.B453R36   1999]
813'.52—dc21   99-34467

El Rancho Rio

Chapter 1

Sometime in the night a shrill wail like jeering, high-pitched laughter woke Mady. For a moment the wicked mockery seemed to encircle her, as if there were malicious faces somewhere near, familiar yet unfamiliar, mocking, too. Then she woke more fully and knew that it was only the night cry of coyotes. Craig Wilson, her husband, had warned her about them and said not to be alarmed.

All the same the sounds were eerie and seemed very near, but the half-dream of half-seen faces disappeared. Craig had said that sometimes, especially at the approach of the cold winter months, coyotes loped out, in their queerly awkward yet speedy gait, from the hills or a dry arroyo. They were predatory; they swooped upon El Rancho del Rio. Sometimes, if they could, they stole fowl; usually the ranch dog drove them away.

As she listened, she heard the indignant bark of the ranch dog. The high-pitched, jeering coyote laughter died away. It was as if civilization, in the way of a domestic dog, had driven savagery back, at least for the night.

Once it was quiet again, Mady watched the amazingly clear starlight change patterns upon the floor, showing now the drapery of the curtains, then the solid outlines of the old Spanish chest across the room. She felt, however, oddly lonely in the cold starlight and in Craig's enormous Spanish bed. He had gone to San Francisco the previous day; he intended to stay only a day or two, but she missed his friendly presence. He would have made short work of Guy Casso and his absurd, inexplicable yet rather frightening visit of the afternoon.

Presently, as the shadows drifted longer across the room, she went to sleep again.

In the morning, so balmy and still that nobody, least of all Mady, recognized it as a weather breeder, she drove to Wilson City and did an errand or two. In the afternoon she decided to take her first ride on horseback without Indian Joe as an escort — a long ride over the ranch trails. As she turned along the arroyo trail toward El Rancho, she found Guy Casso.

Nellie, the delicate little roan mare Craig had given her, shied suddenly and snorted and shied again. Mady pulled her to a halt, but the mare stood shivering and jerking her head. Then Mady saw a man lying among some sagebrush at the very edge of the arroyo along which the trail wound. She thought that he had fallen from his horse.

There was no stray saddle horse to be seen. There was no car, no jeep, no pickup truck, nothing but the sand, sagebrush and bunch grass, the mountains in the west, the craggy hills nearer, and the deep, motionless silence of the land and sky. Not even a jack rabbit or a fat little prairie dog popped out from some hidden lair. It was almost as if the entire world had paused to watch her.

The great rim of the Nevada Sierras was already outlined in black against the western sky, which meant that it was late in the afternoon and the sun was about to drop out of sight with the unnerving swiftness of a Nevada twilight. She thought that she was about a mile from the wider road leading directly to the ranch house. She could not see the house, the trees around it or the cluster of sheds, garages, stables and corrals; a fold of sand and sagebrush not high enough to be called a hill was still high enough to shut off her view. She felt entirely alone in that wilderness of sky and irregular low hills and arroyos. Indeed she was alone, except for Nellie and the man beside the trail who did not move or speak.

She didn't once think of riding hurriedly to the house and sending Indian Joe or someone to see to the man lying beside the trail. Her instinct urged immediate assistance. She slid cautiously down from the saddle and put the reins over Nellie's head, as Indian Joe had taught her to do. Nellie stood still, but she shivered and watched anxiously as Mady crossed down, half sliding, for the trail and rim of sagebrush were at a steep edge of the arroyo. Mady spoke to the man lying there. She said, "Can I help you?" But as soon as she came near, she knew that he was dead. He had to be dead, with the back of his head crushed in. Things seemed to rock around her; this was sheer physical shock at the sight of violent death. She then recognized Guy Casso.

She recognized him, oddly, by his dapper city clothes and something about the overmanicured hand which was flung out into the sandy soil. She had seen him only once before, but it had happened the previous day — so she recognized him.

And in the same instant she recognized

10

something else. It lay beside him. It was the Golden Spike Rail which ornamented one of the tables in the long living room of the ranch house.

Craig had explained its history. When the railroad coming from the East had at last joined the railroad coming from the West, there had been a glorious celebration of all the dignitaries, railroad officials and hard-working crews who had built the roads together. The meeting rails had been joined by a golden spike; and since gold was a soft metal and steel was very hard, a wooden block had been inserted which the spike could penetrate. The continent was spanned by those gleaming rails just over a hundred years ago, on May 9, 1869.

In the course of time the original rails had had to be replaced, and some enterprising person had had them sliced directly down, so although the pieces were only about an inch or so wide, they were completely identifiable as a part of a steel rail. These pieces had been mounted in brass and were distributed as souvenirs. Craig's father had had his initials engraved on one of the broad sides of the rail itself, and on the other side, etched in large letters, the words *Golden Spike Rail.*

The edges of the rail were sharp; the

piece itself was heavy. Craig had told her to lift it, but had quickly warned her and held his hand below hers, so if she dropped it in her surprise at its weight, he could prevent its striking her feet.

Somebody, he said, had given it to his father; the house had many bits and pieces of the early West which added to its charm. Craig's share of El Rancho had included the main house, so it had included the slice of the Golden Spike Rail. Now it lay shining wickedly in the rosy light from the setting sun. It was stained and dreadful. Any officer of the law could and would call it the murder weapon.

Nellie pranced and gave a frightened snort. Someone had told Mady that horses can smell blood and are terrified by it. But Mady was terrified about the man at her feet and the Golden Spike Rail. She again acted instinctively. She was wearing heavy gloves, and she carefully picked the piece of one-time rail out of the sand and sagebrush. She went a little distance from Guy Casso and scrubbed and wiped the piece in the sand. She did it furtively, meanwhile looking all around her. But there was nobody, nothing but sky and wide stretches of silent land and hills. Only Nellie watched her and shivered. When

Mady thought the piece of rail was wiped clean, she went to Nellie. She didn't even try to mount her; she knew that she couldn't without somebody to give her a leg up or something to stand on; she was not an expert rider. The only thing to do was walk home, leading Nellie, get into the house unseen if she could, cleanse the rail more thoroughly with soap and water and replace it on the table — all this before she called the police and reported Guy Casso's murder; the rail alone attested to murder.

The sun was definitely lower, touching the peaks of the mountains. Nellie seemed thankful to get away from the clumps of sagebrush and the murdered man, but she pranced along so nervously that it was all Mady could do to restrain her. She finally gave up and let go Nellie's reins, knowing the mare would merely return to the corrals and that one of the men would see to her. But when she vanished over the slight rise of land, her little heels kicking up sand behind her, Mady was all at once shaken with terror. Nellie had at least been companionship, something alive and near.

And still nothing moved; there was not even a tremor of wind. Mady started to walk faster, glancing from side to side as she went — but she heard nothing and saw nothing move anywhere. She tried to tell herself that whoever had done murder would certainly have fled the place as quickly as he could, but she panted a little as she took the trail upward which, walking, began to seem as steep as a mountain trail.

It now occurred to her that releasing Nellie might have been a wise move. She had an excuse to return home, belatedly, walking: Nellie had shied and thrown her. So it was now possible that she could get into the house without being seen. If she had ridden Nellie up to the long veranda, Manuel would have heard her and come to help her down and send Nellie to the corrals.

Mady was shocked and frightened; her heart was thudding so hard and fast that she felt a little dizzy and confused and kept trying to run and being defeated by the roughness of the trail. But clear in her mind was the thought of Craig and the fact that the piece of rail linked Casso's murder with the ranch. Guy Casso had been Craig's former wife's "very good friend," as the newspapers put it; certainly they had been away on a trip together when Craig's divorce was made final and he was given the custody of his daughter Susan. Guy

Casso had come to see Mady the previous afternoon, had behaved in a preposterous way and had been seen. Guy Casso was murdered on one of the ranch trails. He had been murdered with that easily identifiable piece of rail that Mady now carried, shifting it from one gloved hand to the other.

Craig would logically be the first and obvious suspect.

Mady was not in love with her husband; he was not in love with her. But there was a long friendship, a grateful friendship on her part, and all the same it was marriage.

The sandy trail became slightly steeper. Mady was wearing the regulation ranch attire — blue jeans, a flannel shirt, high-heeled boots with beautifully tooled leather tops. The boots were intended for riding. They grew heavier and so did her heart. There was no possible doubt in her mind that Guy Casso had been killed with that piece of steel, and of all the people she knew, her husband had the most logical reason for killing him. At least, so any jury would say.

She trudged on to the top of the little rise. The trail, as she glanced behind her again, seemed almost flat, so she wondered briefly at her exhaustion. From there the ranch was plain to be seen; it was no more than a half mile away and the trail led, very gently now, downhill. The twilight was descending swiftly. Mady could see the lights from the kitchen windows shining through the double lane of Lombardy poplars. But it was so dark that she could scarcely make out the Joshua trees near the trail. The few she saw seemed to stretch out gaunt, misshapen arms in the growing darkness as if to warn her. She passed the guest cabins, which were now only two dark clumps of shadow beneath the enormous cottonwood trees, and turned into a short walk from the trail that led to the front entrance of the long Spanish ranch house. She would have to report the murder. But first she would clean the Golden Spike Rail thoroughly and return it to its usual place.

The great dining room windows were lighted, too. She caught a glimpse of Manuel in his white coat, moving around the table.

She slid in through the wide front door and tiptoed along the hall to the small washroom below the stairs. Once safely inside the washroom — without being heard by Manuel — she hurriedly, not giving herself time to hesitate, scrubbed the heavy rail. She scrubbed it with paper tissues rather than towels; she thought she was rather smart to remember that bloodstains possibly could be retrieved from towels. Her flannel shirt began to feel unbearably hot. Quickly she dried the rail and flushed away the tissues. It seemed to her that the entire rail was clean. The sharp edge which must have been driven into a man's skull looked bright. Now she had to get it back into the living room without being seen by Manuel. He was faithful to Craig; he had worked for him a long time; he dated from the time of Craig's father's ownership of El Rancho Rio. But he was also very intelligent and later he would connect that battered skull with the rail if he saw it in her hands.

So Mady came out cautiously, listening, and heard Manuel's and Inez's voices from the kitchen. Apparently they were having one of their arguments, which were always carried on in such musical tones that she could scarcely believe in the bitterness of the battles. She tiptoed again but ran for the living room. The curtains were never drawn. The lamps were all lit. She felt as if she were on a stage and everybody in the world could see her, but she went quickly to the table where the rail usually stood and replaced it.

Then she looked at her gloves. They were pigskin and heavy, wet with water and soap but also almost certainly stained with something else. Heavy pigskin gloves are not as easy to dispose of as paper tissues. She jerked them off her hands, then didn't know what to do with them. They had to be hidden first and later, somehow, destroyed, buried perhaps somewhere in the vast stretch of ranch land, sand, sagebrush, cottonwood trees — or even nearer, among the corrals and sheds, the barns, the bunkhouse — oh, anywhere, she thought, and heard the tinkle of ice and glasses coming from the hall. It would be Manuel with the cocktail tray. She shoved the gloves in her pocket, swiftly, moved away from the table and braced herself for what had to come.

Manuel came in the door carrying a tray which glittered with crystal and silver. She said quickly, "Manuel, there's a man — I think he's dead. He's back there along the trail beside the rim of the west arroyo."

Manuel put down the tray. He was Mexican, small, stocky and dark; he was elderly, she knew, but there wasn't a thread of white in his black hair. He said, "Sit down, Mrs. Wilson. You'd better have a

18

drink." He poured something into a glass and brought it to her as she sat down in a deep chair, and only then did she realize that her whole body was trembling.

She said, "What shall we do?"

"Indian Joe will find him and see to him. I'll get on the ranch phone at once. Now then, do please drink this." Manuel eyed her anxiously. "I'm sorry, madam, that you found this man. He can't be one of our boys. No horse living could throw one of our boys. Please, madam, don't shake so. Maybe he's still alive."

Mady sipped at the drink, which proved to be brandy and stung her throat so, she choked. Craig had not known just when he could return home. Yet she had to make sure that he had not returned. She said, "Has Mr. Wilson phoned?"

Manuel, halfway to the door, turned. "Oh, yes. While you were riding. There was a message from the San Francisco office to tell you that he can't be home until tomorrow."

So that was all right. She sipped more brandy. If Craig was still in San Francisco, nobody would believe that he had secretly returned to El Rancho, lured Guy Casso to that deserted arroyo, killed him with the rail and gone back to San Francisco, not even with the speed of Craig's own jet plane. But the rail did link Guy Casso's murder to El Rancho.

Manuel said, "Indian Joe will see to things. Perhaps a doctor can do something."

All a doctor could do was state that Guy Casso had been murdered with a sharp, heavy weapon which was nowhere to be found. Manuel disappeared swiftly. In a moment Mady heard light footsteps running through the hall. Inez cried, "Madam, this is dreadful! Is there anything I can do for you?"

Inez knelt beside Mady, her pretty dark face anxious. She wore her dinnertime dress; no one could call it a uniform, for it consisted of a white blouse with a round low neck and full starchy sleeves, and a wide skirt with a bright red, yellow and green floral design on it. She, too, was Mexican, young and kind.

Mady didn't want Inez to detect the lump her gloves made in her pocket, so she rose quickly and put the empty glass on the table. She thanked Inez and said no, there was nothing she could do, she was going to have a bath and change. She still felt strangely light-headed, as if she were walking through a fog; some of that may have been due to the brandy, but she got herself upstairs and into her own room.

It was a small room but charming. Craig had ordered it decorated for her and had himself specified the lovely old Spanish pieces with which the room was furnished. It adjoined Craig's big dressing room; there was also a door into the hall which was nearer; she was almost running when she reached it and closed the door behind her. A faint lemon-colored light from the sky still lingered outside the windows. She snapped on all the lights and hurriedly stripped off her riding clothes. They smelt of horse; she hoped that someone had found Nellie and seen to her. But what could she do with the pigskin gloves? She finally shoved the gloves, a wet, betraying little bundle, into the attaché case which she used to carry back and forth between Craig's New York office and his home, or her own small apartment when there was extra work to do; she had been Craig's secretary for three years. Then she ran a bath in the enormous pink-tiled bathroom.

She was in the tub, still bewildered with shock, when she remembered that Craig's Aunt Mirabel and his daughter Susan, who had been staying at the neighboring ranch belonging to Craig's brother Boyce, were both expected back that night.

Craig and Mady had arrived home from their long honeymoon world trip only ten days before, and Mirabel had insisted that she and Susan give Craig and Mady at least that much time alone at El Rancho even though their stay there would probably not be too long; Craig's main office, as well as his legal residence for various business reasons, was in New York. On their first night back Craig and Mady had dined at Boyce's ranch, and his wife Edith had done her best to make Mady uncomfortable, but had not succeeded. Now Mirabel and Susan were to come home to El Rancho to stay.

El Rancho was to Mady an enchanting house; it had been built originally in a Spanish style, with thick walls, darkly waxed floors, low ceilings, deep window seats and many fireplaces. It had been added on to from time to time, yet somehow it seemed merely to have grown, so the modern additions were in charming harmony with the rest of the wide-flung house.

The original huge ranch had once been named El Rancho del Rio. Naturally this had shortened itself to El Rancho Rio, or merely, in the family, El Rancho. The reason for its name was the big river — formally El Rio Grande but contrarily always called simply the big river — which wound sluggishly at times, too fast and hard at other times, mainly through Boyce's ranch, although a kind of meandering tributary came down through Craig's part of the property. The whole vast El Rancho had been divided between Craig and Boyce at the time of their father's death. Boyce, being the older, had his choice of the land and cannily, he thought, chose the section which included the best grazing land for cattle. Craig had taken the remainder, which included the old main house and, as a matter of fact, the name.

But then Craig discovered what he subsequently named Wilsonite in the rocky range of low hills — once a silver mine, far to the south of the main house — which were a part of his ranch. And by that quirk of fate and also by Craig's intelligence and hard work, within a few years he became a well-known name and, in a way, a powerful name. He also, without really intending it, became one of the new breed of the fantastically rich.

He was sensible about his money but he made use of it too; he had his own jet plane because it saved him time and energy. He had a leased house in New York; he had a hotel apartment and office in San Francisco. But in his heart he was still a cattleman, a rancher who loved his land — and he loved El Rancho.

Now there would be the inevitable headlines about the Casso murder. And no alert reporter would fail to remember that Rhoda's trip around the world with Guy Casso as her companion was one of the reasons why the judge had awarded Craig the custody of his daughter.

Mady's thoughts went back to the previous afternoon and the mysterious appearance of Guy Casso, the dreadful scene that followed — and the fact that Mirabel and Susan had witnessed it. She could not push from her mind the remembrance of Casso's slim body, like that of a professional dancer, his overhandsome face, his slick black hair, the way his eyes gleamed with a kind of malicious mirth.

With a shudder, she pulled herself back to the present, and wondered what Indian Joe was doing; the body would have to be left where it was, in the sand, for officers of the law to look at. She hadn't thought of that until that moment. Well, Indian Joe and Manuel between them would know what to do.

Sometime during that interval of time while she was going quickly through automatic motions, brushing her hair, selecting some dress, any dress, she really didn't look and choose, shoving her feet into slippers, she made up her mind about the rail. She did not intend to tell even Craig where she had found it, how she had found it and what she had done with it. Naturally she would tell him of her ugly and perplexing encounter with Guy Casso the previous day.

She gave herself an automatic look in the mirror; she had snatched out a dress which was made in Paris; a famous designer had cut those fluid lines and chosen the slate-blue fabric. Craig had grinned and told her she must dress like the wife of a rich man. "Good for business," he had said and then, more serious, added, "Do you like jewels, Mady? Some bracelets perhaps? Or, oh, I don't know. What would you like?"

She had looked at the star sapphire he had chosen for an engagement ring and the pearls which he had picked at Cartier's as casually as she would have picked out a rhinestone pin at a department store and said that she had enough jewels. "More than I ever had in my life, and you know it," she had said shortly.

Craig had laughed again. "No need to get cross about it. I only wondered. Look here, if we go over to London this afternoon we can catch this opening —"

It was all a new world to Mady, almost an unbelievable world.

The world which had come upon her an hour or so ago was unbelievable too. Murder never seems real; it is only a word until one meets murder, lying sprawled in the sand and sagebrush.

Mady began to feel shaky inside again. She opened the door. She had heard nothing until then, but Susan and Mirabel had arrived. She heard their voices. Then Craig said loudly, "Tell the boys to leave the dead man where he was found, Manuel. Call the sheriff while I see Mrs. Wilson."

Craig came then, springing up the steps. He was wearing city clothes. The buoyancy and youthfulness with which El Rancho had seemed to endow him when they arrived ten days ago had gone. He was the Craig Wilson that Mady knew well, sitting at a conference table or dictating quick telegrams and making swift decisions.

"Mady! They say you found him."

"Yes."

"They say it's Guy Casso. Indian Joe looked in his wallet and found his name."

"Yes. It's Casso. There was a message from your San Francisco office saying you wouldn't be home until tomorrow."

"Things got crossed up. I'll tell you later." He had reached her side. He took her hand, searched her eyes intently and leaned over to kiss her. "Mady, you're all right, aren't you?"

She wanted to say no, she felt terrible. Instead she tried to be sensible and said, "Yes."

"Of course, the hellish thing is that it's Guy Casso. All that over again. Well — Susan and Mirabel are downstairs —"

"I've got to talk to you."

There was the flash of swift perception in his eyes which Mady also knew well. "Come on. I'll get into comfortable clothes," he said. She went with him into his big room. He loosened his tie. "What is it?"

"Guy Casso came to see me yesterday. He came into the living room. He pushed me over onto the sofa and — and just then your Aunt Mirabel and Susan came in and saw him."

Chapter 2

Craig looked at Mady for a moment, his face frozen, his eyes blazing. "He came *here? Why?*"

"I don't know. He said the door was open and he just walked in. Craig, it was unbelievable! I'll tell you exactly —"

It had happened about dusk. Mady was in the long living room, with its great sofas and lounge chairs, its enormous fieldstone fireplace, its wide windows looking out toward the Sierras, when a man walked into the room. She hadn't heard his footsteps in the hall; she whirled around when she heard a voice say, incredibly, "Hello, darling."

He stood for a second in the doorway, his handsome, shiny head cocked, as if he were listening, toward the hall. He wore a dapper pin-striped suit and pinched-looking shiny loafers. He had a tiny black mustache and shiny black hair plastered down. His eyes were big, dark and oddly gleeful. He seemed to slither toward her, gracefully. She backed away. "I didn't hear you come in! Who are you — ?"

He interrupted her. He was so close she could smell some sort of perfume or hair oil. "The front door was open. Western hospitality. So I came in. My darling!" His voice raised in a penetrating falsetto. "My darling, I had to see you again."

Mady had backed still further, her legs against the sofa, which was a mistake, for in a second the revolting man proved himself remarkably strong; he clutched at her, pushed her down onto the sofa, and as she called, *"Manuel,"* he began to struggle with her, trying to kiss her, embrace her, she didn't know what. She could only try to fight back, and through the fantastic confusion heard Susan's fluty voice crying, "Why, it's Guy Casso! I didn't know you two were friends!"

He released Mady and stood. She got to her feet and pulled her dress straight. Susan, Craig's twelve-year-old daughter, was standing in the doorway. Mirabel was just behind her. Manuel came running along the hall, and Guy said in that strident voice, "Hello, Susan. You've surprised our little secret."

Mady said to Manuel, "Show this man out! Don't let him come into the house again!"

But Guy Casso gave Mady a mocking bow and said, "Darling. it's wonderful to see you again," and slid with a dancer's grace out past Mirabel, past Susan and past Manuel, who pattered angrily after him into the hall. Mirabel, Susan and Mady stood there without speaking. Then a car started up with a roar outside; Casso had of course arrived by car.

"And that's all there was to it," she told Craig. "I thought he was drunk at first. Afterward it seemed to me that I smelled only that loathsome perfume, no whiskey."

Craig was white. "Did you tell Mirabel that you had never in your life seen him before?"

"Oh, yes. And Susan." She didn't add that Mirabel clearly believed her, but Susan, smiling a little, as clearly doubted it.

"But this makes no sense! I can't understand why he would approach you at all, let alone in such a way. It was malicious, no question of that. He may have guessed that Mirabel and Susan were about to arrive. Maybe he even saw the car leaving Boyce's place and came here, but — no, it makes no sense. What happened after that?"

"We had dinner. Nobody said anything more about Casso. Then your aunt and

Susan went back to Boyce's ranch for the night. One of Boyce's men came to get them. That was all."

Craig said, "Too much. I can't think why he would do that. Wait a minute." Craig started for his dressing room, sliding out of his coat. In a moment Mady heard the shower turned on in his bathroom.

There was a window seat, cushioned in yellow and green chintz; Mady sat there looking out. She could see lights from the bunkhouse and the kitchen beside it. Lights dotted the sheds and barns. It was by then full night. The stars as always seemed very bright and so near that she felt she could put out her hand and touch them. The window was open and the clear night air whispered over her face. She thought she could smell sagebrush. She knew that she could smell the steak the men were having for supper.

If she told Craig about the rail, he would tell the police. If she didn't tell him, she might keep secret something he should know.

He came out of the dressing room; he had got into gray slacks and was pulling a red turtle-neck sweater over his head. His dark hair was wet when it emerged; he had a little gray, a very little, over his temples.

He was attractive, he was good-looking; he was intelligent and strong. Mady wished with all her heart that she was in love with him.

She thrust that thought hurriedly away, deep into the limbo of things which are never spoken and should never even be thought and must not continue to exist. There were times when Craig seemed to her almost telepathic.

This time he was not. He went to a mirror, picked up brushes, and brushing at his hair, said, "He had some motive for all that."

"I thought perhaps it was a preposterous and malicious kind of joke on his part. There wasn't any other explanation. It seemed to me that he was enjoying it — I mean his face was sort of — oh, mean and yet gleeful. I can't describe it. He was a thoroughly horrible man."

"Well, a weak man," Craig said thoughtfully. "Probably deserved murder. Still, I wish it hadn't happened here."

"It seems odd that he would turn up here in Nevada at all. Didn't he live in New York?"

Craig gave his hair another brush. "He might have lived anywhere. He must have come here to see Rhoda."

"Rhoda! you mean — *Is she here?*"

He put down his brushes. "She's here. Arrived this morning. Staying at Boyce's place. I'll tell you when there's time. The sheriff will be here soon. Now, Mady, the sheriff is an old friend but this is an ugly business. I don't want you to tell the sheriff about Casso's visit here or his behavior. I don't want even the sheriff to know that you ever saw him in your life before. Did you tell Manuel who he was when you told him you had discovered him?"

"No," Mady replied, but she was thinking of Rhoda's arrival.

"But you recognized him?"

"Oh, yes. I couldn't see his face, but I remembered his coat, pin-striped, flashy. His hand was out across the sand and I remembered it and the glitter of his fingernails. I knew who it was. But I'm sure I didn't tell Manuel."

"Manuel saw him here yesterday, though. Well, I'll fix it with Manuel. I'll fix it with Mirabel, too. She's safe. And if Susan offers to say a word" — Craig's mouth tightened — "I'll shut her up so fast her head will spin."

"But Susan wouldn't say anything to damage me or you —"

"There's no telling what Susan might get

it into her head to do. I do not intend to have my private life made a circus of. Not again. You're my wife. I'll protect you. I want to protect myself, too. There must never be a word about this visit of Casso's here —" He came to Mady, looked out at the starry night and said, "I can't see what motive he would have in coming to make a scene like that with you." He put a hand on Mady's shoulder. "I wouldn't have had anything like this happen for the world. Manuel told me you walked home."

Mady thought, Why did Rhoda come here? But she answered, "Nellie was frightened. I had to let her come on home."

"You're sure you didn't see anybody at all, any horse, any car? The sheriff will ask you that."

"Not a thing."

"Perhaps one of the boys saw something, or somebody. They'll be questioned. We'll all be questioned. I'll go down now and put the fear of God and a beating into Susan. Seems a shame that Susan lives in a period when fathers really don't beat their children."

"She was very polite last night at dinner. Almost — I don't know — demure."

"Demure like a rattlesnake," said her father. "I was determined to get custody of

34

Susan and at least I've been able to keep her out of the penitentiary. So far," he added. "All right. I'm glad you had the sense to keep your head, send Manuel for Indian Joe, glad you put on that dress and — Don't worry, Mady. Things will be all right."

Mady said, "Did Casso come to see Rhoda? Did he come with her?"

"I don't know but — no, I shouldn't think so. I'll tell you about Rhoda later. Let's go down now."

You don't know about the rail, Mady thought; Rhoda and Casso and the rail seemed to provide a baffling kind of combination. Somebody had to enter the house and take that piece of rail and kill Casso with it. That somebody must have hoped to implicate Craig. Yet she was literally afraid to tell him about it. He had decided not to let the sheriff or any other law-enforcing officer know about Casso's strange visit and stranger conduct. But he might tell the sheriff about the rail, and the rail linked Casso's murder with Craig's ranch and Craig.

He took Mady's hand and they went downstairs together, close as any truly loving husband and wife, and into the living room, where Mirabel sat stiffly in a straight

35

chair, holding a glass in a stiff hand.

Only Susan called her Aunt Mirabel; Craig, Boyce and Edith all said, simply, Mirabel; the ranch hands and Manuel and Inez said Miss Mirabel. She had told Mady firmly to use her name, Mirabel, saying that Aunt Mirabel dated her; she laughed, though, when she said it, for it was clear that Mirabel didn't care what her age happened to be and never would care. She was a tall, strong-looking old woman, very erect, with sparkling gray eyes, jetty eyebrows and white, neat hair; she had firm features, rather like Craig's, and just then her face, too, was stiff and white with shock.

Mirabel said, "Headlines again, Craig. He wasn't worth murder."

"Has the sheriff come?"

"I heard some cars a few minutes ago."

"I'd better go down to the arroyo. Mady tells me that Casso was here yesterday and —"

"I saw him. He behaved atrociously. My advice would be to keep quiet about that."

"I told Mady that. Manuel will do as I say. Where's Susan?"

There was a crash and clatter and running footsteps along the hall. The clash and clatter sounded very much like glass.

Susan came in, ran to her father and clasped him around the waist. Manuel appeared in the doorway and he was furious. His black eyes shot flames. "Mr. Craig, that child —"

Susan shrieked, "Shut up, you old — old Mexican! I didn't mean to drop them!"

"Two of your mother's crystal goblets," Manuel said.

Susan clung to her father and buried her face against him. He said, "Spilt milk, Manuel. I want to talk to you for a moment. Let go, Susan."

Susan clung more tightly. She had red-gold hair, long and straight, held in place by a green ribbon. She had emerald-green eyes and a delicately pink and white skin. She wore a pale green dress, neatly smocked across the yoke and collared in white lace; she wore white socks and black strapped slippers. Her father unclasped her arms and made her look at him. "I want you to listen to me. You, too, Manuel, please. This man Casso —"

"You mean Mother's — secretary," Susan said, all at once sweet and demure and pausing with deliberation before she said secretary.

Rhoda had referred to Guy as her secretary; whether it was fact or fancy, the judge had decided against fact.

Craig said, "He came here yesterday —"

"We saw him," Susan said sweetly. "He was on the sofa. With your new wife. They were wrestling around just like that movie Aunt Edith took me to see."

Mirabel said to Craig's inquiring look. "A few days ago. In Wilson City. Edith said that she didn't realize it was not for children. The usher didn't stop them."

"You can't stop Aunt Edith," Susan said, and added, assuming a bored and sophisticated manner, "It wasn't really very interesting. Nothing new."

"*Susan,*" her father began, stopped himself and said, "Never mind that now. The point is you are not to tell anyone at all that Casso was here. Do you understand?"

"Of course." Susan's green eyes were as clear as river water. "You're afraid of newspapers. You and your new wife, and Casso, an old friend of hers."

"He was not an old friend of Mady's. She never saw him before," Craig said.

Susan said, "It didn't look like that."

Craig seemed to force himself to take a long breath. He said, "Listen to me, Susan. I am bigger than you. I am stronger than you. If you say one word about that visit of Casso's yesterday, you'll wish you hadn't."

38

Susan thought that over. Then she said demurely, "If you beat me, they can take me away from you and let Mother have me."

"But I'll have beaten you first," her father said. "I mean that, Susan."

Susan eyed him thoughtfully.

Craig turned to his aunt. "Did anybody at Boyce's place know that Casso was in the neighborhood?" He meant had Casso and Rhoda met.

Mirabel said promptly, "No. At least — well, I'm sure that Boyce wouldn't have had him on the place."

Manuel said softly, "Mr. Craig, I think the sheriff is here —"

"I'll come," Craig said and vanished into the hall after Manuel.

Mady went to the cocktail tray and took up the wine decanter. She was pouring sherry into Mirabel's glass when Susan said, "You're really all gussied up, aren't you, Mady?"

Mirabel must have caught a slight question in Mady's face, for she chuckled briefly. "Coast slang for dressed up," she explained.

"Of course," Susan said, "that's what I mean. All gussied up. Real cool. You must have got a lot of clothes in Paris, Mady.

When you were Father's secretary, you couldn't buy clothes like that. Yes —" said the child, perching on the edge of the sofa. "I used to see you there in Father's office and think that you had possibilities."

Mirabel had taken a sip of sherry; she choked slightly and put down the glass. "Susan, remember! I will tell your father every single word you say which is in the least impertinent."

Susan widened her eyes and swung brown legs, bare as far as the white ankle socks. She looked like Alice in Wonderland, which was splendid acting on Susan's part. She said, "But darling Aunt Mirabel, that was meant as a compliment. Besides" — she eyed one neatly strapped black slipper — "it's the truth, isn't it?" she said gently. "She *was* Father's secretary. I know all about it. She was engaged to be married to Jim Marsh and he threw her over and she snatched up Father on the rebound and she's never had so much money to spend in her life —"

She stopped on a rather quickly drawn breath as Mirabel rose purposefully. Mady said quickly, "All right, Susan. I hope that you and I can get along. It will be a disappointment to your father if we can't, but —"

40

Mirabel said, "Don't let her off without an apology, Mady."

"It would be a disappointment to you, too," Susan said sweetly. "I'm the real reason my father married you. He thought you'd help Aunt Mirabel bring me up properly."

And that was the truth, too. Mirabel was powerful in her way but not young. Mady said, "Understand this, Susan. I will not let you bother your father. Or me," she said, really very quietly.

The odd thing was that there must have been a ring of something or other in Mady's voice that caught Susan's attention. She was smart; indeed, she was highly intelligent. And as her father had said, so far he'd kept her out of the penitentiary. Mady couldn't help half-smiling as she thought of his baffling words. Susan caught the smile and some of her self-assurance dropped away, for here was something she didn't understand. Mady followed her reasoning. Mady's voice and expression suggested, first, that she hadn't been hurt by Susan's childish — yet oddly adult — effort to do so, and second, that Mady knew something: she had some source of strength which Susan didn't know about and couldn't surmise. Susan sat kicking her legs, eying Mady. Mirabel went back to her chair and sat down, stiff and erect.

But Mady wished that Susan hadn't known about Jim. Probably the whole family knew it; clearly Mirabel knew it, for she had moved to stop Susan; Boyce and Edith certainly knew the story, such as it was. Certainly Susan's mother would have known it and talked of it to Susan. But Mady wasn't prepared for Susan's attack or her mention of Jim. For a second his face seemed to come from somewhere, smiling, coming nearer, almost as if he were in the room.

There had been times, too many of them, when Mady had wondered wearily how long it would be before she could forget him, but this was not one of those times. The present and dreadful problem of murder seemed to shut out everything else, even her inconvenient memory. Mirabel was looking at Susan like an elderly and white-haired hawk about to pounce. The front door opened and there were men's voices in the hall. Craig and the sheriff came in. "The fuzz," Susan muttered darkly.

Mady later learned that everyone living in Nevada did not invariably go about clothed in blue jeans and cowboy boots, but it was her impression at that time and the sheriff did not change it. He was tall, suntanned and sun-wrinkled; he had bright blue eyes and faded brownish-white hair. His jeans were suitably faded, which she had already learned was the *sine qua non* of chic. He carried a rolled and battered Stetson, which also was chic.

His boot heels clattered on the floor. He said in a friendly and casual way, "Hello, Mirabel."

Mirabel nodded. "Hello, Sam. How are you?"

"No younger," said the sheriff. "Still, I can't complain." His blue eyes met Mady's fully and she had an impression that they had already taken her in, top to toe. Craig introduced them, and the sheriff came to Mady. They shook hands; his hand was strong, warm and leathery, rather like Craig's hands after he had spent some time at El Rancho and ridden enough to reinstate the calluses of his youth.

Susan rose with such an ostentatious show of good manners that Mady rather agreed with Craig about a beating. The sheriff glanced at her. "Hello, Susan. Did you get the vet for that dog of yours?"

"Oh, yes," Susan said airily, but quickly

43

added, "sir. The vet knew just what shots to give him."

"Funny-looking dog for this part of the country," said the sheriff in a leisurely way, as if he had merely dropped in for a chat. "How are you going to get him clipped fancy, like the pictures of those dogs?"

Susan's dog was a very large, very black, very waggish French poodle; he was only nine months old or thereabouts but he was enormous. Susan adored him. She now forgot all about being a demure Alice in Wonderland figure; she forgot her assumed manners; she ran to the sheriff. "I thought I'd take pictures for a guide and then use scissors and clip him myself."

The sheriff appeared to consider it thoughtfully. Mady caught a softer look in Mirabel's hawky face, and Craig's face, so like Mirabel's, showed the same faint softening. Mady knew that she was smiling herself in something like reflected pride, for no little girl could have looked more thoroughly engaging than Susan at that moment. The sheriff said, slowly, "Well, I'm not sure that's a good idea. Tell you what. There's a retired marine sergeant come to live in Wilson City. He used to have a lot to do with dogs, those war dogs, you know, guard dogs. Maybe he'd know how to clip your dog."

"Oh!" Susan took the sheriff's hand. Her face was glowing. "That would be wonderful! Will you take me when Sancho needs a clip?"

"Surest thing you know," the sheriff said. "Any time. Now then, young lady, maybe you'd better go out to the kitchen and talk to Manuel. We've got a little grown-up talk here, no use your listening to it."

In a flash the engaging, candid little girl in Susan vanished; she stiffened, lowered her eyes and said, too demurely, "But you're only going to talk about Guy being murdered. I'd like to listen. He was my mother's lover —"

"Susan!" her father roared and caught her by the shoulder. He whirled her around and, Mady felt sure, resisted a temptation to give her a good wallop. "Go upstairs. Your room is ready." He then yielded either to diplomacy or affection and said, "Sancho is there. Inez fed him and Manuel took him upstairs."

"You needn't shove me," said Susan. She went, though, her strapped slippers pattering along.

Craig sighed. Mirabel sighed and sat back in her chair. The sheriff said, "She'll straighten out, Craig. You were kind of a

45

limb yourself, you know, at her age." His blue eyes twinkled. Then he sobered and looked at Mady. "I don't like to bother you, Mrs. Wilson, but they say you found this man. I guess you'd better tell me about it."

Craig came and stood beside her. She began, "I was riding. I was alone. The horse shied and I saw a man lying beside the trail. He was in some sagebrush, right at the edge of the ravine. I thought he was hurt. I got down and went to him and I saw —" Her voice wavered. Craig put a steadying arm around her; she was grateful for it. "I thought that he must be dead. So I came home. I walked because I couldn't get up on the horse again."

The sheriff's blue eyes were thoughtful. "It's too bad you found him, and I'm sorry. Did you see anything that could have killed him? It was something heavy and sharp."

I saw it and I cleaned it and it's standing on the table behind me. Mady thought that so clearly that she was afraid those blue eyes would perceive her thought. She had to answer at once, so she said, "No." It was a flat, out-and-out lie and there was nothing else she could think of at that moment to say.

"Seems strange," the sheriff said. "Somebody sure hit him hard enough to break his head, hard enough to kill him. You'd think the murderer wouldn't want to carry whatever the murder weapon was away with him. Murder weapon," the sheriff said thoughtfully. "That's a bad thing for a man to be caught in possession of." His eyes sought Craig. "I don't like to bring this up, Craig, but maybe you know that your wife — I mean your former wife — is visiting at Boyce's place. Got here this morning. Now, when you got back from San Francisco this afternoon, I was wondering if you happened to go to see her and if you happened to see this Casso fellow."

Chapter 3

Mirabel, of course, had known of Rhoda's arrival. She must have seen and talked to her. She gave Mady a swift and somehow pleading glance. Certainly Susan, too, must have seen her mother.

Craig's arm tightened around Mady. "I got to the house only a short time ago," he said to the sheriff. "I haven't had a chance to tell my wife why I came back sooner than I expected. It was this way." He turned Mady toward him, so he spoke to her directly. "This morning I told our office boy to send off that message saying that I wouldn't be home until tomorrow. Flanker was late in arriving from New York. But then Rhoda phoned to me directly. She said she had just arrived this morning, she was staying with Edith and Boyce and she had to see me at once." He looked at the sheriff. "She was so insistent about seeing me that I had my boys bring me home this afternoon." He turned back to Mady. "You probably didn't hear my plane. The strip is on the other side of the hills, away from the trail where you were riding. My boys, I mean the pilot and co-pilot of course, know when they brought me home. I sent them back to San Francisco right away. They're to pick up Flanker. He is coming to El Rancho in a day or two on business."

The sheriff said, "You mean the Flanker Milling Company president?"

Craig nodded. "We send our Wilsonite ore there to be milled, the Wilsonite extracted. But you know that. The pilots usually stay at the St. Francis. You can phone them there. They'll probably know the exact time of our arrival here. Maybe some ranch hand saw me. When I reached Boyce's place, Rhoda had taken his car into Wilson City. I waited around there until she got back. We talked. We didn't go inside the house. I came home perhaps an hour ago. I didn't have a chance to tell you, Mady. I hadn't told the San Francisco office of my change in plans, so the boy there simply sent my message off as I had told him to do before Rhoda phoned me."

"I saw Craig," Mirabel said to the sheriff. "He and Rhoda walked up and down outside the house. They were still talking but had walked around the end of the house, so I couldn't see them when the car came up to bring me and Susan and her dog here. Boyce had one of his boys drive us. When we left, Craig's jeep was still in the driveway of Boyce's place."

The sheriff said mildly, "I've known you since you were a girl, Mirabel."

Mirabel sat up very straight. "Then you know I wouldn't lie!"

The sheriff smiled a little. "Well, now, Mirabel. I reckon you would tell a good round lie if you thought it was going to help Craig or Boyce."

"I'm telling you the truth." Mirabel looked dangerously hawky.

"All right, all right." The sheriff fumbled in a pocket and addressed Mady. "Mind if I smoke, Mrs. Wilson?"

"Please —" Mady's voice came out in a whisper. The only thought in her mind just then was that in fact Craig had no real alibi for the afternoon and the time when Casso might have been murdered, and she was thankful she had removed the rail and thankful she had told a flat, round lie. She watched the sheriff take out a little packet of papers, extract one of them, shake flakes from a small tobacco pouch into it, pull the string of the tobacco pouch to close it (with his teeth, since both hands were engaged), roll up the cigarette paper deftly,

50

give it a lick to secure the paper and then light it.

Craig said, "Sit down, Sheriff. Want a drink?"

The sheriff glanced at Mady, politely waiting for her, so she sat down hurriedly He then chose a deep chair which happened to be near the table where the rail lay. Mady almost feared that it might assume animate powers and nudge him, saying, "Look at me; this is what you want; look at me."

It didn't. Craig went to the table and poured a drink for the sheriff, who took it without any demur about drinking on duty. He took a healthy swallow, said, "Good liquor, Craig. I guess I'll have to be blunt. Does this mean that you have no alibi for the time this Casso fellow probably was killed?"

Craig replied a little, just a little, carefully. "I don't know when he was murdered, Sam. A ranch jeep was parked near the hangar at the landing strip. I took the jeep over to Boyce's place. I took the cut-off over the hills instead of the main road. Maybe nobody here saw me or the jeep. But — wait a minute — Edith's maid came to the door and told me that Rhoda had gone to Wilson City. She is new; she

51

doesn't strike me as very bright. But she may know what time it was."

"How long did you say you waited to see your — the first Mrs. Wilson?" The sheriff looked around for an ashtray, and by chance, reaching for the nearest one, touched the rail. Hearts do stand still for a second or two; Mady's did.

"I don't know, except the sun started to go down while I walked up and down. Probably neither Boyce nor Edith knew that I was there. But unless Casso was killed while I was in the plane, no, I can't think of any firm alibi. But I really didn't kill him, Sam. I had no reason to kill him."

"Some folks would say that breaking up your first marriage might be a reason," the sheriff said, but very thoughtfully because it was as if he were in fact on Craig's side and wanted to prove that Craig couldn't have killed Guy Casso but wasn't sure he could do so.

He shook off more ashes. "Tell you what. Old Doc Smithers came to see the — remains," said the sheriff delicately. "He'll do an autopsy, but he thinks Casso was killed about three or four o'clock. He can't be sure, he says. I'd guess he'd been dead three to five hours when I saw him. That's only a guess. But it seems to me somebody must have seen Casso arrive." He looked at Mady. "You didn't see a strange car or a horse anywhere?"

"No, I didn't." She wished that she could have quickly and efficiently lied again and said that, yes, there had been a strange car. She couldn't invent a convincing lie that fast, and besides, she had a notion that perhaps she had already lied too much; she was beginning to feel something like the quake and quaver of the ground which she thought must accompany quicksands, and a murder investigation could be nothing but that.

"And you didn't hear Craig's plane come in?"

"No —" Mady thought back over the long afternoon's ride she had taken; there had been the creaking of saddle leather, the thuds of Nellie's small hoofs, the light breeze blowing now and again over the flats or through a tunnel-like arroyo along the trail she took. "That is, I'm not sure. I think I did hear a plane. I did think for a moment that it might be Craig's plane. But I was on that downhill trail, the steep part of it, out where there's a ravine at the west —" She looked helplessly at Craig, for she couldn't possibly identify the exact location, but she was not lying. She had thought she heard a plane, but it was a brief impression and she had as briefly decided that it was a commercial airliner, well to the south.

The sheriff nodded. "Do you know what time that was, Mrs. Wilson?"

"No, but I think it must have been late, nearly dusk." She wasn't sure of that, but the later Craig arrived at the ranch the less likely it was that he could be accused of Casso's murder.

"When did you leave the house for your ride?"

"I think it was about two. I took a long ride."

"Seems odd we can't find the weapon that killed him. Odd sort of murder weapon it must be, too. Gunfire, now that'd seem more likely. Ain't so long since we had more gunplay than we wanted in these parts. But whatever killed him certainly wasn't a gun." The sheriff turned toward the hall, listened and said, "Sounds like the state police. Took their time about looking over the scene of the murder." He rose to his full, lanky height. He leaned directly over the rail in order to drop a cigarette in the ashtray and said, mildly, "These cigarette papers don't seem to hold out like they used to. Sometime I'm going to take to tailor-mades. Want to come with me and talk to these young fellows, Craig?"

"I think I'll have to." Craig started for the hall.

The sheriff said to Mady, "I'm sorry this happened, Mrs. Wilson. Your first visit to the ranch, too. The police will want your statement about finding him, same as I did, but don't let it bother you."

He nodded at her and waved one hand at Mirabel, who, at the announcement of the arrival of the state police, was again sitting very still and straight as if prepared for battle.

Craig and the sheriff went out, the sheriff's heels clicking on the waxed floor of the hall; there were other voices. Then the front door closed and Mady and Mirabel waited.

It seemed a long wait.

"I'm sorry Rhoda came here," Mirabel then said. "She shouldn't have come. Edith shouldn't have let her come. Rhoda arrived this morning. Flew to Las Vegas last night, she said, and hired a car and a driver and came here. Sent the car and chauffeur back to Las Vegas. Heaven knows where she gets the money for renting a car and chauffeur. But she's a spender, always has been.

Craig gave her a handsome settlement, cash and alimony. But then —" Mirabel sighed. "That was before Wilsonite made Craig so rich. You know the terms of their divorce."

"Yes." It had been a simple matter of money. Rhoda had no faith in Wilsonite, which at the time of their divorce was only in the first stages of development. She had had no idea that it might develop as it had, so when Craig offered her an outright settlement of two hundred thousand plus a generous alimony until she remarried, Rhoda had jumped at it, released all communal property claims, taken the flat cash and alimony condition as a complete settlement and left for a world trip with, of all people, Guy Casso.

Mirabel rubbed her nose thoughtfully. "My guess is she knows now that Wilsonite has brought Craig a great deal of money and she wants some more. You know, Mady, I didn't believe in Wilsonite at first. Oh, I gave Craig all the money I had to mine that stuff and for development. But I thought it was a gamble. I had to remind myself that my great-grandfather made his pile when he gambled on finding silver deposits. And then, of course, he got hold of as much free land as he could, homesteaded, bought what he couldn't home-stead. All of it was a gamble. He'd been in California during the gold rush. But he made his pile gambling on silver. He'd seen Spanish houses along the coast. So he built El Rancho in Spanish style."

Craig had told Mady that some of the land had been sold off during one financial panic or another, but it was still one of the great ranches of the West. It had seemed wrong, Craig told her, to divide it when his father died. Yet times had changed and he and Boyce did not always see eye to eye.

The Wilsons had always been known and respected. Wilson City was not a city at all, it was a small Western town, but nat-urally it was named Wilson City. The county was Wilson County. Their cattle brand was one of the oldest in the state.

Presently Mirabel began to talk again. "Sam, the sheriff, used to be the best dancer in Wilson County. We used to have real old country dances around here when I was a girl. I wasn't a bad dancer myself."

Somehow Mady could see her, black hair then, dark gray eyes, vivacious, willful and charming. Mirabel glanced at Mady, read her thoughts, and smiled. "All old women think of themselves as having been great belles when they were young. I wasn't. Too much what they then called a tomboy. I liked to ride, still like to. I could rope cattle. Still can, I expect. I was never much for housekeeping, not till my brother's wife died and all at once there I was, a mother to two boys. But I haven't regretted anything — except letting Craig marry Rhoda. She was a friend of Edith's, you know. Boyce and Edith had been married for several years when Rhoda came out" — Mirabel paused, then went on — "ostensibly to visit Edith. I always thought she came to rope Craig, and succeeded. Rhoda is a year or two older than Craig but still they were too young to know their minds. Susan came along within the first year. Rhoda was bored with the ranch by that time, couldn't bear staying here. She was gone most of the time. Craig was busy with Wilsonite. It was only when Rhoda began to go pretty widely off the tracks, so to speak, running around with men like Casso, that Craig decided he had to get Susan away from her. That is" — Mirabel linked her hands together and looked firmly at Mady — "Rhoda is really only a fool, you know. She drank too often and too much but is not really an alcoholic. There's no real harm in her, just foolishness. But Craig was right. He couldn't let

Susan be brought up by Rhoda. The fact is," she said with the wry twist to her mouth that Mady was beginning to know, "Rhoda wouldn't have brought her up. She'd have left her to maids. Once in a while she might have remembered she had a daughter, but not often. Now she's out of money. That's my guess. Now — Ah, well, that is all water over the dam."

From upstairs there was a gleeful bark or two and some resounding thumps, indicating that Susan and Sancho were having a fine romp. Sancho had been fed but Susan would be getting hungry, so Mady went into the dining room and found Manuel there, standing at a window, his small hands linked together behind his immaculate white coat. "Dinner will be late, I'm afraid," she told him. "But Miss Susan —"

He had turned toward her. "Oh, she's all right. I gave her dinner. You can't see the trail beside the arroyo from here. Only car lights now and then."

Mady said, "As soon as the police leave we can have dinner."

"Yes, Mrs. Wilson."

She went back to the living room. It gave her rather a shock to see Mirabel, tall and erect, at the table where the rail stood, but she was only staring out into the starlight. "They'll certainly suspect Craig," Mirabel said.

"No!" Mady cried. "He didn't do it! He wasn't here!"

"But that's only his story," Mirabel said. "I did see him at Boyce's place. But there's no getting around it. Sam was right when he said that some folks would think that the break-up of a marriage was sufficient reason for murder. I do wish Casso hadn't turned up here the very day before Rhoda arrived. And today again he turned up. Murdered at that!" She went back to her chair. "He really must have known that Rhoda was here and came to see her."

Mady could not help thinking that Rhoda knew Casso, Rhoda knew the rail. She could not believe though that Rhoda had murdered him.

The women heard them coming — the opening of the door, the clatter of footsteps in the hall. Mirabel sat straighter. Mady stiffened her back and her courage, too. But the interview really was nothing like the minute and stern inquiry that apprehension had built up in her mind during that period of waiting.

Craig came to stand by Mady. The sheriff introduced the three men. They were young, thin, yet wiry-looking, all three of them, tanned and trim in their uniforms. They were also polite, their voices soft and drawling and extremely courteous.

They went over the story which Mady had told the sheriff. Nobody seemed inclined to doubt her word, which ought to have given her some sort of twinge of guilt about the rail but in fact didn't.

It was not a long interview. They all thanked her. One of them said that he was very sorry she had been the one to find the murdered man. The sheriff was the last to leave, and he shook Mady's hand.

Craig went with them to the door. He stopped on his return and told Manuel that they could have dinner now and that he was starved. He then came into the living room and poured himself a drink. "No evidence that I could see. They worked very well and very fast. Hard to do when it's dark — I mean, to get the pictures and all that. They'll go to Boyce's ranch and question people there."

"Why?" Mirabel began, and then answered herself. "Oh, they know that Casso knew Rhoda."

"That's no secret to anybody," Craig said, but not bitterly. He only looked very tired. "They'll ask that maid of Edith's when I arrived, I suppose. They're coming back here later."

Mirabel's eyes snapped. "What for?"

"To question the men on the ranch. Sam is trying to establish an alibi for me, I can see that. The fact is I wouldn't have touched Casso with a ten-foot pole, let alone with whatever somebody used to smash in his head."

Mirabel said, "Craig, don't they know where Casso came from? Why? Good heavens, a man can't just drop out of the sky. He's got to come from somewhere."

Craig dropped more ice into his glass with a clatter. "Oh, yes. Sam used the phone in my study. Seems Casso arrived by rented car in Wilson City yesterday about noon. He left in the afternoon — that's when he came here — returned to the motel. The motel manager saw him use the pay telephone, and he spent the night there. He had breakfast and a late lunch at the cafe across the street from the motel. Then he disappeared."

He lifted his glass and sipped with an ease which was a little too easy to be quite real. "The car he rented was found by the state police. It was parked in that clump of cottonwoods just before you get to the entrance to El Rancho. They think that possibly either somebody picked him up there by prearrangement or he walked along the trail above the arroyo to meet somebody who was waiting for him there — and killed him."

Mirabel said, "Rhoda phoned to you from Boyce's place. Why did she drive to Wilson City when she knew you were coming back to see her?"

"She said she had come West without proper clothing. She went to the Wilson City Ladies' Toggery."

"Rhoda!"

"She came West on an impulse, she said. Didn't pack properly. She told me that she didn't expect me to get back so soon. And when she got to the Ladies' Toggery she says she found an unexpectedly good line of sports clothes. So she took her time."

"And you believe her?"

"Well, yes, I do. She says she didn't meet Guy Casso in Wilson City. Even if she had met him, Mirabel, it wouldn't explain Casso's murder. Rhoda is not the murdering type."

"No," Mirabel said, almost regretfully. "But why would he come here if not because Rhoda was here?"

"I don't know," Craig said, "and I can't

see why he pretended he was a friend of Mady's."

Mady leaned forward. "Craig, Rhoda will give you an alibi, won't she?"

Craig unexpectedly laughed. It was a youthful, honestly amused laugh. "She already has. She told the sheriff she met me at Boyce's at about three o'clock. Of course she didn't. It can easily be proved when the sheriff and the police talk to the girls in the Ladies' Toggery. But it was a good effort on Rhoda's part."

Mirabel said shortly, "Rhoda is after something."

Craig said nothing.

Mirabel touched her white hair. "Maybe she wants you back, Craig. Now that she's done with Casso. And very, very done with him, as it has developed," said Mirabel with that wry twist of her lips.

Craig finished his drink and set the glass down beside the rail. "They think the murderer must have been a man," he said. "Let's go in to dinner."

Susan came flying down the stairs as they went into the hall. Her green eyes were shining with excitement. "Father, Father! I know what killed him! Somebody came in here and got it and took it out there and broke his skull with it. And then cleaned it all up shiny and put it back."

Mady could feel an icy kind of chill. She supposed that she stared at Susan with utter horror, for the child looked at her, stopped dead still, said, "Why, Mady! You look so scared! Why —" Her green eyes glittered. "Why, of course, Mady cleaned it up and brought it back."

Mady didn't move. Craig said, impatiently, "Oh, for goodness' sake, Susan! Brought what back?"

"Why," Susan said triumphantly, "that old tomahawk that hangs in your study, of course! It's the murder weapon!"

Mady could almost feel her pulse begin to beat again. Susan, though, kept her green eyes fastened on her, and Mady had a dreadful notion that Susan sensed her relief.

Her father said, "I'll have no nonsense like this. That tomahawk is hanging exactly where it has always hung. Have you had your dinner?"

"If it wasn't the tomahawk," Susan said, watching Mady, "it was something that Mady knows about."

Chapter 4

Her father took her by the shoulder. "Mady has told everything she knows about this murder. I'm sorry it has happened and I'm sorry you know about it." He hesitated. He was swift in his decisions with men. His own young daughter was a more difficult problem. He said, "You are a little girl, Susan. You must trust me. And I'm going to have to ask you to behave as if you were older than you are. Now, then, dinner —"

"Oh, I had dinner a long time ago," Susan said, "but I'll come and watch you eat."

"And listen to everything we say." Her father spoke dryly, but there was the tug of a smile at the corners of his lips. "All right. Come on. You'll not hear anything."

And in fact she didn't hear anything of special interest although her eyes were intent, and so, Mady was sure, were her rosy little ears set below that straight-hanging Alice-in-Wonderland hair. Inez and Manuel came and went silently, like colored figures on a screen, and indeed

Inez in her bright wide-swinging skirt and white embroidered blouse looked rather as if she were part of a musical comedy and about to dance and sing. However, Manuel watched her like a hawk for mistakes in serving.

Mady was already accustomed to the formality of dinner at El Rancho. The other meals were different. Breakfast came up on a tray usually borne by Inez, whose pretty legs were younger than Manuel's, but then taken over by Manuel at the top of the stairs. Craig and Mady ate near the windows of his big bedroom, which looked out over the corrals, the sheds, the ranch, with its grazing lands making patches of green among the arid sections of reddish-gray soil which were mainly alkali flats. Joshua trees grew here, olive-green sagebrush and tumbleweed. The arroyo where Mady had found Guy Casso made a kind of dark slash toward the western hills. Off toward the south a branch of the big river wound its sluggish way and was rimmed with willows. Far toward the south and west a landing strip big enough for Craig's plane had been built; there was a hangar there; neither was visible from the house owing to the irregularly rolling nature of the land. The dark and craggy hills where

Craig had found Wilsonite were barely visible, a low kind of rim with jagged peaks. Wilsonite had been lying there, probably for a million years or so, waiting to be discovered.

Luncheons couldn't have been more informal. They ate wherever they happened to be; and if they were driving over the ranch or visiting the Wilsonite mine, they had picnic lunches. But dinners were served formally. Inez wouldn't have dared splash a drop of wine or drop a spoon under Manuel's stern gaze.

They didn't talk of Casso or the murder or even of Rhoda's arrival. Susan retired at last, disappointedly, saying that Sancho was better company.

"Better take him for a run before you turn in," her father said. "Manuel, will you go with her? Don't go far from the house."

"Scared, aren't you?" Susan slid out of her chair. "Don't be scared. The tomahawk is still there —"

"Susan, I told you!"

"I think old Sam Hawkins is too old for his job. Couldn't he take a look at that tomahawk? They say blood leaves traces, no matter how hard anybody tries to wash it away." She looked bright-eyed at Mady.

"What'd you use to clean it with, Mady?"

"Susan —" Craig made a motion to rise, and Susan fled, all child, white ankle socks twinkling, red hair waving.

Craig watched until Manuel came hurrying from the pantry, where obviously he had heard everything said at the table. He slid through the dining room after Susan and Craig said, "Keep her near the house, Manuel."

Mirabel's black eyebrows lifted. "Of course," she said thoughtfully, "we might have drowned her at birth. But she wasn't a bad-looking baby," she added in the deprecatory way in which one tries to conceal family pride.

Craig gave Mady a very straight look. "Do you think you can put up with her, Mady?"

Mady didn't say, "She's part of the reason for our marriage." She said, instead, "Well, candidly, I'm not sure. I can try."

Craig's eyes warmed; they had always been friends.

Inez went cautiously through the room, carrying the coffee tray, biting her lip tensely for fear she might drop something. Craig, Mady and Mirabel followed her to the living room, where she placed the tray on the table beside the rail.

Mady had to pour coffee and did, and wouldn't so much as glance at the historic piece, but she could almost see it, exactly as it was when she had picked it out of the sand and sagebrush. Her hand with the tiny cups was not too steady.

"I wonder what Rhoda — or anybody at Boyce's ranch — can tell the police," Mirabel said.

It was a paramount question. Nobody spoke for a moment. Sancho then took a hand, or rather four paws, in the situation, for he came bounding in, every short black curl alive, his black eyes dancing, and plunged for the coffee tray. He wagged his tail and put a beseeching paw on Mady's knee. "Is he permitted sugar?" Mady asked Craig.

Craig shrugged. "I suppose so. Try him."

So she offered the dog a piece of sugar, which disappeared without even a visible gulp on Sancho's part.

"Inhaled it," Craig said. "Another can't hurt him."

"Not more than two," Susan said sedately, trotting into the room.

"All right," Craig said. "Now to bed, both of you. Did Boyce's boy bring over your baggage, Mirabel?"

"Oh, yes. In the pickup truck, this

morning. They brought Sancho's cushion, too."

It was domestic and warming and everyday. And the previous afternoon Guy Casso had come and pushed Mady back into the sofa, and while she struggled against him Mirabel and Susan had come and stood, staring, in the doorway. She tried not to think of the sprawled figure in the sand, with his natty clothing, his over-manicured nails and the back of his head.

Craig said, "Bed for you, too, Mady. The sheriff and the police are coming back here after they've questioned Boyce and Edith and the rest of them. They want to talk to the hands here, everybody. No sense in your staying up for all this. I'll not wake you when they leave. Try to sleep."

Mirabel was quick on the uptake; clearly Craig wanted both of them out of the way. She rose. "Goodnight, Craig."

So they went upstairs, leaving Craig sitting over his coffee, the rail which had killed Guy Casso within reach of his hands.

That night no coyotes circled down from the hills to jeer as if with wicked glee. Instead there were lights flashing, it seemed to Mady, all over the ranch. She sat for a long time in the wide window seat in Craig's room with the lights in the room

71

turned off, watching. She had found no better hiding place for her gloves. In the end she washed them again, thoroughly, in the hope of doing away with any slight trace of blood, dried them as best she could, and simply put them back in the attaché case. She didn't feel easy about them. She watched the lights bob here and there from bunkhouse to sheds to the guest cabins among the clump of cottonwoods not far from the house. It was late when the lights bobbed back toward the house, and eventually night silence settled over the ranch. The stars slowly began to slide away out of sight, as if a veil were coming down from the mountains.

There was only the faint murmur of voices from below. Finally she went to her own small room beyond the dressing room but could not sleep. As happened in all old houses, at night the special character of El Rancho seemed to take over, rustle and whisper softly, make itself known.

She didn't hear Craig come upstairs; she watched the way the starlight changed, growing dimmer and dimmer until it was entirely blotted out. Eventually however she slept; when she awoke, late and feeling as if she had been drugged, there was a note from Craig.

It lay on her bedside table. "Glad you slept late. Sheriff is here. Come to my study but have your breakfast first."

It was about nine-thirty, very late by ranch standards. When Mady looked out the south windows it seemed to her that there was an unusual number of ranch hands working around the stables and corrals near the house. The sky was heavy and the rim of the mountains toward the west was touched with startling white against a gray sky.

It seemed too late to expect Manuel and Inez to bring a breakfast tray upstairs, so Mady went down to the kitchen for breakfast and found it a curiously welcoming place, for Manuel gave her an approving look and hastened to make fresh coffee and a fresh batch of batter for flapjacks, and Inez set a place for her at the long wooden table, so scrubbed that it was white. Everything was shining, clean and subtly comforting in its domesticity. The table faced the windows; there were lights turned on in the kitchen that dull gray day.

"It's an early snow," Manuel said, putting down fragrant coffee and a stack of feathery flapjacks. When she asked, he said that Susan and Mirabel had already eaten.

73

The clock on the wall by then showed it to be nearly ten.

As Mady tucked into the flapjacks she wished again that she could get rid of the gloves. She wished, too, that she could get rid of the rail, but its disappearance alone would suggest the use to which it had been put. She knew that Craig had not murdered Casso, first because he said he hadn't, second because he had no motive; he had no thirst for revenge at all. But third, and in its way the most important fact, was the plain truth: Craig would not have been such a fool as to kill a man with a weapon from his own house, easily identified, and then left at the scene of the murder.

Yet Mady wasn't sure that the reasons which convinced her that Craig had not murdered Casso would convince a jury. She drank a second cup of coffee and went to Craig's study.

She knocked, and Craig said, "Oh, come in, Mady." So she did, and he and the sheriff both rose. The sheriff said good morning and Craig motioned her to a deep chair near his own. "We've been talking Wilsonite, industrial spies and foreign spies," Craig said.

Mady settled herself in the low chair beside Craig. The sheriff rolled a cigarette thoughtfully and said, "When you were a kid you were always interested in geology. I can remember your prowling all over that old silver mine that your great-grandfather worked out in his time. Never thought you'd come up with anything like Wilsonite."

"I didn't either," Craig said. "Not really."

"Wish I'd put some money into developing it. Mirabel helped back you, didn't she?"

"Yes, all she could."

"Boyce?"

"No. He didn't have any faith in it."

"Lots of people around here thought you were riding a hobby horse. Well, they were wrong. Now this stuff Wilsonite is an alloy. Tough, but flexible. You had that spur line run out from Wilson City, send the ore by flatcars to the main line and then to the mills."

"Right. The Flanker Mills. They extract Wilsonite."

"And there's nothing secret about it?"

"Nothing. I just happened to be the first to discover its uses, get a patent on its method of extracting, and market it. There are certainly other large deposits to be found."

"That's why you've been buying up or leasing some of the old silver mines around these parts?"

Craig laughed. "So you know about that. I'd like to see what I can find in those old mines. Maybe nothing."

"Maybe something," the sheriff said. "You've got a good head on your shoulders, Craig. Now, you say no spy — I mean no foreign spy and no industrial spy — would take too hearty an interest in Wilsonite."

"Not a chance," Craig said definitely. "As I said, there's just nothing secret about it. Right now I have the market. That won't last. I do have a useful patent. I want to poke around those old mines, yes. I might find something else. Also the price of silver has gone up and methods of extracting silver have improved. I may get something from the mines. But you're barking up the wrong tree, Sheriff, if you think Wilsonite could possibly account for Casso's murder."

"It accounts for the fact that you are a very rich man."

Craig caught the implication at once. "Nobody is trying to blackmail me, Sheriff. There wouldn't be any point in it. I am not a target."

The sheriff said slowly, "Maybe every rich man is a target, one way or another. I've got to ask a kind of personal question. Does your former — does Mrs. Rhoda want more money now that you're so rich?"

Craig looked at Mady. "I want to talk this over with Mady before I decide anything. But I expect you know that at the time of our divorce Rhoda received a cash sum and alimony. She waived any community property settlement. I scraped up everything I could."

"Two hundred thousand dollars plus regular alimony," said the sheriff.

Craig smiled. "I suppose everybody around here knew all about it. I had to borrow from Aunt Mirabel. I was in a kind of low state just then, developing Wilsonite. I needed every penny. But yes, Rhoda is out of cash. I can now afford to give her a larger alimony, and if Mady agrees, I'll do that."

Mady felt an odd sense of something like relief at Craig's flat and frank statement; so Rhoda had come only to ask for more money. She put her hand on Craig's arm. Without looking at her he put his hand over hers. "I think we can call that settled," he said to the sheriff.

"Stick to it, Craig," the sheriff said shortly. "By the way, Mrs. Rhoda did go into that dress store in Wilson City yesterday. But it seems that alibi Mrs. Rhoda gave you, saying she met you at Boyce's place around three o'clock — well, the girls at the Ladies' Toggery aren't sure just when she left the store but they think it was close to four. Give her twenty minutes, say, to drive back to Boyce's —" He shook his head. "I don't know, Craig."

"Well, honestly, I don't know either exactly what time I arrived there. I did have to wait for her. It was late in the afternoon. But," Craig said, "it was a good try on Rhoda's part."

"Mm," said the sheriff, looking thoughtful. He sighed. "As far as I've been able to discover she didn't meet Casso. Yet it does look as if he came here because she's here. Maybe he wanted to make things up with her. Well, I'll let you know how things go. But — I'm an old man, Craig. I've got to ask you to be careful."

"What do you mean?" Craig asked soberly.

The sheriff rose, fiddled with his battered Stetson and said slowly, "I don't exactly know. I've just got a feeling there's something going on here, something more than the murder of a kind of feeble character like Casso."

Craig thought for a moment, eying the sheriff. "All right," he said then. "I believe in hunches, too."

"A hunch can be part reasoning, you know. Part instinct, part the result of experience. Good morning, Mrs. Wilson."

Craig went with him to the door. Mady sat very still in the low chair. Of course Craig could be a target. The rail all but proved that — didn't it?

Craig came back and put his hand under her chin, tipping her face up. "Don't look so worried, Mady. These things always work out somehow. The doctor says Casso was murdered around three or four o'clock. He can't come closer than that. They'll find somebody who came to the ranch and killed him. Now take a ride — no, you'd better not ride today. Don't go far from the house. But get some fresh air. It'll blow away the cobwebs. It's going to snow before we're ready for it. I've got to see what the boys are doing about the stock. I may not be back before dinner. Is that all right?"

Mady rose. "Oh, Craig, of course it's all right."

He put his arm around her shoulders,

went out into the big hall and gathered up a leather windbreaker and gloves. Mady watched him leave, put on her own new leather jacket and went to the dining room, where an enormous bowl of fruit stood on the sideboard. She took a couple of apples for Nellie and went outdoors.

It was strangely, almost eerily, different from the previous day. The air was sharp and cold, as if the wind blew straight down from those snow-covered peaks that looked so strangely white and jagged against the gray sky. She buttoned her coat against the cold, walked around the house and along the lane between the cottonwoods where the guest cabins stood. The cottonwoods loomed up into the gray above; they seemed very high and somehow dry but rugged. The two guest cabins squatted low beneath them; they were fully equipped inside with luxury beds, luxury sofas and rugs, bathrooms and small bar cupboards and fireplaces. Statesmen had slept in them; scientists had slept in them. The presidents and officers of big industrial firms had slept there. Once a prime minister had strolled through the cottonwoods and spent the night in a cabin. The doors were bolted on the outside merely to keep out sand and animals. There were no locks on the inside.

Mady strolled around the end of the west cabin, past the clump of cottonwoods and then back toward the sheds and corrals. She saw Craig's jeep plunge over a sandy rise toward the south. There were still two or three men seeming to be very busy nearby and keeping watchful eyes on anything that moved. One of the hands met her and took off his Stetson with the usual courtesy of the land when he passed. Craig had told Mady that the soft voices and the courtesy of the country were partially due to the fact that in earlier times it was more or less important to assure a stranger of one's amicable intentions. It had been a land, and not so very long ago, where men settled a difference very swiftly and decisively; the difference might be ephemeral but the settling was permanent. In Craig's study there was a gun cabinet, so fully furnished that it startled Mady. He kept it securely locked.

However, he told her that when the ranch hands were moving cattle, riding the fences, in fact most of the time, some of them carried carbines; sometimes there was a calf with a broken leg, sometimes a cow had been hurt, sometimes a marauding animal had crept out of a canyon or down from one of the hills and had to be summarily dealt with. Craig permitted firearms to be carried only by trusted men and proven good shots, but the ranch was enormous to Mady's town-bred eyes and she wondered how anybody ever could know everything that went on in that wide and rugged country.

Craig had told her, too, that there still existed a form of cattle rustling, a very up-to-date and modern form, whereby trucks were driven close to some distant grazing land, fences cut, cattle roped and put on the trucks, hauled swiftly away and then sold to some outlaw dealer. No matter how alert the hands were, fewer cattle were moved in for the roundup than there should be. It was one of the hazards of ranching.

Nellie saw Mady as she approached the corrals nearest the horse barns and came galloping to meet her. Some brood mares looked on with interest when she gave Nellie an apple. Craig had begun to breed a strain of quarter horses, and one of them, a colt, came close to her and then took fright, whirled around with the fantastic agility of a quarter horse, and galloped off to find his mother. Some sturdy, smart cow ponies eyed her over another fence. Horses are gregarious and also very inquisitive. By the time Nellie had finished her second apple, there was quite a circle of longing but friendly eyes near them, watching. Nellie mumbled at Mady's now empty palm with soft lips, sighed gustily and then just stood there beside her.

Mady leaned on the top rail of the corral; she didn't have the courage to hoist herself up on the rail and sit there, leaning her elbows on her knees as seemed to be the custom. She was of course in the tenderfoot stage and didn't want any of the men to see her adopt their time-honored pose quite so quickly. The old ranch dog, Willy, came up to her and wagged his tail when she spoke to him. He was ancient, rough-coated and white-nosed but he could be trusted to announce any intruder and to threaten the coyotes into slinking away to their lairs. He hadn't, apparently, barked at someone who had contrived to come upon his territory the day before; but perhaps he had barked and nobody had paid any attention to him.

It was sharply cold. Mady muttered dog talk to Willy for a while, gave Nellie a pat and strolled back to the house. A few tiny snowflakes fell, stinging her face. Willy went with her as far as the front door, where with a rather mournful look he departed. She had a notion that he knew perfectly well that Sancho had the run of the house and didn't exactly like it, but Willy was not a dog to hold a grudge.

Mirabel, Susan and Mady had lunch together in the dining room. Mirabel had seen some of the state police that morning. "They took the back road, on the other side of the cottonwoods. Maybe you didn't see them. I suppose they went again to the arroyo where Casso was found. Of course, the sheriff was here, too. I saw him leaving. Any news?"

"Not that I know about."

Susan didn't appear even to listen. Indeed Susan, for what developed was her own reason, was remarkably silent and agreeable. Indian Joe appeared as soon as lunch was over; he was to take Susan, Sancho and Mirabel into Wilson City to see the veterinarian.

"It's his last puppy shot," Susan said, shoving her arms into her leather jacket and looking very pretty and very childish in her blue jeans and shirt and high-heeled boots.

Indian Joe said seriously to Mady, "I'm sorry I didn't go riding with you yesterday, ma'am. I'm sorry you found that man and you were all alone."

"I shouldn't have gone out like that alone," she said. "I was too smart for my own good."

He gave her a look of hearty accord but was too polite to say what he thought. He said, instead, "Mr. Wilson told me to ask you to stay in the house this afternoon while I'm gone. Some of the boys are around the place, nearby. But if you feel at all frightened, come with us. Or we can put off the puppy shots. It's not that important."

"Oh, thank you. No — I'm not frightened."

Susan shouted from the car, "Hurry up, Joe."

He waited a moment, and Mady said again, more firmly, "Of course I'm not frightened."

He went rather reluctantly out to the car. And presently the house grew very still. For a while there was a subdued clatter from the kitchen and then apparently Inez went off to her own room and Manuel disappeared to his room off the kitchen. Mady was alone when Rhoda opened the door and walked in.

Mady heard her footsteps in the hall, the little click of high-heeled boots to which she was becoming accustomed. Then a pleasant, light voice said, "Anybody at home?" and Rhoda appeared in the living room door. Mady was sitting there, on the window seat, wishing the rail didn't tug at her as if for recognition. She rose when she saw Rhoda.

She knew Rhoda at once, of course. She looked lovely. Her tight jeans were very tight and her green scarf was the exact emerald-green of her eyes. She said, smiling, "I hoped I'd find you alone. I knew that old Mirabel and Susan were to take that dog to get his shots. I'll say what I've come to say. You're still in love with Jim Marsh, aren't you?" She didn't wait for an answer; her green eyes were bright and piercing. She gave a little nod. "I thought so. I want my daughter and I want my husband back. You want Jim. Let's make a deal."

Chapter 5

She waited a moment, then crossed to the table, stripped off her heavy gloves and dropped them — beside the rail, of course; it was beginning to seem like a magnet. She slid out of her brown suede jacket; it fell in gentle folds on a chair.

She went on, almost casually, lightly, too. "A simple trade. Jim will come out here to see you. You two will make up your quarrel. You tell Craig you made a mistake in marrying him. Trust me —" Rhoda said with a pleasant sparkle in her eyes. "Trust me to get him back again. Then I'll have my daughter, too. For goodness' sake, sit down; don't stand there like a wooden Indian."

Mady got her breath. "I feel like a wooden Indian. What on earth made you think I would listen to you, Mrs. —" Rhoda's name caught Mady in full flight. Formerly, on the occasions when Rhoda had dropped in at the office — Mady suspected it was to ask Craig for money — she had, of course, called her Mrs. Wilson.

She was still Mrs. Wilson, but Mady was Mrs. Wilson, too.

Rhoda laughed; she had a very pretty, musical laugh. "Better call me Rhoda. We're now — well, I suppose we might say relatives. No, that's not right. Connections? Well, it doesn't matter. Call me Rhoda. Your name is Mady Wingate, isn't it? Your father's some sort of teacher somewhere."

A quick wave of homesick affection for her father touched Mady. He was a chemist; he taught at Ambleton University; he lived in a sort of ivory tower, really, but had emerged long enough to talk to Craig of Wilsonite several times, and that was how Mady happened to meet Craig. She had barely finished her secretarial course, and Craig himself had suggested that there might be a place for her in his office.

She said, "My name is Mady Wilson. There's no use in talking to me of Susan's custody. Craig is her father."

Rhoda smiled. "But I'm her mother," she said almost lazily and looked around the room.

She was slimmer than when Mady had seen her those few times in the office; she had then looked a trifle on the lush and slightly blowzy side, but if at that time she had been drinking, too often, too much, as Mirabel had said, it seemed to Mady that she must have stopped it, for now her really beautiful face was slender and fine. She had a fair complexion; her green eyes were deep-set, with long dark lashes and neatly curved black eyebrows. Her red hair was long, too, and done up in a handsome thick coil on top of her head. Her mouth was beautiful now too; formerly it had seemed to Mady a little sullen and lax; she now smiled.

Mady wondered for a fleeting second how Rhoda could ever have taken to a man like Guy Casso.

Rhoda rose with a graceful movement, crossed the room, took an enormous vase of late chrysanthemums in her hands, brought it to the long table and put it down carefully. "That's the place for it," she said coolly.

Mady had an odd and thoroughly childish impulse to say, "But I prefer it where it was."

The vase was now standing beside the rail. Rhoda was looking out the window, but it struck Mady that there was something rather fixed and stony about her face. If so, it was a fleeting impression, for Rhoda turned to her and smiled. "These must be the last of Manuel's chrysanthemums. He always kept a little garden plot back of the kitchen. They'll soon be gone. If I know anything about the weather in this place, winter is here today!" She glanced around the room. "You haven't made many changes in the house, have you? But you haven't had time for that. Now then, we're going to have an understanding, you and I. We'll make a deal."

Mady hadn't worked for Craig without picking up some of his vocabulary. She said, "No deal," and rather astonished herself by her own terse firmness.

But Rhoda leaned back and smiled again; Mady really didn't see how anybody could ever resist her. "But what about Jim?"

"I don't want to hear anything of him." Mady wasn't really lying either, because even the sound of his name still had the power to shake her.

"Oh, now, that's not true. You do want to hear of him and you want to see him and you will see him." She was suddenly as pleased as a girl presenting a Christmas present. "Just listen! We fixed it all up in New York. He's coming out here. Edith invited him to stay there. He says he's got to see you."

Mady stared at Rhoda in utter, stunned disbelief. "Jim! But he can't come here. I won't let him come —"

Rhoda smiled. "But he's coming."

Mady shot up from her chair; she didn't know what she was going to do but she knew that Jim must not be permitted to come to Boyce's ranch. Suddenly a small but surprised question struck her. "I didn't know that you and Jim were such good friends."

Rhoda laughed lightly. "Oh, well — we met at some cocktail party. Actually, it was you and Craig who brought us together. Jim told me how he felt. He is really heartbroken. Your wedding day was a couple of weeks or so away. He only had a case of bachelor jitters. He said that he told you perhaps you'd better put off your wedding for a little and that you fired up and said perhaps it had better be put off forever, and before he knew it you'd thrown his ring at him. He was so upset; he admits that he lost his temper, but he didn't mean it. The next thing he knew you were married to Craig."

"That isn't quite as it happened." Mady was appalled to hear the unsteadiness in her voice. She firmed herself up. "None of it matters. I am married to Craig."

"Well, naturally, when you had a chance at all that money of Craig's, you took it. Who wouldn't?"

Rhoda spoke so softly, so gently that it took a few seconds for the stab to reach Mady. Then she said as she started toward the door, "I'm sorry you came to talk to me. If you want to talk to Craig about Susan —"

Rhoda said, "Oh, but I talked to Craig yesterday. I don't like to hurt your feelings. I'm sure you would have done your best to make Craig a good wife — and hostess. But are you quite sure that Craig doesn't regret this sudden marriage?"

Mady wasn't sure of anything except that she wanted Rhoda out of the house, which had once been her house and where she moved a vase of flowers from one table to another as if it were still her house.

Rhoda rose and took up her brown suede jacket. "Well, as I said, Jim is coming here to see you. Jim is still in love with you. Think over what I've told you. I'll see to it that Craig gives you a good settlement."

"Of course, you know that I'll tell Craig all about this — this preposterous idea of yours. A deal!"

Rhoda laughed. "Of course I know you wouldn't be such a fool. Craig does believe that you are in love with Jim. You know it yourself. If you tell Craig what I've told you, why —" Rhoda shrugged. "Craig will tell you to leave. He'll say go ahead. You don't dare tell Craig that I've had the — the kindness to come and talk to you — prepare you," said Rhoda gently.

"I don't call it kindness," Mady said. "And I'm going to tell Craig —"

"Then I'll say you lie," Rhoda said sweetly. "You can't prove an accusation like that. Craig would believe me. And if you antagonize him in that way, you'll not get a big settlement. Better be guided by me. I know Craig better than you."

"I think you'd better leave."

Mady stood aside so Rhoda could pass her.

Rhoda gave another musical gurgle of laughter. "I never thought to be turned out of my own house! But you do it gracefully, I'll admit that. In your place I think I'd make rather a scene. Oh, by the way, I understand Guy was here. He came to see you, it seems. Susan told me —"

"I know what Susan said. I have no idea why he came here. I had never seen him before in my life."

Mady couldn't tell whether or not Rhoda believed her; her green eyes gazed

93

fixedly out the window. There was now a kind of whitish mist, like a veil between them and the snow-capped mountains. Rhoda said, "It's really dreadful, isn't it? Poor Guy!"

She spoke as if she had scarcely known him, as if she were commenting upon some remote event, something that could not conceivably have anything to do with her. Yet the light from the west windows was cruelly clear; it showed small lines around her eyes and chin; it showed a sudden pallor in her pretty face, which just then did not look so pretty. But she lifted her eyebrows, shrugged and said, "A great shock! But it must have been a dreadful accident. Not murder! Actually, Guy meant nothing to me. I told the sheriff and the police last night."

"You took him with you on a rather long trip." Mady could not resist that.

Rhoda turned sharply to Mady. "Suppose I did! That was ages ago. He was a good dancer. Amusing after a fashion. I thought it most unfair of Craig and the judge to give Craig the custody of Susan because of just — a — a whim on my part. Oh," she was beginning to speak more rapidly, "I realize that it was a mistake. I was bored, I suppose. Craig was always so busy.

94

I — but certainly I did not even see Guy yesterday. And if you or anybody else thinks for a minute that — that I killed him, I didn't." She began to pull her gloves over beautiful white hands. "As a matter of fact," she added with a certain deliberation, "it was lucky that I could give Craig an alibi. Otherwise everybody would think he had killed Guy."

"It isn't such a good alibi. The sheriff says the girls in the Ladies' Toggery aren't sure just when you left the store, but they think it was close to four."

Rhoda's green eyes narrowed. "As if they can be depended upon!" she said after a moment. "I know when I left and when I got back to Boyce's place and met Craig. He couldn't have killed Guy. Goodbye. Think over what I've said." There was suddenly an unmistakable ring of honesty in her words. "I came directly to you to give you a chance to withdraw from your marriage easily and simply." With that, she walked out, drawing her suede jacket around her as she went.

Mady couldn't help following her to the front door. She reached it in time to see Rhoda swing herself into the saddle of Boyce's chestnut mare. She was an expert horsewoman; she wouldn't have had to walk home because she couldn't crawl up into a saddle.

Mady then perceived that Rhoda had drawn the mare up to the step of the long Spanish-style veranda and had mounted from there; this gave Mady a wholly disproportionate feeling of satisfaction. Rhoda went off at a jaunty canter, down the long road between the two lines of Lombardy poplars. Rhoda had been right about the sudden onslaught of winter. It was snowing in small, fine flakes and it was very cold. As Rhoda reached the end of the long drive she lifted an arm to wave at a car which passed her. Indian Joe was bringing Susan and Mirabel and, of course, Sancho back from Wilson City.

The car dashed to a halt at the veranda and Sancho bounced out. Susan tumbled after him. Mirabel stepped down firmly, gave herself a vigorous shiver and said, "When you can't see Old Baldy it means weather."

Mady wasn't sure just which mountain they called Old Baldy, but she looked toward the rim of mountains looming behind their white wall of snow and nodded. Mirabel strode into the house, Sancho and Susan disappeared toward the guest cabins, both running as if the snow and cold had some electric quality which charged them with energy, not that either needed such charging, and Indian Joe said he'd brought the mail and handed Mady the locked leather bag. He drove on past the veranda and around the house. She stood for a moment, taking long and extremely cold breaths and thinking of all the things she could have said to Rhoda. She thought quickly enough now that the chance to say them was gone.

She could have said: Jim was lying to you; his case of what you call bachelor jitters was permanent. He is not heartbroken and never was. He had no reluctance whatever to tell me that he didn't want to marry me, almost in so many words.

She could have said: I don't believe that Craig regrets our marriage. He married me because he likes me and trusts me, but I don't believe that he regrets it.

She might have said: Craig intends to give you a larger alimony, but you want far more than that.

Yet she did believe that if she reported Rhoda's visit and her offer of a "deal" to Craig, it would be a mistake. Instinct told her that; she didn't stop to analyze that instinct. And she did believe that Jim was coming and that she had to stop him.

The cold had crept into her bones while she stood there. She went into the house and put the mailbag down on the enormous table in the hall. It had once been a Spanish refectory table, taken from one of the old missions; it now served as a catch-all. The key for the mailbag hung on a little hook beside a mirror. Mady unlocked the bag and shook out letters, magazines and a letter from Jim.

It was sent air mail; it was addressed to Mrs. Craig Wilson, El Rancho del Rio, Wilson City, Nevada; it was dated November third, which was the previous day. Her heart gave a strangling kind of lunge at the sight of Jim's neat handwriting.

She slit the envelope with her thumbnail and took out a single sheet of paper. "My darling," Jim had written. Guy Casso had called Mady his darling, but that was a nightmare, completely inexplicable.

Jim wrote that he was coming to see her. "I was wrong, wrong, wrong. I have to see you. Edith Wilson has invited me to stay there."

He signed it Jim. That was all there was to it.

He couldn't come! Mady wondered how Edith could have been so maladroit, so careless of Craig's feelings and her own as to invite him.

But it was painfully easy to surmise the reason for Edith's invitation and for her meddlesomeness; she intended to encourage Jim to see Mady, encourage her to leave Craig, encourage the whole preposterous plan which Rhoda must have frankly told Edith, because she and Rhoda were old friends.

Perhaps, too, it was because Edith never really liked Craig. Boyce had had his choice of the ranch land, but Craig had made a staggering fortune from the discovery of Wilsonite in his own section, so perhaps she was jealous, too. It could even be that in some way Edith expected to profit by Craig's remarriage to Rhoda. In any event, Edith was on Rhoda's side.

Mady left the rest of the mail spilled out on the table and went up to Craig's big room, taking Jim's letter with her. She sat down there in the deep window seat. She was conscious of the wind and the fine snowflakes brushing the windowpane and of the darkening gray sky. She read Jim's note again, and all at once she didn't believe a word of it.

She believed that he intended to come and stay at Edith's. What she didn't believe was that Jim felt he had been wrong in breaking off their engagement two weeks before their wedding was planned.

There is perhaps in everyone a cruelly clear-eyed observer who sees things one does not wish to see and tells one things one does not wish to hear. That wickedly astute observer had told Mady, long before then, that she had been too thoroughly besotted with her love for Jim; she had shown it too often and too plainly; she had in effect made herself cheap in his eyes, a bargain easily won.

So, this observer now told Mady, Jim's note could be simply the old dog-in-the-manger reaction. Yet so strange are the quirks of the human heart that she touched the note which Jim had touched with longing fingers. She rose at last, tore the letter and the envelope into little pieces and burned them carefully in an ashtray. She had to prevent his coming.

The sky was darkening more rapidly than it had done the previous day when she had found Guy Casso dead along the trail. The snowflakes hissed against the windowpanes. There was the slight smell of burnt paper in the room. She opened the window to air it away and the icy sweep of cold astonished her. Winter,

Rhoda had said. Weather, Manuel had said. Weather, Mirabel had said. All at once they seemed to be very far away from the protection of cities.

Mady swiftly decided to telephone Jim and tell him not to come. She thought that Craig might be coming back to the house soon, so she didn't use the telephone beside her because he would come to his room to change clothes. She went downstairs, intending at least to send a telegram by way of the telephone in Craig's study. Boyce, Edith and Craig were all in the living room. Craig called to her.

They were obviously having a family conference; Edith and Boyce sat on the sofa, Craig near them. He rose when Mady came in, kissed her and put his arm close around her. "Sorry I was so late. I went out to the mine."

Boyce was like Craig and yet unlike him; brothers often are unlike, but the dissimilarity between Craig and Boyce was one of manner and expression as much as anything; they were both tall, both had firm regular features, rather like Mirabel's strong face; both had dark hair and dark eyebrows. Craig's face was always alert, interested and capable of intense concentration. Boyce was very tweedy, very much the gentleman rancher, but there was an odd kind of slackness about his face and a discontented droop to his shoulders, his mouth, his small dark mustache. Mady knew that Boyce was divided between pride about Craig's self-found place in the world and discontent because it had been Craig and not Boyce who had made such a place for himself. Boyce was not the kind of man to attribute Craig's success to hard work and imagination; he called it luck whenever he had a chance. Yet Mady believed he liked Craig.

Edith was a dumpy, yet sharp-featured little woman, with faded blond hair and flat grayish eyes. She was easier to categorize than Boyce, or at least Mady thought so; it seemed to her that Edith was merely a meddlesome, prying woman, who, like Rhoda, hated ranch life and was jealous of Craig's success.

Craig pulled up a chair for Mady, inviting her to join the family. Boyce went on "— so nobody at our place knows anything. Except that maid of Edith's, whatever her name is —"

"Estelle," Edith said. "And a mistake. I'd get rid of her but it is so hard to get any kind of servant in this godforsaken place."

Craig's eyes flickered toward her. "It is

not exactly a godforsaken place, Edith."

"Oh, you can talk! You have old Manuel and that Mexican girl, Inez. Not that I would trust one of them any more than I would trust an Indian. Why, you act as if Indian Joe were one of the family! I don't see how you can."

"You know, Edith," Boyce said, "Indian Joe grew up with us. What I want to tell Craig is that this maid told the police she wasn't sure just when you reached our place and asked for Rhoda. The maid didn't bother to tell Edith that you had come."

Craig nodded. "The police told me that."

"I was out on the west range. Edith didn't see you at all. I do assure you, Craig, that nobody at my place saw this Casso. Nobody knew he was in the vicinity at all. I'd have got him out of the county if I'd known it."

"Well, it's a free country," Craig said. "I don't see how we could have made him leave."

Edith said, "Rhoda was through with him long ago. Perhaps he came to see Rhoda, but if so, she didn't know it, I'm sure. She's really sorry for that silly trip with him, Craig. It was a long time ago.

And she meant nothing, you know." She slid Mady a glance, swift as a lizard's.

Craig said good-naturedly, "That's water over the dam, Edith."

Edith insisted, watching Mady slyly, watching Craig, "It was only a childish impulse of Rhoda's, taking Guy on that trip. You know Rhoda. She was always so attractive and reckless in a way, I suppose."

Boyce said absently, looking out toward the snowy, swift dusk beyond the windows, "She ought to have given a thought to consequences. Taking Casso on a trip with her! Calling him her secretary! Of course, she was drinking pretty heavily then. I think Rhoda is kind of a pushover really, very pretty but stupid."

Craig said, still good-naturedly, "Reckless perhaps."

"He lost her Susan," Boyce said, rose with a grunt as if he were a much older man than he really was and went to the long window. "Looks like a real one, all right. Old Baldy is completely covered."

Edith said, "We should be getting home. The weather reports say it may be heavy."

Boyce said, "I'm sorry, Craig, that Rhoda came here just now. Fact is she phoned Edith a few days ago and practically invited herself. Edith had to let her come."

"That's all right," Craig said.

Boyce fumbled with some books on the table. Mady couldn't help watching as his hands moved close to the rail, but he didn't touch it. He said, "And there's another thing, Craig. I didn't know about it till it was too late to stop him."

Craig said, puzzled, "Stop who?"

Edith was watching Mady. Boyce said, embarrassed, "Oh, this new friend of Rhoda's. This fellow — I mean — well, he's an old friend of Mady's." Boyce blundered along. "He's — that is — his name's Jim Marsh."

The name was out. Boyce stared fixedly at a book. Edith didn't move; it was as if her whole dumpy little body were sending out tentacles to hear and measure.

Craig didn't move for a moment either. Then he said very quietly, "So you invited him, Edith?"

Edith suddenly began to fluster, as if secretly she were a little afraid of Craig. "No, no. That is, not exactly."

Craig waited, Boyce wouldn't turn; as far as he could, he seemed to remove himself, change into a spectator only.

Edith cried, "Rhoda wanted him! It was

Rhoda's idea! I told Rhoda he could come."

Craig stopped her almost in pity. "All right, Edith. I take it that you expect him soon."

"Yes, tonight. Sometime. If the storm permits. He was to fly to Reno, rent a car there and drive here." Edith was now a little puzzled, even disappointed, as if she had expected a more entertaining reaction from Mady or from Craig.

Mady sat as still as the shining rail on the table. So it was too late for her to stop him. But perhaps the snow would stop him. It was a long drive from Reno. Mady looked out the window, but it was now so dark that she could see only the rushing white movement of snow against it.

Boyce said, "He may not be able to get here tonight. Which way was he to come, Edith?"

"I don't know. If he comes by way of Carson City, the roads should still be open."

"I wouldn't count on it. If he takes the Geiger Grade and gets to Virginia City, he's going to run into heavy snow —"

There was a flurry as Susan and Sancho galloped into the room. Susan flung herself at Edith, clasping her around her waist as if she adored her, as she didn't. Sancho, that mischievous, terrible, happy clown of a dog, flung something up into the air, caught it with his teeth and worried it.

Craig said, "What has he got, Susan? Better take — Why," he went on, going over to the dog, "he's got somebody's glove. Here now, we can't have this, old fellow. Where did he get it?"

He took one of Mady's pigskin gloves from Sancho, who happily permitted it and then stood wagging his tail, eyes gleaming, begging Craig to throw it for him.

So Mady knew why Susan had been so silent and had avoided her eyes at lunch. She and Sancho had taken a good rummage through everything in Mady's room.

Chapter 6

Susan buried her head harder against Edith, and Edith seemed surprised at this display of affection. Craig looked at the glove and said, "Why, this looks like one of your gloves, Mady."

And at that moment Sancho began to claw at his mouth and Mady realized that he had something caught in his teeth, which were remarkably big and strong for a puppy. So she went to him, knelt down, reached into his cavernous mouth and extracted a piece of pigskin snarled around one of those same white teeth. Sancho accepted her assistance with pleasure, thanked her by shoving his head against her arm and gave her an excuse for the wetness of the glove.

"It does look like one of mine." Mady surveyed the remains in Craig's hand. "He's certainly chewed it." She got to her feet, caught a swift glance from Susan behind the curtain of her hair and decided to let her off this time. In fact, however, Mady knew that she was at the same time protecting herself. She said, "I wonder where I left them. I think I put them in an old attaché case — Oh, it doesn't matter."

Susan became very still. Sancho sprawled out his enormous front paws and invited Mady to have a romp with him. Craig said, "He's your dog, Susan. You'll have to buy Mady another pair of gloves out of your allowance."

"No, I —" Susan stopped, thought a moment and said almost dreamily, "I wonder where the other glove is."

This was too much for Mady. She said, "Don't you know where it is, Susan?"

Craig turned sternly to Susan. "How did Sancho get hold of this glove?"

Susan for once looked a little frightened; then she shoved her face against Edith's green tweed jacket. "I expect he just — found it somewhere."

Mady thought she caught a rather beseeching tone in Susan's voice. She said, "A puppy is bound to tear up a few things." And at that moment Manuel came in carrying the enormous silver cocktail tray.

Edith said quickly, "How late it is! We really must be going home, Boyce."

Craig, ever polite, said, "Something to drink first," and went to the table.

109

Mady watched him pour Edith a drink, which rather surprisingly she took neat, and thought, It isn't fair. Jim shouldn't have come without giving me a chance to stop him; Edith shouldn't have invited him. Edith's drink didn't choke her as Mady rather hoped it would; she didn't even cough.

Craig, filling up Boyce's glass with soda water, said in a casual way, over his shoulder, "Edith, I want to make something clear. Your guests and your choice of guests are your own affair. I'll not have Jim Marsh in my house." He handed Boyce the glass and said in a pleasant, even tone, "You do understand?"

Edith saw a chance to stab and did it. She said quickly, "I do indeed understand, Craig. He and Mady — dear me, I do understand."

Craig gave Edith a long, straight look, so very straight that a surge of splotchy color came to her face. Boyce said hurriedly that they must leave. "Wouldn't be the first time we've had a sudden bad blizzard this early," he said. "My boys got in some of the late calves this afternoon, but I don't know about the Dry Gulch range. Have to talk to my foreman. Come on, Edith. Thanks for the drink."

Edith put down her glass, not a drop left. Mady wondered how she could drink it so fast. And as everyone started to leave, Mady walked across the room and dropped the soggy remains of her glove into a basket of enormous sugar pine cones near the fireplace. Susan watched her carefully.

They said goodbyes, luckily brief, for Boyce spoke the obvious truth when he said that there might be a blizzard. Craig walked to the door with them and Mady went with Craig. Boyce's car stood outside; it was already covered with white, so it looked rather ghostly.

The car door banged; headlights made wavering lanes through the slanting lines of snow. Craig went to the end of the long veranda and stood there facing west and then north, actually lifting his nose and sniffing the air. He came back to Mady. "It's getting worse. Go back in the house before you freeze, Mady." His voice was kind, yet suddenly cool and formal. "I've got to see Indian Joe. George is away. George is the foreman," he explained, still with an unusual kind of formality and quite as if she had not taken many letters to George Eldred over the past years. "Feels as if we are in for a bad one. It's the

111

very devil when the snows come so soon. I'll get my coat."

His leather windbreaker lay over the catch-all table in the hall. He shrugged himself into it, said absently yet again with a rather chill formality that they musn't wait dinner, he might be late, and disappeared into the darkness and snow.

Mady drifted upstairs, glanced around her room, which showed no signs at all of the rummage Susan had given it, decided that Susan showed every sign of developing into a good second-story worker and that possibly Craig was right in considering a penitentiary, took a bath, changed clothes and went downstairs, where she sipped sherry with Mirabel. The rail stood on the table near Mady.

She thought of Rhoda's suddenly stony face as she stood at the table, above the chrysanthemums and the rail. Yet Mady could not be at all sure that it wasn't her own guilty imagination that had suggested some kind of awareness on Rhoda's part. Certainly that imagination could not picture Rhoda meeting Casso and somehow killing him with the rail. She could not be certain of anything, except that she began to debate with herself about telling Craig of the rail and the use to which her gloves had been put.

Snow sighed and murmured against the windows. Mirabel took a second sherry and said it was a bad night, which was rather obvious.

"I didn't come down to see Edith and Boyce," Mirabel went on. "I never could bear Edith. Looks of a hen. Brains of a hen, too. Except" — Mirabel thought for a moment — "except she's shrewd, too, when she wants to be. You wouldn't believe how attractive she was when Boyce married her. Came out from the East. On a pack trip in the Sierras. I don't remember how Boyce happened to join the party; anyway, he did. Next thing I knew she was engaged to Boyce — not before she saw his ranch though," said Mirabel with one of her flashes of dry cynicism.

She asked for more sherry. "My third," she said smugly. "They can call sherry an old ladies' drink if they want to. It has plenty of alcohol in it. What did Rhoda want this afternoon?"

Mady was becoming accustomed to the Wilson candor. "Oh, you saw her leaving."

"Cantering along as if she still owned the place. She shouldn't have come here, you know. Susan can go to see Rhoda any time she wants to while Rhoda is here.

113

Which," Mirabel addressed herself to her third sherry, "which I hope and trust will not be long. If Boyce hadn't been worn down by Edith, he'd have had the backbone to phone Rhoda and tell her to stay away."

And Boyce should have had the tact, to say nothing of the good sense, to tell Jim to stay away.

Mady followed Mirabel's example and drank more sherry, with the result that she felt a little better until after dinner and then worse. She hoped the storm would prevent or at least delay Jim's arrival.

Susan had turned up at dinner but was quiet and slid only an occasional guarded glance at Mady. Craig did not come back.

"It's the stock that's the problem," Mirabel said. "They're out on the range now. Trouble is they go with the wind; they get the snow at their backs. So sooner or later they wind up at a fence and just huddle together. This storm has caught everybody by surprise. Usually the stockmen are warned. But the weatherman can't call every shot in time. Things happen here too fast. Well, Craig and the boys will do their best. You'd better go to bed. No telling when Craig will come in."

It was after midnight when he came in.

114

Mady heard him and went down to the kitchen in her warmest dressing gown to fix hot coffee for him, but Manuel or Inez had been ahead of her. There was a thermos of coffee and a great plate of sandwiches. Craig looked tired and pale under the brightly fluorescent lights of the gleaming yet somehow old-fashioned and domestic room. They sat at the enormous kitchen table and he wolfed down sandwiches and drank coffee so hot it steamed. "We'll lose some stock. Can't help it. Some of the boys will be out all night. I've got a good outfit here. Loyal, efficient. Have some coffee?"

Mady got another cup and had some coffee. Craig eyed her. "Don't let this upset you. It's not the first time we've had an early blizzard. Not the first time it has swept down so fast that we couldn't get warnings of it. This morning it didn't look so bad. Mady —" His voice changed subtly. It was formal again. "There's something I have to say. Of course, it's plain as a pikestaff that Rhoda is a friend of your friend Marsh, and why she wanted him to come here."

"Craig —"

"Rhoda hopes that you'll regret your marriage to me, go back to Marsh and —"

115

Craig's face was unreadable. He said rather dryly, "Rhoda is out of money. Susan is our daughter. She feels that with you out of the way, we — Rhoda and I — might resume our marriage. I'm richer now than I was when we were divorced. But that is beside the point just now. I told Edith I will not have this man, Jim Marsh, on my place."

Mady put down her cup so hard it rattled. "Craig, I didn't know he was coming. That is, I did know it but —"

"You knew it," Craig said softly.

"Rhoda told me that he was coming."

"Rhoda! When?"

"She was here today. This afternoon. She —" She offered a deal, Mady thought. She said, "She told me that Jim was coming. And then I had a letter from him. Just a note. It was mailed in New York yesterday. Air mail. I was going to try to phone him or send a wire telling him not to come when I came down this afternoon late and Edith and Boyce were here and I couldn't use the phone in your study. Then Edith said they expected him tonight."

He took another sandwich. "So he's coming to see you," he said flatly. "He said in his letter, probably, that he regretted having left you in the lurch just before your

116

marriage. He said, or implied, that he was wrong, that he is still in love with you and that he wants you to leave me and marry him."

"Not like that. I'll tell you exactly what he said."

"No need. I can guess enough. Boyce was a fool to let him come. But then it wasn't Boyce, it was Edith. And Rhoda."

Instinct was wrong, Mady decided swiftly. "Rhoda came here to — she said to make a deal with me. She said that she would see to it that you gave me a big settlement if I would leave you and go back to Jim —" No, Mady thought then, swiftly too; instinct had been right. She should not have told Craig like that.

Craig's face was hard; his voice stiff. "And I suppose you said no. Very proper, I'm sure." He rose. "I'm tired. I'll have to be up and out at dawn."

They turned out the kitchen lights. They made their way up the wide stairs through the silent house; the only sound was that of the wind-driven snow pushing at it as if it had hands. Craig glanced down at Mady and smiled, his face more friendly and natural. "Don't worry. This old house has taken many a storm, worse than this. The old part of the house even resisted Indian attacks."

They had reached the top of the stairs, where a lamp was lit, and he could see Mady's face clearly. He looked hard at her for a second. "Has Susan been up to any little tricks? She did search your room, I suppose. That's how Sancho got your glove."

Of course Susan had the other glove; she had already made far too close a guess as to Mady's having cleaned off something, not the tomahawk, but something. Mady made up her mind swiftly again, although again it might be a mistake. "It was my glove. Probably she has the other glove. They were both bloodstained."

His face was all at once white. "My God, Mady! You didn't kill that rat Casso!"

"No! Oh, no. But I didn't tell you every-thing."

"If he came after you again, if he —"

"No, no. Listen —"

"Come in here." He took her arm in a hard grip and led her into his room. The heavy Spanish armoire, the great leather chairs looked as if they could withstand anything. He closed the door carefully. "All right. Now —"

As she told him of finding the rail, the movement and life seemed to come back into his face. At the end he sighed and wiped his forehead with the back of his hand. "It's not as bad as I thought. There for a moment I really was afraid that he'd come upon you out there on the trail and that you'd hit him somehow with the first rock you could find and — well, you didn't."

"No. But I washed off the rail. I told you. I washed it as hard as I could but there may still be some traces of blood."

He thought for a moment. "I don't know. If anybody knew what to look for, yes, I suppose some traces might still be found."

"You're not going to tell the sheriff or the police! I was so afraid you would and they'd say that you had reason to kill him!"

"I'll get your glove from Susan," he said in an absent way, as if he hadn't heard her at all. He had heard, however, for he added, "No. I don't think at this time I'll tell Sam Hawkins. I ought to, of course, for clearly whoever killed Casso had to have come into this house, had to know about that piece of the rail, had to get Casso out along a trail on my ranch and contrive to hit him over the head with that thing. But I don't think I'll tell Sam just yet. It narrows things down in a way that can be very unpleasant for all of us."

He shoved one hand across his forehead wearily. "Casso must have come here hoping to see Rhoda. He may have got a notion that he could get something out of her — money is the likeliest reason. But Rhoda told the sheriff that she hadn't seen him. The sheriff asked her about his family, his friends, and she said she knew nothing about him!"

"But —"

He nodded. "Yes, I know. It seems as if she must have known something of him. Yet she says she didn't and I think she's telling the truth. She picked him up in some London night spot, I know that. He wasn't British though. She told Sam that she doesn't know where he was born. He must have had a passport somewhere. Sam says he doesn't know anybody to notify about his murder and doesn't even know what to do with the body."

"But he must have had some sort of identification."

"A driving license from New York. Two or three credit cards. The addresses were different, every one of them. Sam is trying to trace someone who knew him through the addresses he gave, but it looks as if he'd been traveling around." He rose, went to the window and drew back the curtains. "Getting worse," he said. "Like what they used to call a Washoe Zephyr."

"A what?"

"Washoe Zephyr." He came back and lighted a cigarette. "We're quite a distance from the Washoe Valley but still we get something like a real old Washoe Zephyr once in a while. We have a formation of hills, mountains, valleys so sometimes a storm can whirl along the valley like a hurricane. Devilish. The old-timers, the miners, would see their workings, their huts, everything swept away. That's past history. Go to bed, Mady. I'll think things over. I'll get the glove from Susan."

He strolled with her through his dressing room into her room and then said, again with that new and rather chill formality, "You'll remember our bargain, Mady?"

"Our — ? Oh —"

"You were to have everything I could give you to make you comfortable for the rest of your life — money" — he shrugged — "protection. You were to do your best to help me put the fear of God or the law into Susan. I'll live up to my share of our bargain. I expect you to live up to your share of it."

"I didn't want Jim to come."

Craig did not speak of Rhoda or her offer of a deal. He said, "But you're still in love with him," and went out, closing the door behind him.

Chapter 7

The storm kept up all night. Dawn was streaking in when Mady heard Craig tiptoe down the stairs, and she smelled the early breakfast which Manuel, accustomed to life on the ranch, had risen to cook. When she went down, again in her red dressing gown, Craig had already gone. So she sat at the kitchen table, soaking up the comfort and warmth of the room, and devoured everything Manuel set before her.

Susan appeared in the middle of breakfast, sat down opposite Mady and also ate incredibly large helpings of bacon, eggs and flapjacks. Sancho was with her, and she told Manuel crossly that she'd had the dog out and if he didn't believe her he could feel Sancho's coat, which was indeed so wet that the black curls had crinkled up and his usually handsome pompadour lay in wet strings over the sparkling black eyes. Susan gave him bacon, and Manuel saw it but only grunted.

Inez came in sleepily, and Manuel told her it was high time she got busy. Susan and Mady went back upstairs. Once they were on the stairs Susan said, "When did you take your glove out of my room?"

Mady stopped to look at her. "I didn't."

"Somebody did."

"Why did you take the glove from my room?"

"Because I wanted to," she replied.

"Why did you rummage in my attaché case?"

"Because I was curious," she replied, again with true Wilson candor.

"You are not to do that again."

"You didn't tell on me last night. I know why. You were afraid I'd tell how wet the gloves were. You cleaned off the tomahawk and got bloodstains on your gloves, so you tried to wash them and then you hid them, in your attaché case. So you see, you didn't tell my father —"

"Oh, but I did. Last night."

Susan turned wide, sparkling eyes toward Mady. "I see! You got ahead of me. You were afraid I'd tell it. Did you tell the truth about the tomahawk?"

"Susan, I didn't touch that tomahawk. It is exactly where, I suppose, it's been for the last — I don't know how many years —"

"Since Great-Grandfather's time."

"Well, then, since his time. I'd advise you to forget your notion about the tomahawk."

"Then why did you wash your gloves?"

"Because I wanted to wash them," Mady said, stealing a page from Susan's book, and let herself into her own room. She felt slightly battered. She had already discovered that this was not an unusual result of an encounter with Susan.

It was a strange, unreal kind of day.

Mady could see little beyond the swirls of snow beating against the windows; sometimes the dark shape of stable or hay barn or shed would loom up for an instant and then vanish; sometimes lights in the bunkhouse would glimmer for an instant or two and then also vanish behind swift curtains of snow. Once or twice she saw the headlights of one of the ranch jeeps or pickup trucks shine dimly through the wild white whirlwind.

She didn't know whether or not Jim had arrived.

In the afternoon the telephone wires went down and the electric power also went off. Manuel's transistor radio announced that electric wires were down all over the county. He said glumly that it didn't matter about cooking; the electric stove was cut off but there was also a gas stove with a plentiful supply of bottled gas for exactly this kind of emergency. The frozen foods would stay frozen for some hours. But a problem would be heat; the furnace was operated electrically. He snared two of the ranch hands from somewhere and they began stacking logs of wood on the front veranda.

There were several fireplaces in the house: a big one in the living room, another large one in the dining room. Craig's study was a smaller room than most of the others and easier to heat, so as the afternoon wore on and a chill began to creep over the thick floors, Mady and Mirabel and Susan put on heavy woolen socks and grouped themselves around the fireplace in Craig's study.

The lights of course had gone at once. Manuel was prepared for that; he brought out big old-fashioned lamps filled with kerosene, which smelled vilely, and set them at strategic intervals around the house: two in the big living room, one on the long Spanish table in the hall, one in Craig's study. Its soft light seemed to accord with the room, so it came to life in a different and lovely way. It had been the living room of the old part of the house, with low ceilings, white plastered walls where there were now bookshelves and a small but deep fireplace. Craig's big desk stood at the end of the room; there were worn leather chairs, Navajo rugs and an enormous table stacked with newspapers and magazines. Craig's library of books on geology, chemistry and mineralogy, all well worn, was here.

The locked gun cabinet was built beside the fireplace. The tomahawk hung above the fireplace and looked rather dusty. Some ancient cattle-branding irons hung beside it. Now, Craig had told Mady, since the entire herd was purebred they had stopped branding and used tattoo marks instead.

Mady and Mirabel settled down in the study, Mirabel with a book which she didn't read, for both of them kept listening and going to the windows to try to see through the storm. Susan and Sancho soon went out to the kitchen.

Without seeing them arrive, Mady and Mirabel suddenly heard the voices of Boyce, Edith, Rhoda and Jim in the hall. Edith came into the study first, her hen's eyes very bright and red splotches on her cheeks. "We had to come! The power's gone and we have no heat at all and no way to cook. I told Boyce ages ago to get us a gas range, but he didn't."

"You mean," said Mirabel directly, "that you want to stay here? You and your guests?"

"What else can we do?" Edith cried. "There's only that terrible motel in Wilson City, probably ice-cold. We can't stay in our house and freeze to death and starve, too, can we? Surely Craig couldn't be so inhospitable as to send us home again." Her eyes shifted brightly to the windows. "The storm is growing so much worse, I don't think we could get back home again. It was all we could do to make it along the road as it is. There aren't any snowplows out, of course. We're so far from everything here. I suppose we'll lose almost all our stock —"

"Oh, not all, surely," Mirabel said. "We've seen storms like this before and have come through them all right."

Rhoda said clearly and musically in the hall, "Oh there'll be good fires! There's an enormous stack of logs outside. And of course there are those two guest cabins, fireplaces there, too. You and Edith take the first cabin. Jim, you can take the second cabin. I'll stay in the main house. There's plenty of room really for all of us.

Plenty of food too, if I know Manuel. We may not be here," Rhoda said lightly, "more than a few days at the most —"

Mirabel turned to Mady. It was the first time, in fact, that she or anyone had turned to her for a decision from the hostess, the lady of the house. "What are you going to do, Mady?"

She had to say that she didn't know. "Craig should be at home by dinnertime. He'll decide." But all the same she knew that in sheer humanity she couldn't turn these unwelcome guests out of the house, and one of them would be more than unwelcome to Craig.

As she was thinking that she didn't want to see Jim; she didn't want to hear his voice; and she certainly didn't want Rhoda to stay in the house, Jim came to the door of the study and just stood there, looking at her.

He was exactly the same, tall and well built, his light hair ruffled from the parka which he must have borrowed from Boyce; the hood hung down over his shoulders. His eyes were dancing; he smiled mischievously.

Her heart seemed to leap in her throat. She couldn't move; she didn't dare move, and she felt that Jim, Mirabel, even the people out in the hall, taking off their coats, could sense the paralysis that had caught her.

Mirabel eyed him coldly. She said, "I take it you are James Marsh."

He glanced at her. "They usually call me Jim. I expect you've heard of me," he said softly.

Mirabel's eyes blazed. Mady overcame the stifled, painful throb in her throat and said, "May I present James Marsh? This is Miss Wilson, Jim."

The "Jim" came out really quite easily and naturally.

He came across the room, moving with his own special kind of airy grace; with a friendly charm he put out his hand. Mirabel, coolly and precisely, did not see it. She said stiffly, "How do you do." and turned to Mady. "If you want my opinion —"

Mady nodded. Mirabel went on, "I think Boyce can take our unexpected guests back to his place."

Jim's eyes were amused and knowing and mischievous, like those of a small boy who has perpetrated a successful trick. He said to Mady, "Darling, we'll go if you want us to go. I thought it a poor idea to come here myself. But it was really —" He gave a whimsical kind of grin and shrug and shiver and said, "Very cold at Edith's place. Icy. All of us down with pneumonia in another ten minutes. Then of course you'd have to see to us, wouldn't you? Really, nobody could think of anything else to do. But I'll leave if you want me to." His eyes were laughing into Mady's and very confident, yet his voice was ruefully apologetic. "I expect your new husband may not give me a welcome. Is that it?"

Mirabel went out of the study; she was wearing a tweed skirt, too long for fashion but warm, heavy knee socks and three sweaters, yet her departure had all the effect of a queen — and a very powerful queen — leaving a formal ball; she could have been wearing a court dress, train and tiara. Jim smiled when she passed him as if really she couldn't be bothered to look at him.

"She doesn't seem to like me," he said. "Well, that doesn't matter. You like me. Don't you, darling? I've missed you so. I was so wrong, so madly wrong. I only had the — the —"

Mady said, "The bachelor jitters," and was a little surprised at the real yet disinterested skepticism in her voice.

131

"I told you I was wrong. I've gone through hell. I thought it would be better once I saw you —" He paused. His voice became emotional. "But it's worse. How can I compete with a man who can give you the things Craig Wilson can give you?"

She had to end this scene, which, oddly, was beginning to have a farcical touch although she couldn't have said why; whatever it was, it was in bad taste and also against Craig's definite ultimatum. She said, "I'm sorry you came."

"You can't mean that!"

"I do mean it."

She started to pass him, probably much as Mirabel had done, for she was trying to bolster up all the calm and dignity she could summon. But he caught her hand and carried it to his cheek. "I love you so," he said softly. "I never stopped for a minute. Please, Mady —"

As she snatched her hand away, Mady thought that she would never have expected the Wilson habit of blurting out the truth to envelop her so soon. Certainly she felt a shock of surprise to hear herself say exactly what she said, but she uttered it coldly and with utter truth.

"I can't imagine what I ever saw in you!"

It didn't even seem remarkable to her

when she said it. It was like saying grass is green or the sky is blue, a mere statement of fact.

He stared at her. The look of mischievous triumph faded from his face. His eyes widened with surprise. But he didn't believe her. "Oh, my darling, you must forgive me. You're only hurt and angry. I deserve it, but" — he carried her hand to his cheek again — "I love you so much —"

The scene reminded Mady, oddly, of Guy Casso.

It was, it would be, Susan who interrupted this. She cried from the doorway, "Mady! Wait till Father hears about this. Kissing your hand and — Dear me," said Susan, all at once sounding like Edith. "It was only the day before yesterday that your other boy friend was there hugging you on the sofa." She turned sparkling eyes toward Jim and said gently, "You know. Guy Casso. He was murdered. Right here on the ranch."

If at that moment Mady could have strangled both of them she felt that she'd have done it happily. Jim dropped her hand.

Susan said, "Why Jim, I haven't seen you since — why since that day last spring when we met at Mother's apartment!"

Jim said, "I haven't seen you for ages!"

Susan's voice sounded suddenly rather sober. "Well —" she said slowly, "we didn't really meet that day. I was leaving but I saw you go into the apartment house and knew you were going to see my mother. It — wasn't one of her good days."

Susan sounded adult, yet so very, very young and forlorn at the same time that Mady turned back as if Susan were in need. She wasn't; she shrugged away Mady's hand on her shoulder. Jim said, "Poor Rhoda. She had a hard time for a while. But she's stopped drinking, you know."

"Yes," Susan said flatly.

Mady walked between them and into the hall, where Edith was struggling out of a coat. Boyce was hauling off some buckled galoshes and Rhoda was smoothing her red hair before the mirror, her pose, her uplifted arms showing off her lovely figure. There was a stack of suitcases near the door. So they had come to stay for the duration of the storm, no doubt about that.

Mady wondered briefly how long a storm usually lasted. Then she saw Jim's handsome new traveling case which she had given him herself; it had his initials on it and he was going to take it with him on their wedding trip to Puerto Rico. They had figured and figured the expenses of the trip. They had purchased the tickets together; she supposed that Jim had returned them and got the money back.

Rhoda saw her in the mirror and said, "Mady! How awful! Just for a moment I forgot about you, I mean that you are Craig's wife and — oh, I'm sorry. It's your place, not mine, to deal with all of us uninvited guests." She turned fully around; she was beautiful and her eyes were shining. Mady didn't believe that Rhoda had forgotten her, not for an instant. But Rhoda came to Mady confidingly and slid her arm around her. "It's really too dreadful, coming down upon you like this. But there was simply nothing else to do."

Mirabel spoke from the stairs. "It's not polite. It's not dignified. Rhoda here! That man James Marsh, too! It's indecorous! It's unseemly. *Manuel!*" she roared out suddenly. Mady hadn't known that Mirabel could produce so much carrying power in her voice. Manuel came scurrying from the dining room. "Manuel," said Mirabel, "I wish to have my meals served in my room. Inez can do it if you have too many people to see to." She turned then and again with all the majesty of court dress and tiara marched on up the stairs. There was a rather awestruck silence until her shabby tweed skirt and sweaters had vanished around the turn in the stairs.

Then Rhoda said, "You know, she's right. We shouldn't have landed ourselves here."

Edith got out of her coat and was unwinding a plaid scarf from her short neck. "Where else could we go? It's Boyce's own brother's house! She has no right to speak to us like that, the old —"

Boyce put a hand over his wife's mouth. Mady wouldn't have believed it if she hadn't seen it and she wouldn't have been surprised if Edith had bitten him. But perhaps Edith herself was too surprised to take aggressive action, and Boyce took his hand away and said, "Mirabel is right. But I propose we go to the guest cabins. I'm sure Craig will permit us to stay there. I'll come to the kitchen and carry out meals to us. Jim can help —"

Jim had come out of the study behind Mady. Susan was there also, still rather sober.

Jim said, "We wouldn't embarrass anybody for the world. I can quite see that Rhoda — well, the first wife and me — I'm an embarrassment, too, and I wouldn't want to embarrass anybody."

They had, all of them, reached the first-name stage very rapidly. Mady attributed this to Rhoda's influence.

Boyce said, "The guest cabins will be warm —"

She didn't make any pretense of stopping them. It seemed to her as sensible a course as could have been arrived at just then. There was a little half-hearted discussion about how they would share the cabins, which Edith ended by saying that each cabin had two bedrooms and a living room but only one bathroom, and she and Rhoda would share one cabin and the men could have the other. "Are there plenty of blankets?" she asked Mady.

Mady hadn't the faintest idea, she had merely glanced into the cabins, but she said firmly that certainly there was plenty of linen and blankets and that she would see to it that there was wood for the fireplaces. Manuel was still standing in the doorway to the dining room and Mady thought there was just a flicker of approval in his dark eyes; in any event, he said that he would have the men see to firewood for the cabins.

And all at once the whole party, which

seemed as a matter of fact more like twenty people than just four, was getting back into coats and scarves and galoshes and getting luggage — and Jim's suitcase with its shining initials — out the door. The cold wind and snow swept in, chilling Mady. Boyce muttered something about leaving his car out in the blizzard, and Manuel said promptly that there was an empty shed back of the brood mares' stable, and he'd have one of the boys see to that, too. Jim was the last to go; he waved at Mady and his eyes laughed as they had always done and she remembered the hot summer day when she had traipsed all over New York, it seemed to her, to select and buy as nice a suitcase for him as her money would permit.

Susan, practically, went to close the door. "So," she said, "Mother's got a new man on her mind. It's funny. Mother's boy friends are always the gigolo type. I expect," the child said, "that's where some of her money went, don't you?"

"No, I don't know anything about it. We'll not talk like this, Susan."

But Susan went on. "Of course you knew that Jim Marsh was taking her around — probably she paid the bills — while you were still engaged to him."

"But I — no! Susan, really —" Mady stopped. There had been frequent times certainly during their engagement when Jim had had visiting business acquaintances to take to dinner or to the theater. But if he had known Rhoda at that time, Mady was not aware of it. It had not occurred to Mady that he could have been what Susan called a boy friend. Thinking of this, she must have stared at Susan, for Susan suddenly giggled.

"You ought to see your face! Goodness, Mady, didn't you ever think of such a thing?"

"No."

Susan giggled again. "Didn't you wonder how it was that I knew your friend Jim? I can visit Mother, you know, whenever I want to. Jim was very chummy with me. Brought me candy and stuff. Guy never used to do that. I suppose Guy thought I was too young to notice. And then Mother stopped seeing Guy. She said he bored her. But just let me tell you something. You're still in love with Jim —"

Mady said, "Shut up," so unexpectedly and so fiercely that Susan did shut up and looked utterly astounded. It struck Mady that perhaps that was the way to treat Susan; she was by way of being a young bully when she thought she could get her way. Mady waited a moment and in the back of her mind she couldn't help thinking that perhaps Susan's hints were right. Suppose Rhoda was the real reason for Jim's breaking his engagement. Yet, against that, was the fact that now Rhoda openly proclaimed her intention to get Craig back and to promote a renewed romance between Jim and Mady.

There was something out of kilter here. Mady couldn't reason it out. Susan was still looking rather thunderstruck, as if Mady had given her the surprise of her life. Mady said, "I wonder when your father will get back home." It diverted Susan, although Mady was pleased to see that she still eyed Mady rather warily.

Susan said, however, pleasantly enough, "It takes time. We've always fed through the winter. Uncle Boyce doesn't feed much but then his grazing land is better than ours. And of course feeding costs money and Father has plenty of that. But tonight the men are out there, hauling hay." She was all at once rather friendly, telling about the ranch. "They haul out truckloads of hay and dump them where the cattle can find them. They can't graze during a blizzard. The snow covers everything. Water's not a problem with all that snow but feeding is. Cattle are pretty dumb but they'll find the hay unless it storms too much and covers it too fast." She paused and said, "At least they say cattle are dumb, but I've never seen a cow that will take any calf but her own. Funny." The moment of friendliness was gone; she eyed Mady brightly. "They don't intend to be stepmothers! That's it. Nobody likes a stepmother — Oh, dear." She pretended apology. "I didn't mean you!"

Mady felt only rather tired. She said absently, "You have a mother. I don't intend to try to be your stepmother —"

"But you are, you know!" Then the sober, thoughtful look again came into Susan's face, giving her a suddenly and rather sadly adult appearance. "I did see Jim that day — I mean one day last spring. I haven't seen him since. I guess he didn't see me. I was leaving and he was arriving, and my mother — well, she —" Her eyes were precociously knowing, which troubled Mady, who had an impulse to shield her from something, she didn't know quite what. Susan said flatly, "Mother was drinking, passed out cold in her bedroom as a matter of fact. I waited around and —" Her eyes shifted away from Mady.

"Her maid knew how to manage her, so I — well, I did what I did other times. I went down and told the chauffeur to take me to Schrafft's for an ice cream soda. And then to the zoo. I never told my father, of course. Don't tell him — will you promise?"

"All right, I'll not tell him. But she's not drinking now, Susan, you can tell —"

"That's right. She stopped it. She was losing her looks. I don't think she ever liked drinking very much. She just didn't know what else to do. But it's all right now."

"Yes. Sancho wants out."

Sancho could be a problem, as he had been when he came racing into the room with Mady's glove in his teeth, but he was also a great help in diverting Susan. She seized her heavy coat, shoved her feet into long boots, wrapped a scarf over her head and shot out with Sancho bouncing along beside her. It wasn't full dark, but almost. It must have been five minutes before Mady remembered that Craig hadn't permitted Susan to go out alone the previous night. Guy Casso had been murdered and the murderer had to be somebody who knew the house and the ranch.

She was shocked at her own carelessness

and started after Susan, but the door flung open and she ran in, Sancho leaping beside her. Her cheeks were pink. "Golly, it's cold!" She flung off her coat and tugged at her boots. "There are lights in the guest cabins. They must be all settled in. Father's going to be very angry about all this. I mean your boy friend. I don't think he'll mind Mother's being here. Let's have dinner on trays in the living room. It's good and warm in there."

So they did, Susan playing with Sancho and behaving and looking like a nice little girl and not a disillusioned adult. Dinner was reasonably amicable too, although Susan fed Sancho choice bits from her own plate and then demanded more from Manuel, which he didn't approve of, but Mady had a wave of nothing short of cowardice and decided not to risk the fragile politeness between them by suggesting that Susan feed Sancho in the kitchen.

Susan went up to bed, yawning. Mady asked her to stop in Mirabel's room and say goodnight to her, and Susan said happily that she would. She liked Mirabel. And she seemed again quite like a child, untouched by the murder of Guy Casso, half forgetting her impulsive candor in speaking to Mady, and forgetting altogether whatever memories had brought that look of adult and troubled thought into her pretty face.

After she went upstairs, Sancho bounding along beside her, Mady went into Craig's study. She put some logs on the fire; Manuel brought in a tray with whiskey and glasses for Craig's nightcap. She settled herself down in Craig's big armchair, hoping that some careful thinking would help her to reach some logical conclusions. It didn't.

Certainly Rhoda had suggested Jim's coming, and it did seem rather more than likely that Jim had known Rhoda and had been a more or less devoted escort while Mady was still engaged to him.

But the cold fact was that now Rhoda was determined to get Craig back, so determined and so sure of herself that she had come to Mady and flatly stated her intention, the deal she proposed. It would indeed make it easier and simpler for Rhoda if she could persuade Mady to leave Craig. She had expected Jim to conquer any reluctance on Mady's part. Rhoda couldn't really want Jim.

As far as Mady could see, none of this had anything at all to do with Guy Casso's murder.

The logs crackled and shot red flames. The walls of the room seemed to enfold her with a kind of richness and comfort — here where Craig had lived most of his life.

She did think of the reversal of her feelings about Jim, but not very much; it was surprising in its way, but not very important. She'd been a fool, but that was all there was to it. She might have regretted all the emotion she had so lavishly wasted, but that didn't even occur to her.

Mainly she felt released, free as air and very warm and snug, there in Craig's small study, before the fire, waiting for him. She watched the fire, half dreaming. She heard Craig when he came into the hall and stamped snow from his boots.

He came into the study, glanced at Mady and rubbed his cold face. He went to the table, poured himself the stiffest drink she had ever known Craig to take, sank down in the big chair opposite her and stretched out his legs. He looked tired to the bone and yet full of unleashed energy. It was an odd combination, but like Craig.

Craig was her husband. They were at home. Nothing else mattered.

Nothing else mattered at all as long as they were together. She had no special pulse of surprise; she felt only free and happy. She must have been in love with Craig for a long time, but she didn't even wonder about it because it seemed so natural now, as if she had loved him all her life.

Craig set his glass down and looked directly at her. "I told you not to permit Jim Marsh to enter my house."

Chapter 8

The fire crackled and blazed. The Indian rugs scattered over the dark floor had bold designs of white and black and red. The wind and snow whispered relentlessly at the windows.

There was something relentless in Craig's voice, too. Mady said, "But I didn't — he came —" She stopped and said, "I think I'll have a nightcap, too."

Craig rose with one long movement and went to the table. Over his shoulder he said in a quiet voice which yet had an edge to it, "Yes, perhaps you need some Dutch courage."

He came back and put the glass in her hand. She said, "I knew he was coming. I told you. I had a letter from him. But he came before I could stop him. And as for tonight —"

Craig leaned his head back against the chair. "Oh, I know about their coming here tonight. Nobody could turn them out in the storm. I'll get rid of him as soon as I can. Tell me something about him. What does he do? How does he earn his living?"

"Why, I — well, he's worked at different jobs, really. When I knew him he was selling advertising. That was only until he could get a job in a brokerage firm."

"Did he get the job?"

"I don't know."

"How did you meet him?"

Mady remembered that. "It was at a dinner party. I didn't know anybody but my hostess, Winnie Phipps. She had gone to school with me, but then we had drifted apart. I had a job. Winnie was busy with other things. I felt strange. I didn't know anyone at the party. Jim came over to talk to me. He asked me about my job."

"Go on."

"That's all, really. I told him I worked for you. I remember that he said *the* Craig Wilson, and I said yes. Then — Oh, he phoned in a day or two and we had dinner and —"

"How did Rhoda happen to know him?"

"She said that she'd met him at some cocktail party."

She wondered if he would have anything at all to say about Rhoda's offer of a deal. He didn't. He said, "This letter Jim Marsh sent you. You said it was mailed from New York the afternoon of Casso's murder."

148

"Yes. It was on the postmark. Air mail. November third."

"I'm sorry you burned it."

"I didn't want it. I didn't want him to write to me at all."

Craig didn't seem to hear her. He was looking into the fire again. Finally he said, "If you wish to leave me and go back to him, I prefer to make sure that he can support you. That's enough about Marsh for the present. The point now is the murder of this man Casso. I've been thinking about the rail. I've been thinking about what the sheriff said. It does seem likely that somebody tried to frame either you or me. Casso came here, made a scene with you at a time when he may have been sure it would be witnessed by Mirabel and Susan, and thus, conceivably, reported to somebody — me, perhaps. He came here for some reason the next day. He was killed with the rail. This also argues an attempt to frame me or you. He could be called a reason for the divorce from Rhoda. He wasn't the reason, but a jury could look at it that way. A jury could look at that scene with you as another reason I might have for killing him — making advances to my present wife. If the fact of the rail were known, a jury might say, 'Casso was killed on your ranch with a weapon only somebody who knows your house would be able to take away and use.' That limits it to a few people. The servants. The ranch hands. Indian Joe. Boyce or Edith or — Rhoda. Casso's motive for coming here must have had something to do with Rhoda. But I honestly can't see Rhoda waylaying Casso on the trail and killing him. And the fact is — that framing me for a murder wouldn't profit anybody."

He rose, took more logs from the basket and put them on the fire.

He went on, then, thoughtfully. "Even if I were convicted of murder, my money, my property would still be mine. There would have to be ways to manage it but there is no way that it would benefit anybody at all. And suppose all this was really an attempt to frame you. Again, there's no motive. I'm trying to get some information about Casso's past. I'd like to think that his past, which may have been a rather murky one, caught up with him. I'll telephone Seely as soon as the telephones are working again. He'll get in touch with Morrow. They'll run down anything they can find about Casso. I don't hope for much though."

Seely was Craig's executive officer in New York; Morrow was a brilliant and

150

conscientious lawyer. Both were reliable and devoted aides to Craig.

Mady said, "Perhaps they can keep some of this out of the newspapers."

"They can't stifle news. They may be able to keep it to a minimum. I keep thinking that I ought to tell the sheriff about the rail. Well, I can't do anything about it tonight."

"You must go to bed. You've been out since dawn."

"It's a rancher's life."

"Will George come back when he hears of the storm?"

"He couldn't get here now. But Indian Joe is a good straw boss. We've done everything we can do. I doubt if we'll lose much stock. I've been breeding white-faces — pure-bred Herefords; they are reasonably hardy. Funny, though. I mean, this ranch. It's something different. I mean — Oh, I care about Wilsonite and I care about all the stir and commotion of business. I care about all the money Wilsonite is making, too. But the ranch is something else. Something different."

"I know."

He glanced quickly at Mady.

She said, "I remember the big mural of El Rancho that hangs in your office. You

151

used to look at it so often, so —" It seemed to her there was surprise in his eyes. She went on hurriedly. "I mean, when you were dictating letters or trying to make up your mind about something or — you would stop and look at the mural of the ranch and — one time you pointed out to me this house and the corrals. And the grazing lands and the river."

He smiled. "I didn't know that I was so transparent. I wish that we could have kept the entire ranch in one unit. Yet it made sense for Boyce to take the part he wanted. Or Edith wanted. Boyce does whatever Edith nags him into doing."

"He slapped her tonight."

Craig sat up. "You don't mean it!"

"It wasn't a slap exactly, but like one. She was going on about something Mirabel said and Boyce put his hand over her mouth. She was surprised."

"Good for Boyce! What did Mirabel say that got Edith so worked up?"

"She said it wasn't dignified for Rhoda and Jim, too, to stay here. She said it wasn't seemly and that she'd have her dinner upstairs. It was quite clear that she didn't intend to sit down at the table with any of them."

Craig suddenly chuckled. "I can see her.

152

She's a very powerful woman!" He rose. "I'm going to eat before I go to bed. Want to come along?"

Mady jumped up and followed him to the kitchen; for an absurd moment she was very happy because he had suddenly seemed more like himself; he had asked her to come along with him. Manuel had left food keeping warm in an oven. Mady poured coffee from a thermos. Craig adjusted the wick of the lamp, which was smoking. The wind and snow whispered against the windows even more insistently there.

She wished she could say, "Craig, I'm in love with you. I was a besotted fool; I clung to my own ideal of Jim and he isn't like that at all. I don't know when I fell in love with you, but I did and I never want to see Jim or hear of him again."

It was impossible to say it; Craig was her husband but he was not in love with her; he was kind; he would protect her, he had said so, and he would do whatever he said he would do. But she couldn't make him love her. He had immediately seen through Rhoda's motive in bringing Jim to the ranch. He had shown no indignation, no emotion whatever when Mady had told him of Rhoda's offer to her. Yet all the same, in his heart there might still linger a far deeper love for Rhoda than he had ever even pretended to have for Mady.

Rather against her own judgment Mady made one effort. "Craig, about Jim — I didn't want him to come here. I told you. I don't want to marry him —"

It was a mistake. Craig's face and eyes became chilly again. "That's sensible of you, since you are married to me."

Mady could feel color surge up into her cheeks. "I'm only trying to tell you —" She stopped, feeling as if she were thrusting against a stone wall.

Craig said, "I really think you are better off as Mrs. Craig Wilson than you would be as Mrs. James Marsh. But, as they say, money isn't everything. I'm going to bed."

"It isn't money! It has nothing to do with money —"

He leaned over to blow out the lamp and gave her his hand to lead her to the hall. His gesture was merely a courtesy and he released Mady's hand as soon as they reached the lighted hall. They went upstairs and Craig said goodnight politely but with finality as he opened the door of her room and turned away toward his own.

There were candles on a table that gave a wavering light, so the shadows of the great Spanish chest seemed to move. The room was cold; heavy red curtains were drawn across the windows but they stirred a little when there was an exceptionally wild gust of wind. She crept under the blankets and pulled up an enormous eiderdown which Inez must have dug out from some closet. After a while she crawled up high enough to blow out the candles and then sank back into the chill blackness. There wasn't a sound except the push and thrust of the wind and snow.

Anybody has the right to be a fool once in a while, but nobody needs to always be a damned fool; she thought that in so many words. It was no comfort to tell herself that she wasn't the first woman to make a fool of herself over what Susan called the gigolo type.

However, she had been fortunate — Craig had rescued her.

Craig had been a good employer; he had paid generous salaries; if crisp and impatient at times, he had never been unfair. He had always shown a kind of friendly impersonality toward Mady and the other people in the New York office until the day after Jim had told her that he didn't want to marry her

She had been taking a letter; Craig had

stopped in his dictating and said, "Am I going too fast?"

"What — ? Oh — I'm sorry —"

Craig had looked at her and she had looked at her shorthand, which had lagged behind Craig's words. Craig said, gently, "What's the matter? You look as if you'd been crying all night."

She had been crying; she was sure that her heart was broken, and her pride was certainly in the dust. To her utter dismay she felt the tears rolling down her cheeks again.

Craig had said, "See here, we can't have this." He had risen, walked around the desk, and Mady felt his hand on her shoulder. It was a comforting kind of warmth. He took out his handkerchief, turned her face up toward him and wiped away her tears. "You don't cry much, do you, Mady?" he'd said. "Neither does Susan. But once in a while — There now. Feel better? Suppose you tell me about it. Or wait, I'll guess. It's something about this man you're going to marry, isn't it?"

He knew about her coming marriage; she had asked for time off for her honeymoon trip with Jim. But she was going to continue working; Jim had said it was a sensible plan until his affairs were more settled.

So she told Craig there wasn't going to be a wedding. She must have told him what Jim had said to her: that they would always be good friends; he would never forget her.

Craig stood looking at the ranch mural for quite a long time after she had finished her dismal little tale. He then told her to go into the luxurious washroom adjoining his office, wash her face and fix her hair (so nobody in the outer office would see that she'd been crying; she knew that) and then go home and sleep, because he was coming to get her at nine o'clock that night and they were going out to have dinner someplace where there was a good dance band.

So she did. Three weeks later he asked her to marry him. He needed a hostess. Mirabel was getting a little too old to see to things; she'd never really give up, but she needed help. And he needed help about his daughter. He knew Mady; he knew her father; he knew that he could depend upon her.

He said that by this time Mady should know something of him. He said that really they had a good foundation for a marriage if she could see it that way, but he told her not to make up her mind at once.

It was a bargain. They were married. Love had not been a part of their agreement.

And that night Craig had talked quite coolly of her leaving him and marrying Jim. Now Mady had a rival, and a formidable one, in Rhoda. True, Craig had looked at Mady for agreement when he told the sheriff that he would arrange a larger alimony for Rhoda. Yet it was a formal and polite gesture, one due his present wife.

But Craig had hurried back from San Francisco to see Rhoda, almost the moment she had telephoned to him and asked him to come. That haste hadn't struck Mady until now, in the cold darkness of the night. Had it been impatient haste, eager haste, loving haste?

Her thoughts began to whirl around hazily. The wind howled a little now and then, reminding her of the coyotes and their wicked laughter. She wondered to what lairs they had slunk, waiting for the storm to pass.

She didn't think that she had slept at all, but she had, for the small sound that awakened her did so gradually, as she came slowly to full and puzzled consciousness. Someone, somewhere, was wailing. No! She sat up. Somewhere a dog was whimpering. A dog — Sancho, of course!

She fumbled around, found kitchen matches stuck into a china mug and struck one. She lit a candle on the bedside table. She heard Sancho whimper again. It was the sound of a dog who has been shut up somewhere and doesn't like it.

Little alarm bells seemed to ring in her head. Sancho always slept in Susan's room, on her bed. Indeed, there had been some slight altercations with Inez concerning muddy paw prints left on the blanket cover.

He whimpered again.

Chapter 9

So Mady got out of bed and bundled herself into her red dressing gown, for the house was now icily cold. She took the candle and hurried along the hall to Susan's room. A candle had been lighted there, too. Its wavering glow showed a tumbled bed, but no Susan and no Sancho.

But Sancho had heard Mady; he gave a bark which said as plainly as words, Come and get me out.

So she did. He was easy to find. He was shut up in a broom closet, down the hall. He bounded out, leaping at her. Susan wouldn't have shut him in the broom closet. Mady went back to Susan's room, and only then did she see the sheet of Susan's drawing paper that lay on the floor. It had words scrawled on it in heavy black crayon. The huge words were clear enough in the candlelight and utterly unbelievable: "Sancho got out. I'll get him back. Don't come after me. Mady."

It was a short message and unbelievable because Sancho hadn't got out; he was inside the house, and as he brushed against her, Mady could feel that his thick coat was dry. The signature was unbelievable because it was her name; "Mady" was scrawled in huge letters which could be anybody's handwriting.

The point was that Susan, of course, hadn't obeyed this fake message from Mady. Anybody knowing Susan and her devotion to her dog would have known that she wouldn't stay in bed. She'd go out into that storm, in the middle of the night, to rescue the dog.

By this time Mady was running to Craig's room. He was asleep, his head on his arm. She called him, she shook his shoulder until he sat up blinking, rubbing his eyes, and then took in the sense of her words. Mady had dropped the scrawled note. He saw it on the bed, read it, and she told him where she had found it. Sancho whimpered and nuzzled against her.

"I'll find her. She can't have gone far." Craig was pulling clothes on, snatching the first things he could find. "We'll find out about this note later. Get on the phone to the bunkhouse, tell the boys — Oh, I forgot, the wires are down. Well, I'll find her. Go back to bed —"

But she followed him as he ran down the

stairs. He snatched up a heavy coat. He caught up a flashlight from the table and flung open the wide front door. Snow swirled in. Craig and the rays of light vanished.

Of course he would find Susan. She couldn't have gone far. Craig had thought of help from the ranch hands sleeping in the bunkhouse. Mady ran up to her room again, snatched up clothes as Craig had done, heavy slacks, sweaters. She ran downstairs, carrying the candle. There were overshoes in the hall closet; she shoved her feet into the first pair she could find. She took one of Craig's sheepskin-lined coats. She could not find another flashlight, but she was sure that she could grope her way around the house, using her hand against the wall of the house as a guide, then take a direct line which would arrive at the bunkhouse. It seemed a clear enough plan. Sancho bounded out the door with her, and she didn't know that until she felt his nose against her hand, but then all at once he was gone. Craig had disappeared entirely. She could not even see his flashlight; there was no light anywhere. She felt her way along the veranda and around the corner of the house, and then the wind and snow fell upon her.

Mady had never been in a blizzard before. She hadn't the slightest idea of its full force. Almost at once she lost her bearings. She was then in a complete void of blackness, cutting wind, snow, and before she knew it she was floundering in drifts.

She tried to backtrack. She tried to find the walls of the house. She was completely lost. She called to Craig, and the wind snatched her breath away. She screamed, and it only hurt her throat. If she kept moving, she would perhaps get too far from the house. If she stood still, how could anybody find her in time?

In time, Mady thought, already half dazed. That meant before she was literally frozen.

She screamed again for Craig, for anybody, and her groping hands touched an arm.

She couldn't see any face. There was only a kind of black blur beside her. Then a most shocking thing happened, for the arm gave her a sudden hard thrust. She went over backward, stumbling, falling into smothering snow. The arm was gone.

There was nothing at all. The cold and weight of that feathery-seeming snow seemed to bind her within itself. She tried to get up on her knees; she tried to stand

and could not get a foothold; she screamed and the scream was swept away by snow and wind.

But Indian Joe heard it. Mady had a vague glimpse of an enormous flashlight waving near. Then Indian Joe found her, scooped her to her feet and half carried her to the house. She felt a dull surprise that he could find his way so directly; but they did reach the veranda, they did reach the house — and Craig and Susan and Sancho were in the hall.

She slid out of Indian Joe's strong clasp, wavering rather dizzily, and Craig came to catch her. Indian Joe said, "She'd fallen in the snow. I just happened to hear her scream."

Mady said, trying to get her breath, "Somebody was there. I felt his arm. Then he shoved me backward into the snow."

Craig turned to Indian Joe. "Go over to the guest cabins. See if you can find a snowy coat — pants, boots, anything." Two ranch hands came bursting into the hall. They had on coats lined with sheepskin and were carrying flashlights. Craig said to them, "Go with Indian Joe, will you? We want to find anybody on the place who shouldn't be here. But take a look for wet clothing first, Joe. See if anybody in the guest cabins has been out in the snow."

Mirabel spoke from the stairs. She was a kind of blur to Mady's eyes, all white and red and yellow. "See to Mady, Craig. Bring her up here to bed."

Susan crouched down beside Sancho, her chin so solid and firm that Mady guessed she was trying not to cry. Her voice was unsteady. "It's my fault. I woke up and I thought somebody had come into my room, so I lit a candle and there was a piece of my sketchbook paper. Sancho wasn't in my room, just like it said on the paper. Mady had signed it and told me to stay in my room, but I had to find Sancho, so I went out and then I got lost. But Father came with his flashlight. I could see the light and I screamed for him and then Sancho came too —" She was cold and shaking and frightened.

Mady said, "No harm done, Susan."

"It's all my fault. Father said you didn't write those words in crayon and I ought to have shown it to him, and never should anybody go out in a blizzard —"

Craig said, "She's right. Neither of you should have gone out. You don't know anything about the kind of blizzards we can get. I told you to stay here, Mady —"

"I thought I could find the bunkhouse."

"I went around the other side of the house. I know my way. I roused the boys and came back, and Susan saw my flashlight."

"There was somebody," Mady said. "There was an arm and it came out of the darkness — as if — as if I had surprised him —"

If she kept on she would begin to cry; Susan would cry; there'd be a fine yelping scene. Mady stopped, and Craig said, "I'll get you to bed. You, too, Susan. Get up there and get yourself warm."

Mirabel said firmly, "Bring Mady upstairs. Come with me, Susan."

Susan ran up the stairs, Sancho after her. Craig put his arm around Mady, half-lifted her upstairs, got her into her room, out of her snow-wet clothes and bundled down under blankets before he asked, "Mady, whose arm?"

"I don't know." The unpleasant tremor which shook her voice and indeed her whole body was subsiding.

"Didn't he say anything?"

"Nothing."

"Could you tell anything about the — oh, his coat sleeve? Texture of it? Anything?"

"No. It was so quick. I only knew that

somebody was standing near me and I knew I had touched his arm. I — I think that he was surprised. He pushed me back so quickly."

"Could you see him at all?"

"There was a kind of solid something, black. I couldn't possibly have seen who it was."

"It must have been a man."

"Oh, Craig, I was a fool to go out like that."

He leaned over and pushed her tousled hair back from her face. "Well, it's all right now. The snow is so strong, you see. It takes a man's strength to get through, and even then —"

Mady thought he might be going to hold her in his arms, even kiss her and tell her he was glad she was safe and he would keep her safe. Then someone shouted from below. "Mr. Wilson! There's somebody here —" It was Indian Joe's voice.

It was thus that Mr. Banner — Walter Banner — added himself to their group of refugees. Mady could hear the men talking clearly enough to know what had happened. Indian Joe and the two other hands had found him, or rather Mr. Banner had found them. He had seen their lights. He had stumbled and fought his way through the drifts and almost fallen from exhaustion. He had shouted for help. He was still gasping for breath. Mady heard Craig say, "I'll get you a drink."

Mr. Banner's voice was rather high-pitched and to Mady's ears had a very slight accent which, however, she couldn't identify. He was breathless and stammering from cold. "My car —" he said. "The snow caught me. I didn't realize — didn't know — I kept on the road as long as I could, but then the fence posts, everything, disappeared. I had to stop. I was afraid to let the engine run. I was afraid of carbon monoxide. I couldn't see lights anywhere. I got colder and colder. But then I thought there was a flicker of lights from this direction. So I decided to try it and I walked — at least I managed to get this far — Oh, thank you."

Someone must have brought him a drink. The gasping voice fell silent.

Indian Joe said, "He says he fell in the snow and couldn't get up again. He said he'd started out from Las Vegas early this morning. He intended to drive to Reno. He said they'd told him the snow might get worse and make for dangerous driving but he couldn't believe it. So he came on." Indian Joe's voice was rather dry.

"Nearly killed myself," Mr. Banner said and then introduced himself. "Name is Banner. Walter Banner. I'm just a tourist, driving around, aiming at the West Coast. Never thought of anything like this."

Mirabel came in. Mady saw then that the kind of blur she had seemed to see around Mirabel when she came down the stairs was in fact a bathrobe made, apparently, of Indian blankets; it had boldly geometric designs in red and yellow and black on a white background. Her white hair was on end. Yet she still — remarkably — looked like a perfect lady. "There's somebody half-frozen downstairs."

"I know. I can hear them."

"I was at the head of the stairs. I listened," she said with Wilson candor. "Wanted to find out all I could about this stranger. We don't really like strangers around here — especially after somebody was murdered on the place. Mady, who pushed you into the snow?"

"I don't know. I couldn't see anybody."

"Could it have been this man? This stranger?"

"I don't know. I didn't really see anybody."

Mirabel looked stony white. "You do realize that if Indian Joe hadn't come along and found you, you could have frozen to death."

Mady swallowed hard. "Craig would have found me. Craig would have had everybody looking for me."

"But it might have been a little late. I don't mean to scare the life out of you. But —" Mirabel rubbed her nose vigorously, "This is a bad business. I don't see why anybody would do that to you. Or why anybody would get Susan out on a night like this. And as to that, why Guy Casso would come here to get himself murdered. Not, of course," she said reluctantly, as if she didn't wish to admit anything that could evidence any possible decency in Guy Casso, "not that he intended to get himself murdered. I'm going to see what Craig is going to do about this Banner. I don't like the sound of his voice, I'll tell you that." She whisked out of the room, back very straight, encased in all those brilliant colors. Mady heard her on the stairs. "Why not make him up a bed on the sofa in the living room, Craig? I'll get blankets."

Craig replied, "He can use the foreman's cabin. The boys will show him. Mady might like something hot to drink."

"Of course!" Mirabel said. "I'll get it

right away."

There was a commotion in the hall, men's voices, but Mady could distinguish only a few words; then apparently Indian Joe, the new and uninvited guest and the other two hands all left. She heard the heavy bang of the front door. After a few moments Craig and Mirabel came upstairs. Craig came into her room.

"Mirabel fixed some hot milk laced with whiskey."

Craig sat on the edge of the bed and waited until she had downed every drop of it. The candle flame flickered a little, stood straight and then flickered over Craig's intent, tired face. "There's a traveler, got caught in the storm."

"Yes, I heard."

"Says his name is Banner. Could he have shoved you into the snow?"

"Anybody could have done it. Even you," she said a little foggily. "Although of course I know you didn't."

"I didn't," Craig said. "If you're going to talk like that on about three ounces of whiskey, you'd better sleep it off." But then he grinned a little, adjusted her pillows in a gentle way and kissed her — altogether too gently, she thought, yet she felt very warm and very, very sleepy.

171

But the next morning when Mady saw Mr. Banner she had an uneasy notion that she had seen him before, but she didn't know when or where.

The house was warm again, which was cheering. Obviously some electric wires had been rescued, and she thought of the valiant and half-frozen crews of workmen who must have labored in the blizzard during the night. It was still snowing. Mady looked out at the swirling gusts of wind and whiteness. When she went downstairs she found that apparently Mirabel was still adamant about the uninvited guests in the cabins, for narrow paths had been shoveled between house and guest cabins, paths which were quickly being eradicated by the snow but had made passage between cabins and main house possible.

Craig was in his study talking to Indian Joe and called to her to come in.

Indian Joe looked embarrassed when she tried to thank him for pulling her out of the snow the night before. "Nothing, Mrs. Wilson. I just happened to find you."

Craig said, "Joe says that all the coats in the guest cabins were snow-wet — still wet likely from their trek over to the cabins from the house. So there's no way of telling whether one of them was worn again during the night."

Indian Joe shook his head once. "All of them damp. They were all asleep by the time I got there last night. Or pretended they'd been asleep," Joe said thoughtfully. "May not be so. Bedrooms are on the sides of the cabins, living rooms between. One of them could have come out without rousing anybody else."

Craig shook his head. Indian Joe eyed him for a moment. Then he said, "But this new visitor, Mr. Wilson, he's lying. I got out to his car this morning. It was out on the road, as he said. We managed to hitch a tractor to it and drag it to that empty shed back of the brood mares' stables where we put your brother's car. Banner had made a big fuss about leaving his car out in the snow. Wouldn't hurt it. But it has more gas than it would have if he drove straight from Las Vegas."

"You mean he must have come from Wilson City?"

"It's the only place fairly near where he could fill up the gas tank. They'd have told him not to keep going in the storm."

"Do you mean that you think he intended to come here? He made the blizzard his excuse to stop and ask for help?

Why, Joe, what reason? Nobody here knows him."

"Maybe not. But somebody pushed Mrs. Wilson over in the snow. It strikes me that she might have stumbled against Banner and he acted quickly, surprised, not stopping to think. He wouldn't have been able to see her. He wouldn't know who it was. And then of course he wouldn't want to admit it. And — Look here, Mr. Wilson, I think I may have seen his car. I may have passed it on the road two days ago, the same afternoon Casso was killed. I was going to town to get some parts for that cranky pickup truck. Mrs. Wilson had decided to ride alone that afternoon. I can't be sure what time it was. About three or so, maybe earlier. I didn't pay much attention. But it's either the same car or one like it."

"Did you see him?"

Joe sighed. "I didn't see anybody; that is, I didn't take any notice. It was at that narrow part of the road where it goes down to the Wilson Creek bridge. I was edging out to make room for the car. I have a kind of notion there was more than one person in it, but I couldn't possibly say for sure."

Craig said, "Maybe he murdered Casso."

It was against Indian Joe's nature to

shrug; his face was still as a stone. He said, "No evidence, Mr. Wilson."

There was what might have been called anti-evidence; Mr. Banner, a complete stranger to the ranch, could not possibly have entered the house, taken the rail from the living room and taken it and himself out along the narrow arroyo trail.

Craig looked at Mady. "I think Joe should know about the rail."

She started to say, "Oh, no." She thought, But he'll tell the sheriff. Craig guessed what she was thinking. He said, "Joe is like a safe. You can tell him anything."

Indian Joe said quietly, "You mean the Golden Spike Rail? Yes, that could have done it. I saw the wound in this man Casso's skull. Something heavy with a sharp edge made it. Then it was Mrs. Wilson who brought the rail back here." It was not a question. Indian Joe had merely made an obvious leap of conjecture.

Craig said, "She thought it best."

Indian Joe, wooden-faced, said, "Heap smart squaw." There wasn't even a gleam of laughter in his eyes. He went on. "No use in letting people think you killed Casso, Mr. Wilson. The police needn't know this. But whoever got that rail had to come into the house. Manuel doesn't know anything about it?"

"If he does he'd tell me."

Indian Joe agreed. "Oh, sure. But that rail's been standing there on the table as long as I can remember. Many people have seen it. Not so many people could come into the house and take it."

"I suppose a stranger might merely happen to think of it as a murder weapon," Craig said.

Indian Joe shook his head once but firmly. "A stranger wouldn't merely happen into the house. The rail does narrow things down," he said with the first trace of feeling Mady had seen in him. He looked at nothing with very dark and bright eyes. "Your brother. Mrs. Boyce. Your first — I mean Mrs. Rhoda Wilson."

"Myself," Craig said.

Indian Joe looked scornful. "But maybe that was the intention, to frame you. And you've had guests, people around here, people from way off. I'd trust all our boys though."

"I do."

"Besides," Indian Joe said, "I can't see why any of them would take such a crack at this Casso man. Wouldn't even know him."

"I can't see why either." Craig gazed at the fire. Then he raised his head. "I think we'd better tell Joe the whole story, Mady."

Indian Joe's face could not be said to show interest, but she felt that all his senses were tense and alert. She nodded at Craig.

"It's not much of a story," Craig told him. "But puzzling. This man who was murdered, Casso, came here the day before he was killed —"

Mady had heard of cigar-store Indians. She had even seen one in Wilson City; Indian Joe could have given him points on utter immobility as Craig went on with the story.

Casso's visit to El Rancho, his preposterous conduct there, his airy departure, the fact that Mady had never seen him before in her life — Craig told it all to Indian Joe. Joe listened and asked no questions and showed no expression whatever in his face.

He knew of the paper with Mady's name scrawled upon it which she had found in Susan's room. "Somebody had to know the house, know Susan's probable reaction," Craig said, and Indian Joe nodded once.

There was a pause. Then Craig went on: Jim Marsh had come to Boyce's ranch at the invitation of Mrs. Boyce. He did not need to tell Joe that once Mady had been about to be married to Jim; Indian Joe appeared to know that, too, for he became sufficiently mobile to nod again.

When Craig had finished, the only thing that Indian Joe did not know was Rhoda's visit to Mady and her offer of a deal. Craig did not tell of that. But perhaps Joe had guessed something of the reason for Jim's arrival at the same time Rhoda had returned.

If so, he did not speak of it; he said only, thoughtfully, "I'd like to know exactly when that rail was taken out of the house."

"I can't remember when I last noticed it," Craig said. "I've been trying to think, but I'm so used to it, I simply can't remember when it must have disappeared."

"Manuel might know."

"We'll ask him." Craig went to the hall door.

"Get that young Inez in here, too," Joe said.

They both came, Manuel looking old and cross, Inez pretty and worried.

It was Joe who questioned them, and he

did it neatly, yet directly, too. They had been talking of the murder weapon, he told them, and it had occurred to Mr. Wilson that the rail could have been used for that purpose; so, he asked, did either of them know if the rail had at any time been taken out of the house.

Inez shook her head and looked frightened. Manuel glowered and said the rail had been on the long table in the living room every morning since he had come to work at El Rancho and he'd have known it if anybody at all had taken it away. He looked personally insulted at the idea that any object belonging to El Rancho could have been put to such an ugly use. He then said he had work to do and left. Inez scuttled after him.

"I'd trust Manuel's memory," Joe said.

"Well, but — he's getting old. It's possible that someone took it — oh, any time — and Manuel didn't notice its absence."

Joe didn't even reply to that. He said, "The first Mrs. Wilson wants to get Susan away from you."

Craig nodded.

"So," Indian Joe went on, "this Casso comes here, tries to put your wife" — his dark eyes went to Mady — "in a false position, not a good position, with witnesses,

Miss Mirabel and Susan. Somebody gets Susan out in the storm last night; could be made to look as if neither you nor Mrs. Wilson is capable of taking care of the girl. A judge might be inclined to doubt your reliability as to the care of Susan. Somebody who could get into the house, who knew Susan well enough to know she'd go chasing out after her dog, come hell or high water. That could be kind of a bad count against you, in a way. But," said Indian Joe, "that's a possibility maybe but not — it's too — I don't know, too devious. The only person who would do that would be Mrs. — Mrs. Rhoda. No, it seems to me more likely that somebody tried to — well, to get rid of Susan."

"No!" Craig cried violently. "Why would anybody do that? Oh, I thought of it, of course! But that can't be the reason —"

"I hope not." Joe was very sober. "But Susan is a very smart girl. She's got good sharp eyes and a good head. Maybe she knows or even guesses something about Casso's murder that's got somebody scared —"

"No!" Craig cried again violently. He took a quick breath. "No, it is not a possibility, Joe! Rhoda — Susan's mother — wouldn't hurt Susan. And if Susan knew anything at all she'd — she'd tell some-body. Besides she'd act — oh, different. She's taken the whole thing in her stride. Hasn't touched her in the least. I don't mean that she's inhuman. But she's had a child's reaction. It's all part of a grown-up world, remote from her, nothing she has anything to do with. She's a sensible child — when she wants to be," he added rather gloomily.

"Yes," Joe said. "Yes, she is. But I think maybe we'd better keep a close eye on her, Mr. Wilson. Shall I bring Banner here for you to talk to? Maybe you can get some-thing out of him."

"All right," Craig said.

Indian Joe permitted himself a kind of polite gesture toward Mady and went away.

Mady said, "You told him everything."

"If I can't trust Joe, I can't trust myself. He's been on the ranch since he was a kid. His father worked for my father. We grew up together, he and Boyce and I."

"Indian Joe always calls you Mr. Wilson."

"That's his idea. When an Indian makes up his mind to something you can't change him — that is, if it's Joe. You see, he feels that now I'm his employer and, especially

181

around the outfit, he should say Mr. Wilson. But sometimes he forgets and only remembers all our years together, school, everything."

"You went to the same school?"

"Oh, sure. That is, Joe went first to the reservation school, before his father came here to work and brought Joe with him. When we grew to university age my father sent all three of us to Harvard. Joe had the best grades. Boyce came home after a couple of years. I transferred to the Colorado School of Mines. Joe" — Craig looked suddenly youthful and natural — "Joe got a master's in philosophy. He's about the only really happy man I know. He likes the ranch. It's about time for George to retire. Joe will then be foreman. It's not good enough for Joe but it's what he wants. If a man does what he wants to do, I don't see what else he can ask for in life." He paused, deep in thought. Then he roused himself. "That business of getting Susan out in the storm — Rhoda wouldn't have done that. It's too dangerous. But there were only Rhoda and Jim Marsh, Boyce and Edith — and of course Manuel, Inez, the ranch hands on the place last night."

"And Mr. Banner."

"Yes. But — I don't see how he could have got into the house, found his way to Susan's room, got the dog shut up in the broom closet, scribbled that note to Susan — all that without ever having been in the house before."

"Anybody could have lured Sancho into the closet. He's a puppy. He's had only kindness. He trusts everybody. Craig, how did *anybody* get into the house and into Susan's room? The door must have been locked."

"Oh, it was locked. I saw to that. But the fact is that I've never had new locks put in the house. As far as I know the locks haven't been changed since — oh, I think it was my grandfather who had the old big locks removed and more modern locks installed. But there must be keys around — any number of keys. Anybody who has ever worked here or been around here could easily have a key. As soon as I can I'll have new locks and heavy bolts put on the doors, but that is literally locking the barn door too late." He sighed. "Boyce, of course, would have a key. Perhaps Edith — oh, anybody."

He didn't say, naturally, that Rhoda would have had a key sometime. Rhoda could not have led her own daughter out

183

into a killing blizzard. Craig said abruptly, "Have you had your breakfast?"

Mady hadn't even thought of it. So she went to the dining room, which was empty, through the shining pantry and back to the kitchen, where, again, she sat at the cleanly scrubbed wooden table and Manuel fed her flapjacks and coffee and orange juice and she was very thankful indeed that the electricity had come on again. It was cozily warm and pleasant in the big kitchen and she stayed there until she heard Indian Joe return.

Mr. Banner was with him and looked rather breathless; he wiped a glistening, swarthy face. "Quite a blizzard," he said, saw Mady and looked very blank.

And all at once she felt an odd kind of tingle that wasn't familiarity with his face or figure but was like it. Craig stood in the study door and introduced them, and Mr. Banner bowed smoothly. In spite of his breathlessness and his blankness Mady felt that she had seen that bow before somewhere, too.

Chapter 10

They settled in the study. Mr. Banner was short, fattish, yet very lithe in his movements. He had a vaguely European countenance. He was glossy in an odd way, in spite of the sheepskin coat he had probably borrowed from one of the hands, and had a smooth, rather affected way with his fat hands. He had big brown eyes which looked very, very polite and blank, and yet she had a sense of a lively intelligence scurrying around behind that soft gaze. His manner was not pleasant — or rather, it was overpleasant, ingratiating and smooth. Mady did not like Mr. Banner.

And she couldn't for the life of her remember where — or even if — she had ever seen him before.

Craig was very polite but very Wilson and direct in his approach. "You've been here before, I mean near the ranch, haven't you, Mr. Banner?"

The soft brown eyes widened. "Why, no, Mr. Wilson. Never been in these parts before."

Indian Joe was standing opposite Mady, as it happened, just below the tomahawk which Susan had chosen as a murder weapon. His eyes did not flicker.

Craig said, "I had an impression that your car was seen on the road between here and Wilson City — let me see, wasn't it the day before yesterday?"

Mr. Banner spread his plump yet somehow strong-looking hands and shrugged. "Not my car, Mr. Wilson. Perhaps one like it. But day before yesterday — oh, yes, I was trying my luck at the game tables in Las Vegas. Had no luck but it was entertaining. I'm only a tourist, you know. Thought I'd enjoy just treking over the continent, taking my time, heading generally for San Francisco. I didn't expect anything like this storm!"

"Where," Craig said flatly, "did you last get gas for your car?"

"Where — ? Oh!" Mr. Banner didn't smile but something moved a little behind his eyes. "Why, I carried an extra can of it in the car. Five-gallon can. Put it in the tank not very long before I began to realize what a fool I had been to undertake this drive. But then I never in my life saw a blizzard like this."

Craig didn't glance at Indian Joe, and

Indian Joe looked thoughtfully at the tomahawk, which may — or may not — have been the property of one of his relatives long ago. Yet Mady felt the exchange of thought between them. It was as if they said to one another, "It's a good story. More to this man than he looks."

Craig waited a moment, as if to request speech from Indian Joe, who also waited and then said, "I didn't see the can in your car, Mr. Banner."

Mr. Banner's eyes seemed to move again. "It was very kind of you to put my car in a shed. It must have been difficult!"

"Tractors are powerful. Do you remember what you did with the empty gasoline can?" Joe spoke as smoothly as Mr. Banner, and Mr. Banner said at once, "Empty can? Now what could I have done with it? I don't remember — threw it away, I suppose. I was upset — scared by the storm, I have to admit. I really don't remember anything about the can."

Craig said, "Oh, well, it'll be found when the snow is gone."

Mr. Banner looked slightly smug and very blank again, as if that would be a long wait — as indeed seemed likely.

Craig said, "I hope you're comfortable in the foreman's cabin."

"Very. I had breakfast with your cow-boys. So kind. Thank you —"

There was a long pause, during which Mady had a notion that Indian Joe and Craig silently communed again and decided there was not much use in trying to question Mr. Banner further just then. Craig said casually, but changing the subject, "I don't think we're going to lose much stock, do you, Joe?"

"We'll lose some. Not many. The boys are out again with the jeep and tractor, trying to spread more hay."

"I ought to have got that helicopter we talked of last spring."

Indian Joe shook his head. "It wouldn't have done much good now. Nobody would want to take a helicopter with hay in it up on a day like this. Couldn't find his way."

"It might help though. I'll get one before another winter." Mr. Banner was sitting with his hands folded in a contented way. Craig turned to Indian Joe as he said, "Thank you, Joe. See that Mr. Banner is taken care of."

He didn't say, "Watch Mr. Banner like a hawk"; it wasn't necessary. Mr. Banner bowed and thanked and good-morninged his way out with Indian Joe, who stalked along beside him looking very tall and wiry and alert.

Mady said when they'd gone, "I think I've seem him somewhere. But I don't know where. I don't know when. I can't associate it with anything at all."

"New York?" Craig suggested.

"I don't know — perhaps. No, I'm not sure."

"In Wilson City?"

She shook her head. "I went into Wilson City the day after you went to San Francisco. The day Casso was killed. In the morning. I don't remember seeing Banner."

"Think hard," Craig said. "Indian Joe thinks Banner's car may have been in the neighborhood that day and he thinks there were two people in the car. The second person might have been Casso. Did you see either of them in Wilson City?"

"No — no, I'm sure I didn't." She had taken the car Craig had given her; it was a Lincoln Continental; a gray-blue two-door with a black top. She was accustomed to the third-hand jalopy she had bought and used around the campus before she went to work for Craig. She could scarcely believe the birdlike smoothness of this car, with its leather upholstery, its easy control, even her new name, which was on a little plate near the glove compartment, Mady Wilson.

When he was in New York Craig leased the services of a stately Rolls Royce and uniformed chauffeur, not always the same man, at what Mady had considered a ruinous cost, for sometimes one of the office accountants had left checks on her desk for Craig to sign and she couldn't help seeing the costs of the kind of living that was Craig's.

Even the house was leased, furnished. It was luxurious; it was staffed by some kind of domestic service which was efficient but rarely seemed to send the same servants twice — one never knew who was going to cook dinner or open the door. There was nothing personal about the New York house; it was very different from El Rancho with its traditions of living, the effect of generations, gathering up this or that and adding to the house, so it seemed to have grown that way and had its own being. Mady had never liked the New York house.

While she was in Wilson City she had posted a letter to her father. She remembered the postmistress who asked her in a very friendly way if she enjoyed ranch life.

She had stopped in the one drug store to replenish toothpaste, taken a chance or two at the row of slot machines, lost her nickels and dimes, decided that whoever called the slot machines one-armed bandits was right, upon which the slot machine suddenly rolled up some cherries and rolled out a fistful of dimes, felt better about the whole thing and had driven home. She had seen various people in Wilson City; but she couldn't remember Mr. Banner.

She shook her head. "No, no, I'm sure I'd remember him."

Craig said, "Don't press it. Maybe it'll come to you. I hope they get the phone lines up soon, but it's a hard job in a storm like this. One good thing, the fellows at the mine are all right, plenty of food and some old-time coal stoves. They probably are having long sessions of poker. No use working when the flatcars can't get out from Wilson City. I'm going to see how things are going. Don't go out in the snow again, will you?"

"Craig, Joe could be right about Susan's having seen or heard something which might identify whoever murdered Casso."

Craig's face took on a rocky kind of firmness. He put his hands on Mady's shoulders and looked very straight into her eyes. "Really, Mady, I can't believe that that child knows anything at all about the murder."

"She knows that somebody was in the house last night and contrived to get her out in the blizzard."

"Yes, yes. I can't think of the murder and that thing that nearly happened to Susan as being two unconnected events. Yes, someone could have attempted to abduct Susan. The sheriff was right when he said a rich man was a target. But I'll see to it that nothing happens to her. Or to you," Craig said and suddenly was gone.

That day it began to seem to Mady that the fact of murder had got its ugly talons into all of them.

The faked note left for Susan clearly indicated that whoever had lured her out into the blizzard knew Susan, knew them all and knew the house. It did not seem likely that the attempt either to lose her in the blizzard or to abduct her had nothing to do with the murder. It was almost as if something or rather somebody lay secretly in wait, ready to spring.

At first perhaps, immediately following the murder of Guy Casso, the shock itself had operated to induce a kind of disbelief, as if they said to themselves that this thing cannot have happened, and happened to us.

They had to accept it now; it had happened, and happened to them, and Susan might have lost her life.

And Mady did not forget the arm which, taken she thought by surprise, had reacted by thrusting her back and down into smothering, cold darkness.

So that day it seemed to Mady that everyone was a little different, everyone, that is, except Mirabel; she sat erect and stony, playing double solitaire and glancing out the windows now and then.

Susan, however, was silent and so pale that once or twice Mirabel asked her sternly if she felt all right.

Susan replied curtly. Yes, she felt all right; no, she didn't have a sore throat; no, she hadn't taken cold. But she sat on a hassock near the dog and soberly leaned her head on her hands. She didn't rouse until Rhoda came.

Rhoda had waded through the snow along the narrow path and was out of breath and tired when she came into the house. She pushed open the heavy front door and walked in, closed it with a hard bang and began stamping snow from her overshoes. She was shaking her coat when Susan and Mady ran into the hall, Sancho bounding and barking along with them.

Rhoda said flatly, "Hello."

Neither Susan nor Mady spoke for a moment. Mady glanced at Susan. She had her mother's lovely coloring, red hair, emerald-green eyes, yet just then she looked exactly like her father, hard and firm when he made some decision. She set her lips; then she put her arms around her mother's waist.

"What's the matter?" Rhoda said irritably.

Susan hugged closer.

Rhoda looked down at Susan's red head. "Look here now, Susan. I want to know the truth about last night. You did write that note yourself and sign Mady's name to it, didn't you?"

Susan shook her head violently.

"Well, then," Rhoda said, "exactly what happened? Come on now. The truth."

Susan put up her head. "I'm not in the habit of lying."

"Tell me what happened."

There was the faintest pause. Then Susan, putting two and two together, swiftly said, "Who told you that anything had happened?"

"Oh, heavens, child. Indian Joe told us last night. He came to the guest cabins. He asked if we knew anything about it — or if we had seen or heard any stranger. I didn't come to see you then. Joe said you were all right. Now tell me your story."

Susan said slowly, "I woke. I thought there had been some sound in the room. I lighted my candle. I couldn't find Sancho. There was a paper, a piece torn out of my sketchbook, on the floor. Somebody had written big letters in my black crayon all over it. It said that Sancho had got out and I was not to go out at all and it was signed Mady."

Rhoda looked at Susan for a moment; then she said, "Why did you go then?"

"Why?" Susan cried. "Sancho is my dog!"

Rhoda sighed. "I see. That is, I don't see who would do such a terrible thing. Now I want to talk to Mady. Privately."

Susan waited a moment; then she turned. Mady could see her face, and again it wore a look so like Craig's in its firm decision, so like Mirabel, too, that she could scarcely believe Susan was the young child that in fact she was. "Mother —" She paused.

Rhoda said, impatiently, "Well, what?"

"Mother," Susan said unexpectedly, "I do love you."

"Why — why, of course you do," Rhoda said. "You're my daughter, aren't you? Now run along."

Susan didn't run; she walked slowly away, Sancho trotting after her, looking oddly serious, as if he sensed something he didn't understand and didn't like.

Rhoda said, "Honestly, I've never understood that child. She's all Wilson. Let's go into Craig's study."

Mady followed her. Rhoda closed the door, went to Craig's armchair and sat down.

Mady saw that the ugly claws of murder had sunk into Rhoda, too. She had seemed at first almost casual about it. Now she was quite different; in the cold light from the windows, she was pale, her eyes darkly shadowed, so she looked haggard and old. Even the fine lines in her lovely face were sharper. She couldn't have slept much, not after learning of the attempt either to murder, to lose, or to abduct Susan; she looked as if she had never slept and never would sleep again. It was a strange and horrible thought that struck Mady.

But Rhoda was still beautiful. And she

was still determined. "I thought we'd better have a frank talk. Jim told me that you were through with him. He said you told him so when he arrived. Did you?"

"Yes."

"It gave him a shock."

"Oh, no, I don't think so."

"You were very cool and flat about it. But of course he didn't believe you."

"That's too bad."

"Oh, now, don't be angry. Jim came with me from the cabins as far as the door just now. We had — we had a talk. I know and Jim knows that you didn't mean whatever it was you said —"

"But I did mean it!"

Rhoda went on as if she hadn't heard Mady. "I don't want to hurt you, Mady. That's why I have been so frank with you. I'm giving you a chance to act for yourself. You are in a weak position. You're clinging to Craig. You are breaking up a family. I am Susan's mother. You heard her say that she loves me. It is only right that Craig and I should marry again and make a home for Susan. She shouldn't be shuttled around like this —"

"You broke up the marriage long before I ever knew Craig."

Rhoda went straight on. "I am in a very

strong position. I was Craig's wife and I loved him — I always loved him; I was only — I don't know, silly and very stupid. I didn't know what I was doing when I asked for a divorce —" Her words and voice sounded forced.

Mady waited.

Rhoda said, "What are you going to do? Withdraw with dignity? Behave well, let us keep together as a family? Or stick it out and hang onto Craig? And his money? I feel sure that Craig will make a handsome settlement on you. Much more," said Rhoda, suddenly sounding sincere, "than he did for me."

"He had no money then. You know that as well as I do. He had to borrow money from Mirabel to give you two hundred thousand dollars —"

"I signed away my property rights to get it."

"But you wanted the cash. And you have your alimony, too."

Rhoda said dully, "You're only interested in Craig's money. But I do think that at heart you want to do what is right. Don't stand in the way of keeping our family together. Think of Susan and Craig and me. I was wrong, I know that now. But I'm sorry. I love Craig. I want him back and I want my daughter all the time, not just visits with her — and it's wicked of you to cling to Craig!"

"He's my husband," Mady said.

Rhoda waited a moment. "Think of Susan then."

"I am thinking of Susan. She is a very nice girl." Mady was vaguely surprised that lightning did not strike her dead on the spot. "She needs a real home."

"You think you can give it to her! You heard her say she loves me! How wrong you are to separate mother and child!"

"But you did the separating." Yet even as she said it, Mady knew that Rhoda had a very powerful argument on her side.

Rhoda eyed her. "You're not doing such a good job of taking care of Susan. Whatever it was that happened — nearly happened — to her last night proves that neither you nor Craig takes care of her as you should."

There was powerful truth in that, too. But Mady adopted the liberty of plain talk herself. "Rhoda, why would Casso have come here except to see you? Are you sure you didn't see him that day you arrived?"

Rhoda's lovely eyes shifted away from Mady. "I've answered that question a number of times. The answer is still no.

And I don't think it is your business to question me."

"I don't think it's your business to try to break up my marriage." They were beginning to sound like two children bickering. Mady said, "There's no use in quarreling about this. I am Craig's wife."

"Not for long," Rhoda said. "I'll see to that. I know that Craig really still loves me. He loves Susan and I'm her mother and you haven't a leg to stand on and you know it."

And of course that might be the truth, also. Rhoda rose and went out into the hall. She shrugged herself into her coat and sat down to shove her feet into the high buckled overshoes. She then walked out of the house without another word. She tugged at the door to close it. Mady went automatically to push from her side of the door, and had a glimpse of her turning away into the onslaught of snow and wind. When Mady turned, Susan and Sancho stood just inside the dining room door and Susan was blushing.

Susan was not the only one who could put two and two together. Mady said, "People don't listen at doors."

Caught in the act, Susan reverted to her more normal self. "They do," she said, "when they know they're going to be talked about. Did you mean it when you told her I was a nice girl?"

The contagion of Wilson candor caught Mady. "Sometimes," she said guardedly.

"Well —" For a moment Susan looked a little daunted. Then a gleam came into her eyes. "If I were you I wouldn't be so sure of myself. My mother gets what she wants, and right now she wants my father back. His money, too. And she thinks she wants me." All at once the gleam was gone. Again her pretty face took on a sadly adult look. She said tonelessly, "Not that she really does want me. I'm too much of a bother. She has other things to do. But she is my mother." She had a queerly defiant look, quite as if she were arguing Rhoda's case against some accusation. "She doesn't always mean what she says. Especially if she's drinking. I mean — I mean *when* she was drinking. She doesn't drink like that any more. She stopped. You can tell that. But she — nobody can blame her for — for anything!" she cried, tossed her red hair back and ran for the stairs, whistling for Sancho.

Mady was tempted to follow her, try to get her to talk, and if she knew or guessed anything at all about Guy Casso's murder, to tell Mady what it was.

Of course she couldn't; she wouldn't overstep her slender authority, if indeed it could be called authority. If Susan really had some bit of knowledge and really understood it for what it was, she would almost certainly have told somebody, and that somebody had to be Craig.

But there had to be some reason for luring Susan out into the blizzard with so wickedly conceived a bait.

Mirabel was in the living room; its great windows were still veiled in swirling white. She snapped off the radio as Mady came in. "Weather report," she said briefly. "Stockmen's warnings all across the county. It's a bad one. What did Rhoda want?"

"Craig." It occurred to Mady that life was certainly made simpler by the Wilson habit of direct questions and direct answers.

"Don't give him up, Mady."

"If he wants her, I can't help it."

"Why, you little fool," Mirabel said, her face as stern and craggy as any mountain. "Of course you can help it. You can simply stick it out and refuse to give him up. If you like him you can show it, can't you? All sorts of ways. I don't know what the young are coming to! They think they know so much and really know so little. And that," Mirabel said, "applies to you." She sat down. "Besides, there's Susan. Rhoda was a foolish and a careless kind of mother. Didn't give a hoot about Susan, if you ask me. Now she is relying upon Susan as an argument for getting Craig back."

"It's a strong argument, no matter how you look at it."

Mirabel was powerful and adamant. "I have looked at it a great deal more closely and a great deal longer than you. Rhoda has her good points. But she's no more stable than water. She says one thing one day and another the next. She'd as soon lie as look at you. She's very easily influenced. Anybody can lead her by soft words —" Mirabel thumped the table beside her with her wrinkled but strong old hand. "She's beautiful. And she has a certain kind of charm. But she refuses to face anything she doesn't want to face. She can fool herself, shut her eyes to anything she doesn't want to see. I don't object to her seeing Susan occasionally — not that she has wanted to see her often until lately, when apparently it occurred to her to use Susan as an argument to get Craig — and his money — back." She broke off and stared at the curtain of snow. "I believe that's Boyce. And that young Marsh. They must be going to the bunkhouse."

Her eyes were old but sharp as an eagle's; Mady could barely see the shapes of two men trudging single file through a very narrow path in the snow in the direction of the bunkhouse.

Mirabel looked at her watch. "It's about time for another weather report."

It was close to noon when Mady went to Craig's study again and tried the telephone, but the instrument was still as blank as the puzzling Mr. Banner's soft brown eyes.

Again she tried hard, as Craig had told her to do, to remember when and where — or even if — she had ever seen Mr. Banner before, and could not. Yet there had been an immediate sense of something familiar, something not quite recognition but near it.

Craig did not return, but late in the afternoon there was another visitor, Edith. She came plodding through the path, which by then was almost drifted over, stamping inside the house without knocking, unwinding scarves and shaking out her coat and going into the study without removing her heavy boots. "I came to see Craig," she said. "I want to talk to him."

Mirabel was in the living room; Susan, again unwontedly quiet, was upstairs with Sancho. Mady told Edith that Craig had gone out to help the ranch hands.

Edith sat down and puffed. "More than Boyce would do," she said. "Heaven only knows what that foreman of Boyce's is doing. We'll probably lose every head of stock on the place."

"I hope not."

Edith eyed Mady narrowly. "You don't know anything at all about us or about ranching, do you?"

"I'm learning fast," Mady said and meant it.

Edith shrugged; her little eyes snapped. "I have something I just might tell Craig."

"I don't understand."

"Just tell Craig that I might do him a good turn. I just might. Craig is a generous man, isn't he?"

Mady again did her share of putting two and two together, swiftly and surprised. "I don't think he'll buy information."

"Oh, don't you? He would if —" Edith broke off and said fretfully, "You ought to be thankful this house is heated. Those guest cabins are cold as charity. Of course"

— she reverted to whatever her theme was — "Craig has not been exactly generous with Boyce and me. When he discovered Wilsonite on the part of the ranch that came to him, he didn't give Boyce a penny."

"Boyce didn't believe in Wilsonite. He didn't put up a penny for its development." Mady wasn't going to let Edith provoke her to anger but she couldn't resist that.

Two pink spots came into Edith's cheeks. "Boyce didn't have the money to back any of Craig's wild schemes. We barely make out with the ranch. Boyce is not a cattleman. Craig ought to help him. And I think he will when I talk to him. Very, very generously. It's worth something. And believe me, it will cost me something."

Mady rose, closed the door of the study and came back to speak softly to Edith. "Edith, if it's something about the murder, something you know or — or guess —"

Edith's little eyes seemed cloudy and rather undecided. "I wouldn't call it — well, it's only a conclusion — that is —" Her eyes sharpened. "I'd rather not talk to you about it."

"You said conclusion. You mean that you know something that has some bearing upon the murder?"

"It's as plain as the nose on my face. I'll say that. There could be only one reason for — Oh, never mind. You're not going to coax it out of me. I'll talk to Craig."

"But, Edith, wait. If you've found out something or heard something or — in any way have made some sort of guess about the murder which might be the right guess, why then — Edith, that's very dangerous."

"Dangerous!" Her hen's eyes opened brightly. "Dangerous to the murderer, not to me!"

"But, Edith — Well, then don't tell anybody. Don't let anybody know —"

"I've told you." She thought for a moment and then said with a strange effect of sadness, "I told you that it will cost me something. But I'm going to tell Craig just the same." She rose.

Mady actually caught her arm. "Edith, stay here until Craig gets home."

She seemed to think that over. Mady could make nothing of her face, but she thought there was a certain indecision which struggled against resolve. If so, resolve won. Edith said briskly, "No. But tell Craig what I've told you. You might prepare him for a high price." She rose and started winding herself up in scarves again.

Mady resorted to a point-blank question. "Do you know who murdered Lasso?"

Edith pulled a scarf closer over her head.

Mady said rather desperately, "Do you know — have you guessed *why* he was murdered?"

Again the look of indecision came into Edith's face. She said after a moment, "I don't have to be told things. I can reason for myself. I'm going now."

She trundled out of the room through the hall and left.

The snow and wind fell upon her and the open door, and again, as when Rhoda had gone, Mady pushed the heavy door shut and then got a mop from a closet off the kitchen and cleaned up the little drifts of melted snow on the lovely floor with its wide dark boards. Manuel didn't try to stop her. He was looking harried, preparing baskets of dinner for Boyce and Jim to take to the guest cabins.

Mady listened for Craig. She wished that she had been able to get more information from Edith or to keep her there until Craig returned.

Mirabel engaged her in some prolonged games of Russian bank. Susan came and leaned over Mady's shoulder, advising her about openings she had not seen. "Susan is a good card player," Mirabel said.

"But Aunt Mirabel usually wins," Susan said.

Yes, Mady thought, a nice girl — sometimes. But almost immediately she gave a kind of normal, Susan-like whoop, shouted to Sancho and ran to the kitchen, where a hubbub arose like an explosion. Mady could hear Manuel's angry voice, Inez's voice and Susan's shrieks.

Mirabel said calmly, "Let them fight it out. You haven't told me what Edith wanted."

"She wanted to talk to Craig."

"She wants money, of course. That's Edith for you. Did she have any special excuse for asking for money?"

"Yes," Mady said slowly, "I think so. But I don't know what. That is, she seemed to feel that she had seen something or heard something — or only reasoned out something which Craig might pay her to know about."

Mirabel eyed her for a moment. "You mean about Casso's murder? Could be anything," she said finally. "Could be wrong. But Edith is shrewd. It could be something. Well — I think I'll take a rest before dinner. I'm not as young as I once

209

was." But she marched out of the room as vigorously as a twenty-year-old.

It was dinnertime, fully dark and still snowing when they found Edith.

Chapter 11

It was probably as easy a murder as had ever been done. The snow and wind had covered all tracks. The snow supplied curtains of invisibility. The snow prevented fixing even the time of her murder. Carbon monoxide from Mr. Banner's car did the rest.

Craig had barely returned to the house when Boyce, Jim and Rhoda came, the men helping Rhoda along a path which by now was almost obliterated. Mady had had no chance and no time to tell Craig of Edith's visit and of her offer to sell what had to be evidence if Craig was prepared to pay the price for it. Mady was in his room; Craig had just started to change his clothes when they heard the voices in the hall. Boyce's rose above the others. "Craig! Where are you, Craig? Edith's gone. We can't find her anywhere!"

Craig ran down the stairs. Mady followed, and afterward it seemed to her that she must have known what had happened, but of course she didn't. Nobody living the kind of lives most people live can seriously consider the possibility of murder. But Mady had once found murder. And Edith had come to trade something to Craig for money.

Rhoda, it developed, had discovered Edith's absence. She had not seen Edith all afternoon; but she had thought only that she was sleeping, for Edith's bedroom door was closed.

After lunch Boyce and Jim had struggled to the bunkhouse simply because there was nothing else to do. Mr. Banner had joined them for a while. Then Boyce had come back to the cabin and lounged around on his bed, reading old magazines. Jim had returned, too, borrowed a warmer sweater from Boyce and gone into his own room, where he turned on a radio. Rhoda had heard it.

Nobody knew where Mr. Banner had gone; it was assumed that he had returned to the foreman's cabin. Rhoda, she said, had taken a long nap herself. It was only when dusk came on that it struck Rhoda that Edith was taking a very long sleep; she knocked at the door, opened it and Edith was not there. Rhoda had waded over to the other guest cabin; Boyce and Jim were there. They thought Edith must have gone to the main house.

She *had* come to the main house, Mady thought, with a cold kind of knock at her awareness, in the late afternoon. Mady also thought, strangely, that there was not a solid alibi among them.

The darting course of her own fancy shocked and frightened her. She watched while Craig bundled himself again in a heavy coat and a cap with enormous ear flaps; she watched the three men go out into the snow, which shone like tiny diamonds where the rays of light from the open door streamed out into the night. The door then closed.

Rhoda slid out of her coat. Mirabel said they could only wait. Mady was sure that they, too, were afraid of what might be found.

It was a long wait; it probably seemed even longer than it was. Craig came back at last, hurrying along the hall, searching for a new battery for his flashlight. Somehow, Mirabel, Rhoda and Mady all got into the hall at the same time, and Craig glanced at them, said, "Nothing yet," and found the battery in a drawer in his study. He was jamming it into the enormous flashlight when Indian Joe thrust open the front door. Mady saw his face and instinctively knew what he was going to say. Craig came running out of the study, and Indian Joe said it. "We found her. She's in that man's car. Mr. Banner's. The engine was running. When I got near enough the shed I smelled it, so I looked."

"Is she — ?" Craig began, and Indian Joe said, "Yes. No way to get the sheriff or the police here now."

"Sheriff?" Craig said.

Indian Joe nodded. "No doubt about it. Big bruise on her temple. She was dragged into the car, left there in a huddle. Engine started. Car doors, shed door, everything closed up tight. No use trying to do anything for her now."

Craig took a long breath. "We can't leave her there."

Indian Joe agreed. "The law says leave her. It doesn't seem right. How about taking her to the cabin Shorty used to have?"

"All right. I'll come with you." Craig turned to Mady. "Try to keep Susan out of this till we know what to do."

He went out with Indian Joe. Mirabel stood like a stone.

Rhoda didn't faint but she slipped down on the stairway and put her face in her hands. Mady started upstairs to try to soften things for Susan, but Susan knew. She was hanging over the banister and she had heard every word. "She was murdered," Susan said.

There was no use in trying to evade. "She was found in the car that the man who came last night —"

"I know — Mr. Banner. Engine running." Susan looked hard at Mady. "Somebody hit her over the head, dragged her into that car, started the engine, shut the door of that old shed. Maybe Uncle Boyce did it."

"Susan! Don't say things like that!"

"She was a nagger. Nearly drove Uncle Boyce out of his head sometimes. She was a snooper, too. Read other people's letters. All the same —" Susan's lips quivered a little. She bent over to pat Sancho, who stood, troubled, beside her. "All the same I wouldn't have wanted anybody to kill her."

"Susan —"

Susan lifted her head. "It shows that whoever murdered Guy is still around. He tried to get me last night out in the snow. And he pushed you down in the snow so you wouldn't know who it was. I'm scared."

"So am I," Mady said truthfully. "Let's go into your room and have a game of Russian bank."

"You are trying to distract the child — me." Susan's green eyes were uncannily clear and also firm. "There's one thing you have to admit. Only a man could have done this."

"I don't see how a woman could have killed Casso — or your Aunt Edith."

Susan searched Mady's eyes with that clear and steady gaze, seemed to believe her and gave a slight shrug. "All right," she said, "come on," and led the way into her room, Sancho still at her side.

Her mood had changed; she reverted as swiftly as a shadow to her normal self. "I get tired of Russian bank. It's the only game Aunt Mirabel likes. Want me to teach you poker?"

"All right."

Mady had come to Susan's room intending to try to give some support to the child; actually, it worked out the other way. Susan was cool, self-controlled and matter-of-fact.

They set up a card table, Susan laid out poker hands and gave Mady brief but, as she later learned, excellent lessons.

"Of course," Susan said, "poker is the

real reason why my father married you."

"Poker!"

"It was why old Sissypoo fired me from school. Father was kind of desperate for somebody like you to help see to me."

"You mean Miss Siskins." In fact, Sissypoo was not a bad name for her. Mady had encountered her once, when she came to talk to Craig about some heinous activity or other on Susan's part.

Susan said airily, "I only taught some of the girls how to play. It wasn't my fault that they lost money to me. Wasn't my fault at the school before that either. Only" — she looked pensive — "that time it was craps and the girls didn't have enough money with them, so I had to take their I.O.U.s and one of them told on me. The headmistress made me give back all of the I.O.U.s before she told my father she didn't think her school was the right one for me."

"Well, Susan, you'll have to go to school somewhere," Mady said helplessly.

Susan set her lips and her chin. Then she yielded. "All right. I don't want to be another Uncle Boyce. I like to read and — But I want to go to school right here in Wilson City. I want to live here at El Rancho. Now listen, Mady, you've got a

217

good pair. I think that, because you drew three cards. The averages are against your drawing the third card for your pair. And while I think of it, never, never draw to an inside straight. Card games are made up of averages." She explained it lucidly.

"You ought to be good at mathematics," Mady said, and Susan nodded complacently yet, Mady thought, truthfully.

"Yes, I am."

"How did you learn card games?"

"Indian Joe, of course. And the boys in the bunkhouse. They're very good players. Of course, at first they used to let me win. I'm a girl and the boss's daughter. I soon stopped that." She looked searchingly at Mady. "I expect you took dancing lessons, or music lessons or something. What's the difference?" She looked now entirely natural, as if for the moment she had forgotten whatever it was that sometimes brought that adult and troubled shadow into her face. She grinned, her eyes danced. "Let's make a bet on this hand. No fun unless we bet."

"What kind of bet?" Mady asked cautiously.

"Well, it's this way. Aunt Mirabel chooses my dresses. At least she has up to now. She lets me wear blue jeans and shirts here on the ranch, but at dinner and in the city — Oh, you've seen. She's still making me wear baby clothes!" Susan snorted rather like Mirabel. "I'm going on thirteen. I'm too old for those sissy dresses. If I win this hand, you'll be on my side about clothes. How's that?"

Mady tried to think back to herself going on thirteen. She couldn't remember what kind of dresses she'd worn. She said, "All right. But you'll win."

"Of course," Susan said smugly. "It's betting on a sure thing. Not exactly fair but —" She had started to deal; she stopped, listened and put down the cards. Her face hardened. "There they are. You want to go down and hear what happened? So do I, but they'll not let me."

"Are you going to listen from the top of the stairs?"

"Of course," Susan said matter-of-factly.

There wasn't really any way Mady could stop her. Besides, she had a growing respect for Susan's recuperative powers, as well as her basic common sense. So she went down and into the living room where they were all talking. Rhoda was saying, "I wasn't alarmed. But then at dusk when she still didn't come out of her bedroom, I looked —"

Mirabel told Rhoda to take it easy.

Craig went to the fire and put on more logs. The house was warm, yet it seemed as if a pervasive chill had entered it.

Boyce was in the dining room. Mady heard the clink of ice in a glass. Craig said, "I'd better see to Boyce," and went out. Rhoda just sat as limp as a doll, her face drawn and lifeless. Certainly none of them looked quite natural. Even Jim, who had known Edith so little, looked stiffly sober. He took the drink Mirabel handed to him as absently as she — efficiently, yet in a rigidly controlled way — handed out glasses to Indian Joe and the two ranch hands who had come into the house. The two men swallowed their drinks, asked if anybody needed them any longer, then trudged out and back through the snow to the bunkhouse. Indian Joe remained.

They had gathered in the living room probably because Manuel had set out the tray of glasses and whiskey on the table there. The rail still stood where Mady had replaced it. At least it had not been used a second time for murder.

Craig returned from the dining room with Boyce, who was unsteady on his feet. Craig shoved him into a corner of the sofa, and Boyce tried to sit up with dignity, but his eyes and, when he tried to speak, his voice were blurred.

They were an odd-looking company. Craig was in a heavy flannel shirt, heavy boots and jeans; his fleece-lined coat lay on the floor. Boyce was the tweedy gentleman rancher still, but a very disheveled one. Jim wore an assortment of clothes apparently borrowed from Boyce, flannel shirt, heavy sweater which was too big for him, khaki trousers which were soaked to the knees from the snow; boots borrowed from somebody, too. In spite of it he looked rather elegant, as if he were wearing the assortment of ill-fitting clothes for a masquerade. But he also looked rather glassy and frozen. Rhoda downed her drink, held out the empty glass and didn't seem to have the strength or will to rise and pour another for herself.

Indian Joe put his swarthy finger on the first and obvious action. "We can't get the sheriff or the police here now, Mr. Wilson," he said. "The way I see it we've got to do what we can ourselves. Whoever killed her is here on the ranch. No way to leave safely, no way to get here safely. Shall I get this new fellow, this man Banner, in here and question him?"

Boyce came to a little and said, "Banner

did it. His car."

"Did Edith know Banner?" Craig asked him.

Boyce considered it, tried to shove his hands in his pockets, missed and said blearily, "Can't have. Never saw him before. Can't have known him."

Indian Joe said, "I made a mistake, Mr. Wilson. The key was in the ignition and we started Banner's car when we hauled it off by tractor and put it in the shed. I ran it in the shed myself as soon as we got it to the door. But then I left the key in the ignition the way Mr. Banner had left it. I shut up the shed doors to keep the snow out and never thought of the key again. Never thought of anything like this. I should have taken out that key. It made it easy for the murderer to start the engine."

"Nobody would have thought of anything like this," Craig said. "Did Banner know that the key was still in the car?"

"I don't know. We can talk to him."

Indian Joe did not sound very hopeful of discovering anything at all in a talk with Mr. Banner. Neither did Craig, but he said, "We'll talk to him now. Talk to the boys in the bunkhouse, too. One of them may have seen something —" He didn't say what.

Boyce was determined to go with them. He mumbled, he staggered, but he heaved himself up and made a fairly straight line for the door and his coat. Jim started after them, and then said to anybody who was listening, "No use my going, too." He looked at Rhoda's empty glass, took it to the table and replenished it.

Rhoda all at once began to sob wildly. Mirabel waited a moment as Jim went to Rhoda and put the refilled glass in her hand. "Here," he said. "Here —"

Mirabel took over. "Come now, Rhoda." She spoke sharply, and Rhoda looked up, her face ghastly white and her mouth pulled wide with sobbing. Mirabel said, "You'll terrify Susan. Now pull yourself together and come upstairs with me. Wash your face. You'll feel better."

Mady didn't think that washing one's face was likely to improve anybody's state of mind just then, but Mirabel's sharp command did rouse Rhoda and she went out, almost running, with Mirabel.

It so happened that Jim and Mady were left alone for the first time really since Jim's arrival.

She was only vaguely aware of his presence. She wanted to talk to Craig and she had had no chance to talk to him alone.

She did not know and couldn't possibly make a reasonable guess about the identity of Edith's murderer, but she was dreadfully sure that she knew why Edith had been murdered. Edith was a foolish woman perhaps; Mady knew her very little but she had sensed in her a kind of mixture of cunning, shrewdness and bitterness over life in general. It was possible, indeed it now seemed probable, that whatever conclusions she had drawn were correct; it also seemed logical to believe that in some way her murderer — and thus Casso's murderer — had known what those conclusions were. "I don't have to be told things," she had said, "I can reason for myself."

It seemed likely that that belief had cost Edith her life.

Jim said something. Mady had forgotten his presence. "What?"

Jim said, "Why did I ever come to this place?"

It needed no reply. Mady went to the fire and stirred it up with the huge iron poker.

Jim said, "I never dreamed of anything like this. Murder and the sheriff and police and this horrible snow. Now maybe that you've seen what it's like, you'll come to your senses and let me take you away."

Mady felt only a kind of sharp impatience. "Oh, don't talk like that!"

Jim sat down and eyed her and said at last, softly, "I don't believe you've changed. You still love me."

"I don't. I don't know why I ever thought so."

"You can't deceive me. I know you too well. You only want to keep me dangling awhile. Pride. You want to punish me."

"Don't be fatuous!"

"I understand you better than you understand yourself. I hurt you. I admit it. I was wrong. I am sorry. But it was mainly because all at once I was afraid I couldn't — couldn't support you. Couldn't take care of you. Yes, I'll admit it, I was scared. But I came to my senses. Now I want you to come to your senses."

"I did!"

Jim rose and came toward her. "Mady, my darling —"

Mady lost her temper. "I told you! I really can't understand what I ever saw in you. I mean it!"

"You mean that you've had a taste of money and you like it. Well," he said waspishly, "you'd better get all you can out of Craig because Rhoda is going to get him back again."

225

"Not if I can help it!" She said it shortly, almost absentmindedly, listening for Craig, thinking of sharp-faced Edith with her hen's eyes, her tragic knowledge.

Jim laughed. "You don't have a chance against Rhoda. Besides, there's Susan to consider. I came out here because I'm still in love with you. It was Rhoda's idea for me to come. She thought it would help her. She knew that once I was here and explained everything to you —"

Mady interrupted. "She thought that I'd leave Craig and run back to you. And she'd get Craig to marry her again! You may have thought so too but —" Mady stopped. She was struck by an inconsistency. "Why, Jim, you're not at all in love with me! Why did you lend yourself to such a plan?"

He turned away and walked to the glittering black window which reflected him and Mady and the lights of the room and also the rail standing there, shining. The vase of chrysanthemums still stood beside it, bright in yellow and bronze, still sturdy, withering only a little. She must remember to tell Manuel to take them out the next day.

She thought that, absently, and then an ugly yet reasonable surmise stabbed its way into her mind. "Why, you thought that

Craig would give me a big settlement, as he did when Rhoda divorced him! No, you thought he'd give me even more than he gave Rhoda. He's very rich now. He wasn't rich then. You thought I would make him give me — oh, a really big sum of money. And you intended to marry me and get that money."

The fire crackled. Jim's image and Mady's stood still in the shining window. Then he gave a pleased chuckle. "Why not, darling? Craig is rich. You and I can use some money. Why, he can set us up for life and it won't hurt him. That's settled then —"

Mady said, "No!" like an explosion, and then heard the front door open and men's voices and footsteps in the hall. She ran to the door. Craig was helping Boyce, who was frankly staggering. Indian Joe held Boyce's other arm. They got him into the living room and sat him in a chair. Mady went to Craig. "I've got to talk to you," she said in a low voice. She thought that only Indian Joe's acute ears could have heard her. Jim had gone to assist Boyce, who was demanding a drink in thick accents. Craig gave Mady one look and led her to his study. He closed the door. "What, Mady?"

"I think I know why Edith was murdered."

He opened the door and called to Joe, "Will you come in?"

Joe came in as quietly and swiftly as any of his forebears might have moved, and again closed the door.

Craig said to Mady, "You don't mind if Joe hears whatever it is —"

"I think Edith knew something about Casso's murder. I think she had discovered it only recently. She wanted money from you —"

She told it all, word for word, as accurately as she could. Indian Joe stood perfectly still. Craig sat on the edge of his desk. Both listened carefully.

Mady concluded: "You had come into the house, Craig, a minute before Boyce and Jim and Rhoda came to look for Edith. I was waiting to tell you what she had said when they came. I think that's why she was killed."

Craig made her sit down near him; he put his hand over hers. "You couldn't have stopped it. Edith would never have told you whatever it was she thought she had discovered. She didn't give you even a hint? I mean a person, a conversation, any sort of evidence?"

"Not a word. But she wanted money."

Craig said, "Poor Edith. Boyce —" he went on, "is upset now. Shocked, of course. Drinking too much. That'll go on for a while. But it isn't as if there was much love lost between them. I think Edith was always disappointed in her marriage. She expected something more glamorous." He rubbed his hands over his tired eyes. "What do you think, Joe?"

"Same as you," Indian Joe said. "Mrs. Boyce got hold of something, and it was something that she thought would be valuable enough to get you to pay for it. She said it would cost her something. That could have meant that it would cost her money, or it would be hard for her to do, hurt somebody she liked. She liked Boyce — I guess. But I can't see Boyce killing her. Or Casso. You said she used the word 'conclusion,' didn't you, Mrs. Wilson?"

Mady nodded. "She said it — whatever it was — was as plain as the nose on her face. She said she'd rather not talk to me about it. But she would tell Craig."

Indian Joe said, "And then you asked her if she knew who murdered Casso?"

"Yes. And she wouldn't say, so I asked her if she knew why he was murdered. She wouldn't answer that either. And when she left she said that she didn't have to be told things. She could reason for herself. That's all."

Indian Joe said, "It looks as if she reasoned the right way. And somebody knew it and killed her and — Is that phone working yet?"

Craig took up the telephone as they had all done, it seemed to Mady, for days and days. There was no dial tone. He put it down again. "The sheriff couldn't get here anyway. Or the police. We'll have to do the best we can. There's no avoiding the fact that the murderer is here on the ranch. It was easier to think or at least hope that whoever killed Guy Casso merely chose that trail hoping to escape being seen and to get away, somebody who knew Casso but nobody connected with us. Of course, the rail was always an argument against that. Whoever killed Casso had to know about the rail, had to have reason to think he could enter the house and take it and get away without being seen. And of course," Craig went on, "only somebody accustomed to the ranch could enter the house and contrive to get Susan out in the snow."

Indian Joe looked at Mady. "You didn't happen to tell anybody that Mrs. Boyce had been here or what she said, did you, Mrs. Wilson?"

"Why, no — that is, anybody might have known that she came here. But I didn't tell —" She stopped short. "Yes, I did. I'd forgotten. But it was only Mirabel."

There was a short pause. Then Indian Joe turned to Craig. "Have you talked to Susan yet, Mr. Wilson; I mean — well, just suppose she does know something about Casso's murderer."

"I can't believe that she does," Craig said, but he looked very white.

"Not," Indian Joe said wryly, "that she'll tell you anything she doesn't want to tell. Not Susan."

Craig thought for a moment. "We'll have to try."

There was a kind of deep silence, as if the whole house were listening, waiting for someone to speak. Mady said at last, "I take it that none of the ranch hands know anything about Edith's murder?"

Indian Joe flickered an eyebrow, which, from the taciturn Joe, was practically a long statement to the effect that the ranch hands had seen or heard nothing at all that was evidence.

Craig was more explicit. "All of them working. Banner was in the kitchen most of the afternoon. Cook left him there while he went to take a rest. Cook says Banner was still there when he came back to the kitchen to cook supper. No evidence. Mady, have you remembered if or where you saw Banner?"

"No. I'm not sure I've ever seen him before. I could have seen somebody in — oh, a movie or on the street, or somewhere. I can't even find a connection. How soon can the sheriff and the police get here?"

"The snow is dwindling, about to stop. They can get here as soon as a passable road is cleared. They'll get the phone working as soon as it's humanly possible —" Craig stopped as the study door opened and Rhoda came running in. She flung herself at Craig; she put her arms up around him. She sobbed against his shoulder, "Craig, take care of me. I'm so frightened. Take care of me."

Mady did what Mirabel had told her not to do. She walked out of the room. Indian Joe stalked after her, gave her a look of infinite scorn and said, "Squaw very damn foolish. Ought to stay and fight it out with Red Hair."

There was not even a glimmer of humor in his dark eyes. He meant what he said.

He went out the front door and banged it hard after him.

So Indian Joe knew, or easily guessed, Rhoda's intention to remarry Craig.

Chapter 12

Indian Joe and Mirabel agreed. But all the same, if Craig wanted Rhoda, then let him have Rhoda, Mady told herself. Mirabel was all wrong about fighting for Craig; so was Indian Joe. If Mady had to fight for Craig, she didn't want him. But even as she thought it, she knew that she was lying to herself. She went back to the living room before she remembered that Jim and Boyce were there.

Jim stood at the window, his back to the room. Boyce was a sodden hulk on the sofa, so red-faced from the cold and from drinking that she thought he'd have a stroke then and there and didn't care. However, she didn't think, in spite of Susan's opinion, that Boyce would have murdered Edith.

Jim turned around. "I've been thinking," he said directly to Boyce, ignoring Mady, "nobody on the ranch has a real alibi for the time of your wife's murder. Isn't that right?"

Boyce didn't hear for a moment; then

the words seemed to penetrate the haze of shock and of whiskey. He lifted his red face and blinked at Jim. "Alibi?"

"Alibi," Jim said impatiently. "Listen. You don't have an alibi. I don't have an alibi. Any of the fellows on the ranch could have drifted out, any time, or come in from whatever they were doing —"

"Feeding," Boyce said thickly. "Hard to feed in a storm like this. Have to take out hay and —"

"But that's my point. Nobody knew anything that was going on this afternoon, all the time."

Boyce blinked and said, thickly again but making a point, "They don't know when Edith was killed. How could anybody have an alibi for any special time when nobody knows what that time was? Understand me?"

"Yes, of course. But my point is —"

Mirabel came in. She gave Mady such a sharp glance that Mady was sure Mirabel knew Rhoda was with Craig, and went to Boyce. "Give me that glass," she said firmly. "You'd better get some food into you."

Food, Mady thought rather wildly. It was long past dinnertime. She went out, past the study door, still closed, and did pause for just a second to hear the soft murmur of Rhoda's voice inside. Her hand itched to open the door. She went on into the dining room, and there such courage as she still had failed her entirely, for the long table was formally set for dinner — plates, crystal goblets, wineglasses, candles, the entire array of silver. They could not possibly sit there, all of them, facing each other over that table.

Manuel had heard her footsteps on the polished floor and opened the pantry door. He looked old and gray. Inez peered over his shoulder; her enormous black eyes were full of question. Mady said, "Manuel, I don't think it's a good plan to have dinner as usual. Besides, it's so late."

"Oh, it dried up long ago," Manuel said. "We can manage something hot though. On trays?"

"Yes," she said thankfully. "How about Miss Susan?"

"She came down to the kitchen. The dog, too. They're all right. She went back to her room — unless," said Manuel, revealing his knowledge of what went on in the house, "unless she's listening on the stairs."

Probably she was doing exactly that. However, Mady felt again a kind of tingle of alarm. It was hard to believe that Susan could have any evidence about Casso's murder; yet somebody had lured Susan out into the snow and had done it adroitly.

"Trays, fine. Thank you." She ran up the stairs, but Susan was in her room, this time making sketches with crayons and looking less pale and adult. Her model was Sancho, who, Susan said, pretending to be cross, wouldn't mind her and kept moving and she didn't know why she had such a bad dog. Sancho knew the word bad and looked serious. So Susan hustled over to tell him she hadn't meant it, he was a good dog.

Mady said, carefully, "You'll not take Sancho out alone, will you?"

Susan pulled gently at Sancho's ears and he lolled out a red tongue. "I'm no fool. Somebody killed Aunt Edith. But that man who came last night and got lost in the snow, Mr. Banner — well, he couldn't have known Aunt Edith. And you don't," Susan said with logic, "kill somebody you don't know." She paused to consider that and added thoughtfully, "Not as a rule, anyway."

There were footsteps on the stairs; Susan ran to the door and looked down the hall. She turned back to Mady. Her look, her mood changed in that split second of time. She was now pale and unchildlike. She gave Mady one green glance and bent over to pat Sancho. Somehow Mady was sure that she was thinking hard. Craig and Indian Joe came in.

Susan did not look up. Craig did not look at Mady; there was again in his attitude a subtle sense of remoteness. That was because of his talk with Rhoda a few moments before, Mady thought swiftly and with a mixture of anger and apprehension. Rhoda had looked so beautiful; she had flung herself into Craig's arms; she had said, pathetically, that she was afraid.

Craig said, "We want to talk to you, Susan." Indian Joe leaned against the door which he had quietly closed.

Susan shook her red hair over her face. "I know what you want. You're going to grill me."

Craig sighed. "Listen to me, Susan. You're a little girl. I'm your father. There are times," he added, lapsing into naturalness, "when I'd like to give you a good walloping. But I'm not going to grill you, I only want to ask you some questions."

"You want to know who got into my room and wrote on that paper out of my sketchbook and who shut Sancho up in the closet and — and why!" Susan lifted her head, shook her hair back and said defiantly, "It was somebody who wanted to scare me or — or to leave me out there in the blizzard and — I know that! But I don't know who it was and you can't make me say I do because I don't. But I do know that it had to be somebody who — who doesn't like me," she ended up with a childish, frightened little shake in her voice.

Indian Joe said, "Come here, Susan." He sat down in a rocker which was far too small for his long legs. Susan hesitated; then she went to him. "Now, Susan," Indian Joe said, "it's not nice to have to ask you these questions. But we want to know some things about the afternoon that man Casso was killed. All right?"

Susan considered it. Finally she said, "Well, what?"

"We've talked to your Uncle Boyce and to Miss Mirabel and to your mother."

"So did the police," Susan said.

"Yes — well — your uncle says that he was out on the ranch during the entire afternoon."

Susan nodded. "Yes, he was. I saw him leave. He took the jeep."

"Yes. Now, your mother arrived that morning."

"Of course," Susan said. "You know that. She had rented a car in Las Vegas. A chauffeur too. She got there late in the morning."

"Yes, I know. Then she phoned your father in San Francisco."

"She's told you that. She wanted to talk to him. I heard her at the phone."

"You know why she wanted to see him?"

"Oh, well, it wasn't hard to guess. She sort of spends, you know. Uncle Boyce thought it was very extravagant for her to rent that car in Vegas and so did Aunt Edith — but my mother only laughed."

Indian Joe said smoothly, "I expect she had a good talk with your Aunt Edith."

Susan drew back. "What do you mean a good talk?"

"They hadn't seen each other for a while. It would be natural for them to have a kind of talk, wouldn't it?"

"I suppose so," Susan said reluctantly.

"You didn't happen to hear any of it, did you?"

Susan's face flushed. "You shouldn't say things like that! That's not nice!"

"Well, did you?"

"No! No, I didn't!"

"Now, Susan —" Indian Joe said quietly, and Susan sighed.

"Oh, all right. But they didn't say anything much. Aunt Edith said that Father wouldn't like Jim Marsh's coming. And he *didn't* like it. But Mother said that Mady wanted Jim to come —"

Craig didn't look at Mady. Indian Joe went on. "Then what did they say, Susan?"

"One of them shut the door," Susan said, rather disappointedly even now.

"Oh," Indian Joe said after a moment. "But then your mother phoned Mr. Wilson —" Susan nodded. "And then she borrowed Boyce's car and went to Wilson City?"

Susan nodded again. "Yes."

Joe said, softly, "Why didn't you go to Wilson City with her?"

"Because — because" — Susan lifted her head and eyed Joe defiantly — "because I didn't ask to go, I expect! Anyway, Uncle Boyce *did* go out with the jeep and was gone all afternoon. Aunt Mirabel put on riding clothes and took out that new mare of Uncle Boyce's —"

Neither Craig nor Indian Joe moved; there was no sign of tenseness in either face, yet Mady knew that this was news to them as it was to her.

Susan knew it, too; her green eyes sparkled. "Didn't she tell you that? Why, she must have forgotten. She said she hadn't tried that mare yet, and she wasn't too old to stay on a horse's back, and off she went. I didn't notice which trail she took. But she got home about half an hour before my father came and had changed and had got herself ready to come over here."

"Your Aunt Edith didn't go to Wilson City with your mother," Indian Joe said so softly that it was not like a question.

Susan said, "No, she didn't. I don't think my mother wanted her."

"Why not?"

"Why, I — well, you know you get sort of tired of Aunt Edith. I mean" — color came up into Susan's cheeks — "I know all about that *de mortuis* — *de mortuis* whatever it is —"

"*De mortuis nil nisi bonum*," said Indian Joe gravely. "Second-year Latin?"

"First," Susan said. "Second comes next year. If Father can find a new school for me."

"Your Aunt Edith," Joe hinted.

"Oh, well, yes, you see, a person did get tired of her. My mother was one of her oldest friends, but Aunt Edith was — oh, well, everybody knows it. She was a nagger and a — a snoop," Susan said. "She read other people's letters and — well, while my mother was in Wilson City, Aunt Edith went through her suitcases. Every single thing. I went to my mother's room to see what Aunt Edith was doing and she said she was unpacking for my mother. But she looked embarrassed."

There was a rather long pause. Then Indian Joe said, "Go on, Susan. What next?"

"What next? Why, Aunt Mirabel came back from her ride, I told you. Then my father came up in a jeep and I knew that he'd come all the way from San Francisco in his own special private personal plane just to see my mother. And then she came home after a while and they walked up and down and talked and then went around the house out of sight, along the drive, talking. Then the car came to take me and Aunt Mirabel here. So we came. And my father came too, just a few minutes later, and you told us about the murder." She leaned against Indian Joe.

"Is that all, Susan?" Indian Joe said gently.

Susan lifted her head defiantly. "Certainly that's all. I don't know anything at all about that murder. I don't know anything at all about Aunt Edith's being killed that way. I don't know a thing about —

about any of it!"

Craig said, gently, "Susan —" and put out his hands. She went to him slowly. He took her hands. "Susan, I want you to stay with me. Live in my house. But if you want to live with your mother, I'll not stop you. You're old enough now to make your own choice."

Susan looked into his eyes a long moment. Then she said in a whisper, "All right."

"You mean you want to live with your mother?"

Susan lowered her head. "I —" she began, "I — I don't know. That is —" Again she lifted her head to look directly at her father. "She's not drinking any more, you know. She stopped that. It wasn't very nice sometimes. She'd — she'd say or do things she didn't mean — but she's stopped that, you know."

"I know," her father said.

"So — oh, I don't know. I've got to take Sancho out!" Susan cried.

She let go her father's hands and ran to Sancho, snatching his collar. He knew what she meant and bounded for the door.

Craig and Indian Joe both shot up. Craig cried, "Wait, Susan — I'll go with you —" Indian Joe said, "Wait for me, Susan!" He

244

turned to Craig. "Miss Mirabel's a strong old woman," he said flatly, "but I don't think she'd kill anybody. She might want to —" He didn't quite smile, but almost, and Susan shrieked from the hall below, "Hurry up, Joe!"

Joe disappeared. Craig said, "If Mirabel knew anything about Casso's murder she'd tell it. Mirabel never liked Edith but it's preposterous to think of Mirabel's killing Edith."

Mirabel said from the hall, "What are you talking about?"

Craig went into the hall. Mady followed him. Mirabel was standing there, her hand on the banister. Mady couldn't help observing what a strong and perhaps ruthless old hand it was.

Craig said with true Wilson frankness, "Susan says that you were riding at the time Casso was probably murdered."

Mirabel stared; then she gave a booming laugh. "I was! I tried that new mare Boyce just bought. They fooled him too. Told him she knew all five gaits. She doesn't. She's downright spooky, too. Can't keep her steady." Her eyes were very keen and searching. "H'mm," she said. "You want to know where I went, how long I was gone and whether I killed Casso. Well, I didn't."

Craig put his hand on her arm. She shrugged it off. "Now wait a minute. I'm strong. I saddled that spooked mare myself. I haven't forgotten how to ride either. I can still stick on a horse's back. But I took the trail that winds down along the river. Used to ride it when I was a girl. Had some trouble with that mare; everything she saw scared her. But I could manage her all right. I got her back to the house and changed and got ready to come here. And if you want to know why I didn't tell Sam Hawkins about this — or the police either for that matter, they didn't ask me. Not," said Mirabel, "that I'd have refused to tell them. I did not kill that man, Craig. And I didn't kill poor Edith. Oh, I think exactly what the rest of you think. It isn't likely that two murders would occur in the same place and have no relation to each other. Murderers aren't that numerous, and thank heaven for that," she said with energy. "You'd both better come down and have something to eat. Manuel's got food set out in the living room."

She went ahead of them down the stairs.

Rhoda was in the living room. Jim and Boyce had gone.

"I sent Boyce and young Marsh back to

the guest cabin," Mirabel said flatly. "They'd had some food. No sense in their hanging around here. But Rhoda —"

Rhoda gave Craig an appealing look. "I can't stay alone in that cabin where — Edith and I — no, I can't stay there."

Mirabel said dryly that Rhoda could have the small room next to her own. "It's not as comfortable as it might be; bed needs new springs," Mirabel added. "And I don't approve of your visiting here, Rhoda. But" — she looked very grim — "this situation is, I trust, unusual."

Joe and Susan and Sancho came back into the house, Sancho and Susan galloping along the hall and into the living room to see what, if anything, had happened while they were out on their walk. Mirabel called to Joe, telling him to come and have supper.

Rhoda poured coffee and then apologized to Mady. "I'm so sorry. I seem to forget. I should have waited for you —"

Mirabel said, "Eat your dinner, Mady. That casserole stuff is still hot."

Rhoda sat back; her lovely hair glowed redly above the yellow turtle-neck sweater she wore; her dark slacks outlined her slim figure. When Manuel and Inez came to clear off the tables and remove the trays,

Craig and Indian Joe went into Craig's study.

As it developed, Indian Joe spent the night in the house, sleeping on the sofa in the living room.

That night, however, the gun cabinet in Craig's study was broken into and a revolver was removed. This was not discovered until noon the next day.

That night, too, stealthily and swiftly, the thaw began.

Chapter 13

A gentle wind came softly from the Pacific, wafted itself across California and over the Sierras and settled upon El Rancho Rio. The blizzard had either spent its force or its own winds had driven it away. Mady was still awake when she began to hear a small, regular sound from the eaves above the windows and after a while identified it as the steady drip of melting snow.

So at least, she thought in her ignorance, they would no longer be cut off from the world, shut in with murder.

She tried not to think of Edith. She did think of Rhoda, who had gently, pathetically, established a foothold actually in the house itself. Yet it would have been inhuman to oblige her to stay in the guest cabin which she had so recently shared with Edith.

All the same, however it had come about, Rhoda was now in the house and, Mady was sure, had every intention of staying there.

Her thoughts seesawed back and forth: if

Craig wanted Rhoda back, she wouldn't stand in his way; that was her resolution at one moment. The next moment it seemed just as certain to her that both Indian Joe and Mirabel had given her sound advice: if she wanted Craig, and she did, then she must fight for him.

A question was: How?

Another question was: What had Rhoda said to Craig after she had flung herself into his arms? Certainly his manner to Mady had changed subtly, as it had done when he heard that Jim was arriving. He was polite, kind and chill. Certainly he had told Susan that if she wanted to live with her mother he would now permit it. Up to then he had never been willing to allow Susan to live with Rhoda; he had not in fact even liked her visits to her mother, visits which according to Susan sometimes were not visits at all, when Rhoda was in no condition to bother with Susan. So Susan had had the chauffeur who drove the leased Rolls Royce take her, as she said, to the zoo or to Schrafft's for an ice cream sundae or just for a ride. She had never reported these changes of plan to Mirabel, Mady was sure, or to her father. If Craig had known, he would have asked Mirabel to accompany Susan — or even

Mady, for that matter — or he would have forbidden the visits altogether.

Yet Susan hotly defended her mother against the slightest hint of accusation. Susan was perfectly aware of Rhoda's apparent indifference to her daughter; yet the child had a strong streak of loyalty.

She was torn, of course, between her father and mother and her own common sense; she was inconsistent and changeable; her moods could not be predicted and yet made a firm kind of pattern. She would speak of Rhoda with the coldest kind of perception and the next moment fling her arms around her mother and say that she loved her. The fact was, of course, Susan was a child, but a child who had been forced into a kind of precocity about some things.

Mady didn't hear Craig come upstairs and he did not come to her room. The house was very silent, so the drip of melting snow seemed louder in that stillness and certainly steadier.

By morning the thaw was well established. The sky was a blazing, warm blue. The sun was dazzling white on the dwindling heaps of snow.

When Mady went downstairs, Mirabel met her in the hall. The telephone was still not connected, she said. But Boyce and Jim had borrowed a jeep with a snowplow fastened in front of it and — "They took Edith home," Mirabel said. "Craig will get the police and Sam Hawkins as soon as possible. Go and get some breakfast."

So they had taken Edith back to the ranch she hated. Mady went back to the kitchen again, and Manuel told her crossly that she was late, but he had expected her so he'd made some fresh batter for flapjacks. From the wide kitchen windows she could see the bunkhouse and some of the corrals; men were out, forking hay into a jeep. She didn't see Craig anywhere.

She was in the hall when Jim returned. He didn't knock at the door; he simply opened it and walked in, and when Mady started to walk past him, he said, with that mischievous, small-boy twinkle, that he had come back to see her. "I saw Craig leave this morning, off in the direction of the mine, Boyce told me. So as soon as we got to Boyce's place and — and the boys carried Edith into the house and all that" — he did look a little sober just then — "I came back. I've got to talk to you."

"You may as well go back to Boyce's ranch and stay there. I'm not going to talk to you."

"Well, really!" Jim said in an injured tone. "I'm not going to hurt you."

Mady took a long breath. "Let's have this clear, Jim. You act as if I would really try to get money out of Craig for a settlement and then turn around and marry you. I would never think of such a thing!"

Jim looked a little taken aback by her vehemence, but then he put out a confident hand. "Darling, it's me. We understand each other —"

She pushed away from his hand. "We have no understanding at all and never will. I'm Craig's wife —"

"But Craig wants Rhoda back," he said softly.

"That is not true!" Mady said it with all her force but she was not at all sure that she was right.

"Oh, yes. And —" There was the laughing, half-teasing look in his eyes that once she had found almost irresistible. "And Craig knows that you are still, really, in love with me."

"No!"

Jim shrugged. "Rhoda had a talk with him yesterday. You're the only obstacle to reuniting the family. She told Craig that you had married him on the rebound, as you did. She said you had regretted it."

So that was what Rhoda had told Craig the previous afternoon, and had told him so convincingly, so earnestly that Craig must have believed it.

"But I don't regret it!"

"You sound as if you mean that."

"I want you to go back to New York as soon as you can. Besides everything else, I could not possibly consider taking any money as a settlement from Craig. No matter what might happen at any time, he owes me nothing."

"You are so stubborn," he said. "I always knew that. But we never disagreed before now."

"This is my home," Mady said. "I'm asking you to leave. I don't want to send for someone to throw you out, but I will if I have to."

"Really," Jim said. "Really —" He tried a new tack. "I thought we could always be friends —"

"You thought wrong! Now please go!"

He went to the door, stopped, turned back and all at once looked like the Jim she thought she had known so well. "All right," he said, "I was wrong to come here. I give up. But there's one thing I want you to do and that's get out of this place, get out of this horrible thing, whatever it is that is going on here. I don't know these people. I don't know what it's all about, but whatever it is, you should not be entangled in it. It's dangerous, Mady. Leave now, leave today, make an excuse if you have to. I'll not urge you to break up your marriage. You have finally made me believe you. But I do urge you to leave here now. I'll take you to Wilson City in Boyce's car —"

"You can't," Mirabel said dryly from the living room door. "This thaw will make the roads completely impassable. I'm surprised that you could even get to Boyce's place. Since you did, I advise you to return and stay there."

"I'm going." Jim hesitated, then said politely, "Please believe me, Miss Mirabel, I wouldn't have come here at all if I hadn't believed — if I hadn't hoped that Mady — But never mind that. If she is happy, then the only thing I can do is accept it. I'll wait and perhaps —"

"I wouldn't wait," Mady said.

"I was going to say I'll wait until the roads are passable. I'm sorry I came. I apologize for — for jumping to conclusions, as I seem to have done. Rhoda told me — But never mind that. Do you mind," he said to Mady, "if I go over to the guest cabin? I seem to have left my shaving gear there."

Mirabel looked a little thoughtful. Mady said, "No, of course not." Jim waved at her and went out.

"H'mm," Mirabel said after a moment. "Sounded very frank. Very decent, as a matter of fact. I may have misjudged him."

"You didn't hear all that he had to say," Mady said snappishly, feeling obscurely that somehow Jim had twisted himself and his manner around, and she didn't like it.

"Oh, yes, I did," Mirabel said. "Every word of it. You were here in the hall. Not a place for a private conversation. Is there any truth to what he said about Rhoda and Craig?"

"I don't know."

"Why don't you ask?"

"Ask Craig! I couldn't —"

"Dear me, little Miss Fancy Manners! Can't ask her own husband if he wants her to leave him so he can get his first wife back." She turned around, her back erect and rigid, and strode into Craig's study, and they then discovered that the gun cabinet had been broken into during the night.

"We'll see if the phone is working yet," Mirabel said, took up the phone, which was still dead, looked past Mady, and after a frozen moment, put down the telephone.

Mady looked then, too. The door of the gun cabinet was of wood, but it had a modern and substantial lock which now was broken. The door hung only a little off center, a fraction of an inch ajar. There were two hinges, both of them torn out but apparently shoved as nearly into place as possible. Mirabel strode to the door and bent to examine it. "H'mm," she said, "prized out the hinges. Put them back very carefully so it might not be noticed. Broke the lock, of course. Somebody wanted something out of this, obviously a gun. Let's just see —" She took a letter opener from Craig's desk; it had a huge turquoise on its handle which gleamed brightly blue as Mirabel's strong, old hands prodded carefully and adroitly at the door of the cabinet. It came further ajar; she caught it and pulled carefully, and reached inside the cabinet. Mirabel clearly knew every gun it should contain, for she leaned close to peer inside; she groped around with her hands while Mady held the door. "A revolver is gone," she said in a very low voice and glanced over her shoulder. "Shut the hall door, Mady."

Mady went to close it and for no reason moved very quietly. When she came back

Mirabel had pulled out a drawer below the cabinet and was searching again, this time among boxes of shells. She straightened up. "I can't be sure. I don't know whether or not any shells have been taken. But a revolver is no use unless it's loaded. Well, I think we'd better try to arrange this door as it was."

They adjusted the door again, very carefully, but anyone who happened to look that way could not fail to see the broken lock and hinges.

Mirabel stood deep in thought for a moment. Then she said, "Craig went out early this morning. I heard him go downstairs. Indian Joe must have gone even earlier. So neither of them were in this room this morning. Craig would have seen the cabinet. This must have been done during the night. Indian Joe slept on the sofa in the living room. I can't see how anybody could get in the house and break into the cabinet without Joe's hearing him. Still, it must have happened then. All we can do is tell Craig about it." Mirabel sat down as if suddenly she felt tired and old. "I don't like the idea of a revolver floating around. Try the telephone again, Mady. Craig must have gone to the mine. If the telephone is connected we can reach him there."

There was still only complete silence from the telephone.

"Well," Mirabel said, watching as Mady put down the phone, "we'll simply have to wait. Where's Susan?"

Mady was suddenly terrified. She ran to the hall and up the stairs, and Susan was squatting on the floor of her room, trying to teach Sancho to roll over, which he obviously did not propose to be taught. She looked up quickly and as quickly saw something in Mady's face. "What's the matter?" She bounced up. "What's wrong?"

"Nothing. I — only wanted to make sure that you were here."

Susan eyed Mady for a moment, looking as stern and unyielding as Mirabel. "Something's wrong. But you don't want to tell me what. Of course I heard you talking to Jim. Heard every word of it. Did you mean what you said?"

"Yes."

She studied Mady. There was again the fleeting look of adulthood in her face. She said only, however, almost nonchalantly, "A good thing. If I were you I'd stick to my father. But — oh, I don't know. If my mother really wants him back and he wants her back — well, what can you do about it?"

Mady answered her as she would have answered an adult. "I really don't know that I can do anything about it, Susan."

Susan's face closed in; she said, "Probably not," and leaned over to tickle one of Sancho's enormous puppy feet. "You know that my mother went to the guest cabin, the one she shared with Aunt Edith, a while ago?"

"Why, I — no, I didn't. I haven't seen her this morning."

"So probably she and Jim —" Susan scrambled up and went to a window that had a view of the cottonwoods, the drive and the two log cabins. "There they come now," she said, pressing her face against the glass.

Mady went to watch, too. The jeep was plowing along, its snow shovel sending up showers of snow and slush. Rhoda, a green scarf tied around her head, was sitting beside Jim, who was intent on driving. Neither seemed to be speaking. They passed out of Mady's range of vision as they approached the long veranda, and the roof cut off the view.

In a moment the jeep came into sight again, chugging along; this time it went down the long drive which led to the main road and to Boyce's ranch. Jim sat in it alone. They heard the heavy front door open and close as Rhoda came into the house.

"Mady," Susan said suddenly, "if they've — oh, quarreled or something, I mean if Jim says anything that's not nice about my mother, you'll not believe him, will you?"

"What do you mean, Susan?"

"Oh, just that. Nothing really. But you'll take her side, won't you?"

Mady put her hand on Susan's. "Tell me what you're talking about, Susan. What would Jim say that could be to your mother's disadvantage?"

But she squirmed away from Mady. "Nothing! Goodness' sakes, don't look so serious! I just meant that it — well, it looked to me as if they'd kind of had a quarrel or — or something was wrong. Didn't it look like that to you?"

"They weren't talking," Mady said slowly. "But, no, I didn't think of anything like a quarrel."

Susan said airily, "Forget it." She knelt down beside Sancho. "Now come on — roll over — like this —" She turned Sancho over, who thumped down and rolled a mischievous eye at Mady.

Mady went downstairs. Rhoda's bright green scarf and suede coat lay upon the refectory table in the hall. Rhoda herself was in the living room, kneeling down, thrusting some of the enormous sugar pine cones under the logs in the fireplace. She reached for matches; her hand shook. Mady said, "You must have got very cold in the guest cabin."

Rhoda gave a little start, glanced at Mady over her shoulder and tried to light the cones. "It was icy," she said. Her voice was unsteady. She looked so pale that there was a greenish tinge to her fine skin.

"I saw Jim bring you back to the house."

"I shouldn't have gone to the cabin. I left some clothes there, sweaters and things —"

A pine cone caught and burst into rosy flame. Rhoda said, "But actually, when I got there it seemed so dreadful, so — well, anyway, I didn't even bring back my clothes." She huddled over the fire, which was now leaping and crackling. She was Mady's rival, her very formidable rival, yet for an inexplicable moment Mady felt sorry for her.

Then she heard the heavy front door open and close again. Craig came along the hall and saw them. He said, "Mady, will you come in the study?"

She followed Craig into the study. She

knew that Rhoda had turned to watch her go.

Craig was standing at the gun cabinet, examining it. "Look at this!"

"I know. Mirabel and I found it. She says a revolver is gone."

"It's gone all right." He examined the hinges and lock. "I didn't know it until I came in the room just now and saw it." He turned around. "Mady, this young Marsh. You said you had a letter from him saying that he was coming here?"

"Yes, of course. I told you."

"You said it was dated November third."

"Yes, it was. I remember noting it because I hoped that I had time to stop him."

"But then," Craig said, "you burned the letter."

"I didn't want it."

He gave her a long look, walked across the room, closed the door to the hall and came back to lean against the big desk. "Mady, I find it hard to believe that Marsh's arrival here and Casso's arrival were sheer coincidence."

Mady said slowly, "But, Craig, Jim couldn't have killed Casso. The letter was dated the afternoon Casso was killed. Jim wasn't here then."

"I expected you to defend him."

"I wouldn't defend him! I don't see why he would murder Casso, and facts are facts. The letter really was dated that afternoon I found Casso. It was sent air mail, and then the next day after it was sent Jim arrived —"

"But you burned the letter," Craig said.

Chapter 14

"I didn't burn it to protect Jim. I didn't burn it to try to give him a sort of alibi. It *was* dated November third!"

Craig said, "I know you. Your faith in people dies hard. I can tell that you are still in love with young Marsh." She started to speak, but he stopped her. "Wait, Mady. I also know that you are loyal. You married me and you'll stick to your bargain. I don't want that kind of loyalty —"

"Craig, you must listen —"

"Not now. We'll talk this out later. I only want you to know that I'll not hold you against your will. When all this is settled — we'll talk about it then. Marsh was here this morning. Don't bother to deny it —"

"I wasn't going to deny it!"

"One of the hands saw him, in the jeep. Saw him leave, too. Reported it to me. You see, there aren't many people around here who could possibly have known Casso, let alone kill him. Very few people who could have got hold of that rail. If Marsh were actually in New York at the time of Casso's murder, then he couldn't have murdered him, that's obvious. Banner is a stranger. He might have known Casso. It is hard to believe that he merely happened to come to El Rancho. Besides, Indian Joe thought that he saw Banner's car — or one like it — with two persons in it, the afternoon Casso was killed. The other person was not Casso, apparently, for the police found his rented car. There must be a reason for Banner's return. Yet I can't see what Banner would gain by killing Casso one day, here on the ranch, and coming back through the storm the next night. Indian Joe questioned him again this morning. He denies ever having known Casso. Sticks to his story: he's only a tourist and got himself lost in the snow. He wants to leave as soon as the roads are passable. I'll make him stay until the sheriff and the police can get here. I'm going now to get Indian Joe and tell him about that revolver." He rose.

When he had gone, Mady sat down in his armchair. There seemed to be no possible way she could break through the barrier between her and Craig.

As she sat there, Rhoda came in. "Where's Craig?"

"He's gone to talk to Indian Joe."

"Oh." She slid into a chair opposite Mady. She looked half frozen, almost blue with cold. "Edith came to talk to you the day she was killed. Edith was — was one of my oldest friends. We didn't always get along, but all the same we were friends. Why did she come to see you that morning?"

"She came to see Craig. He wasn't in the house."

"Didn't she tell you why she wanted to see him?"

"No."

"Well, but — didn't you guess? Did she know something about Guy Casso's murder?"

"I didn't know. She wouldn't tell me."

"But she — if she knew something —" Rhoda leaned back. It was as if she were talking to herself. "Surely she'd have the sense not to try blackmail. Surely she wouldn't go around telling that she knew anything or suspected somebody."

Mady said, "But she was killed. If you know anything about it, Rhoda, you'd better tell Craig."

Rhoda rose; her hand clung to the chair back as if she barely had the strength to move. She said swiftly, however, "But I don't know anything about it! I'm only —

267

only shocked and frightened."

Mirabel had said that Rhoda would refuse to think of anything she didn't want to think about, that she would shut her eyes to anything she didn't want to see. This time Rhoda looked as if, just perhaps, she was forced to look at something she had had no intention of acknowledging, even in her thoughts. She said after a moment, "You won't tell me what Edith told you?"

"She didn't say anything that was evidence about Casso's murder."

"I see." Rhoda stared at Mady, but as if she didn't see her and instead saw some unwelcome vision; she put one hand unsteadily across her face and turned rather blindly toward the door. She left Mady alone. There were light footsteps on the stairs and then only silence. Mady went into the hall and called Susan, who came from the dining room, munching a cookie. Sancho was with her.

"Here I am," she said. "Want something?"

"No, it's all right."

"You wanted to be sure that I'm all right," Susan said with her natural, yet sometimes uncanny, perception. "Well, I am. Aunt Mirabel is in the kitchen. We're having coffee. Want some?" she said as politely as any well-brought-up little girl.

Mady thanked her and said no, and Susan went back through the pantry. Mady was still waiting in the study when Craig and Indian Joe returned. Joe nodded at her in an absent way and went with Craig to examine the gun cabinet. He finally straightened up, whistled in a mournful way and said glumly that it only went to show that the only good Indian was a dead Indian.

"Must have been done last night while I was in the living room," he said morosely. "I didn't hear a thing. Somebody came in the house, somebody came into this room, somebody pried out those hinges, broke the lock and took the revolver and — How about shells?"

Craig pulled open the same drawer that Mirabel had looked in. Both men bent over it. Craig said, "I can't tell for sure."

Indian Joe took a leather-covered key ring from his pocket, opened it and showed Craig the keys. "George gave me his key to the cabinet when he left on his vacation. The other one is mine."

Craig dove into his own pocket and extracted the silver ring with a small gold nugget fastened to it. "Mine is here," he

269

said, sorting them over. "House key, too. But the house keys —"

Indian Joe permitted himself a sad kind of grunt. "There's no telling how many keys there are to both front and back doors. Or where they are. No telling how much ammunition for that revolver should be in that drawer either, not till George gets back, and he may not know. We don't keep a close check on things like that. Maybe we should. But," said Indian Joe, as Mirabel had said, "a gun's not much use unless it's loaded."

Craig said, "We'll have to assume that whoever got the revolver loaded it. What's your idea, Joe?"

"Same as yours," Indian Joe said again. "Somebody took that gun because he's scared of his life, wants to protect himself — herself — that's one way of looking at it. But another way of looking at it is intent to murder. The question is, who took it?"

"Obviously it was somebody who can come and go in the house."

Joe nodded. "Somebody who can come and go in the house and knows the house took that rail, too."

"Not many people."

"Not many. But none of our outfit had anything to do with Casso's murder."

"I don't see how any of the boys would even know Casso," Craig said.

Joe nodded again. "I know every one of those boys. I may not know all about each one, but almost. I don't think one of them has been east of, say, Chicago. Maybe not even east of Las Vegas. Of course, come to think of it, Vegas is quite a town. Quite a big city. Tourists coming and going, people everywhere, nobody pays much attention to other people. Hard to trace anybody there — motels, big hotels, cars from everywhere. People could meet in Vegas and nobody be the wiser."

"What do you mean, Joe?"

Joe's face turned wooden Indian. "I'm only thinking. It does seem to you and to me that Mrs. Boyce knew something about Casso's murder and that she was willing to sell her information. So she was murdered. She may have tried blackmail, but the argument against that is that nobody around here but you has got much money. It looks to me as if Casso's murderer found out that Mrs. Boyce knew whatever she knew — or thought she knew — and had to kill her. And now that gun —"

"We can look for it," Craig said, but rather hopelessly.

Joe agreed. "Big place to search, Craig.

271

Your ranch, Boyce's ranch." He had slipped and said "Craig." He noted his own slip, said in an absent way, "Mr. Wilson," and then he was silent.

"Banner?" Craig suggested.

"Maybe." But Indian Joe shook his head in a morose and gloomy way. "Somebody had a key to the house and got in. Somebody is very scared. There could be shooting. This is a big place to search, Mr. Wilson. I'll do my best." He started for the door and then turned back. "You might question your — Mrs. Rhoda Wilson. She's got something on her mind."

She had, indeed, Mady thought fiercely. But Joe did not mean what she meant. He said, "She was downstairs last night. I think she's fallen off the wagon. She was in the pantry drinking when I went back to the kitchen for coffee. That was two o'clock. I noted the time. She said she was restless and couldn't sleep, but she was kind of unsteady and — well, anyway, I waited till she went back upstairs. She took a bottle with her," said Joe and stopped, his dark eyes fixed upon the tomahawk in a thoughtful way. After a moment he said, "It was after that that I drank the coffee Manuel had left for me," and without another word he went out.

Craig frowned. "But Rhoda wouldn't — couldn't — have put anything in his coffee to make him sleep! Rhoda wouldn't want a revolver! She wouldn't break into the cabinet!"

And Rhoda came swiftly in from the hall. "Craig, I couldn't help hearing you! I wouldn't even think of — why, of putting anything at all in anybody's coffee! But it's true, I did go down to the pantry last night and I did mix myself a little drink. I couldn't sleep. I kept thinking of Edith. But that was all! I tell you I'm through with drinking and have been for a long time!"

It struck Mady that there was something like hysteria in her manner, something like desperation, yet she was all at once her most gentle and charming, too, so there was an appeal about her that was in its way full of pathos. She was Mady's rival, but at that moment Mady had a twinge of pity for Rhoda. It was a contradictory kind of feeling and it vanished very swiftly, for Rhoda drove straight to attack.

"Craig, I must tell you this, even if it is not nice to tell. I had another talk with Jim Marsh this morning. We met by accident at the guest cabin. He told me that he had talked to Mady and she had told him again

273

that she was in love with him, she hadn't changed. But —"

"*I did not say that!*" Mady cried.

Rhoda went straight on, advancing to Craig and putting one hand on his arm pleadingly. "She wants to leave you, Craig. But she thinks she shouldn't —"

"*That is not true!*" There comes a moment when sheer self-defense is more important than anything else. Mady cried, "I told Jim I never wanted to see him again, and I don't! I don't want to leave you, Craig, and neither Jim nor Rhoda is telling the truth."

Craig sat on the edge of his desk, picked up a coin-silver cigarette box and turned it absently in his hands; it was set with bright blue turquoises which gleamed in the light. He didn't look embarrassed at two women coming to a hammer-and-tongs quarrel over him, but he didn't look anything; he was only very quiet.

Rhoda would not give up. "I'm pleading for myself, Craig. But also for my daughter —"

"You can have Susan if she wants to live with you," Craig said, still examining the silver box as if he'd never seen it before. "I told Susan that. She's old enough now to choose for herself."

"But" — Rhoda caught her breath, then rallied — "but, Craig, I'm your wife. I'm really your wife —"

Mady said, "I am his wife." And she thought, we're like children again, all but pulling each other's hair.

Craig moved the lid of the cigarette box up and down.

Rhoda said softly, "Please don't turn me away. Mady only has a feeling of loyalty to you because of that marriage ceremony. I admire her for it. I still feel that I'm your wife. There's our daughter."

Mady forced herself to speak slowly and carefully. "Jim lied when he said that I wanted to marry him. I don't. You, Rhoda, and Jim together made up this plan. You called it a deal —"

"Why, Mady!" Rhoda looked shocked. "How can you lie like that?"

Craig said, "Do you know Marsh well, Rhoda?"

"Why, I — not really. Except — in an odd sort of way you and Mady drew us together. He was heartbroken when their engagement was ended. When you and Mady were married — well, I had wanted a divorce from you, yes, but I guess I never thought you'd marry somebody else. It was only then that I — I came to my senses. So, yes, Jim was sure that Mady was still in love with him and had only married you on the rebound. And I — yes, I did hope that Mady would leave. I felt I was still your wife —"

Mady said, clearly, "I did not lie. You came here the day after Casso was murdered. You called it a deal. I was to leave Craig and then you'd marry him again —"

"That isn't true!" Rhoda said, still softly. "I wouldn't do that!"

Craig put down the box and got to his feet. "Do you know Banner, Rhoda?"

"Banner?" Rhoda's green eyes were bright and still. "You mean that — that little man who got lost in the blizzard?"

"You didn't happen to see him while you were in Las Vegas?"

"See him!" Rhoda laughed thinly. "Why, I wouldn't remember it if I had! Besides, I was there only overnight. The plane got in and I went to the hotel and hired a car for the next morning, early. I started for home — oh, it was very early. I knew it was a long drive and — Banner! Good heavens, Craig!"

Craig said, "Banner says that he was in Las Vegas. I wondered —" He stopped as Indian Joe and a ranch hand came to the door.

Indian Joe said, "I brought Dancy to mend the cabinet."

Craig said, "Come in. Morning, Dancy."

The man they called Dancy nodded politely at Craig. Rhoda's gaze went swiftly to the gun cabinet. She gave a little scream. "Craig! What happened? That door!"

Susan came jauntily into the room, Sancho beside her. She had heard Rhoda; she gave the gun cabinet one swift look. Then she whirled around, her long red hair flying, put both arms around her mother and glared at Craig. "She didn't do it. She didn't break into that gun cabinet. You mustn't say she did —"

"I didn't say she did," Craig said.

Indian Joe didn't appear to hear what was said and all at once again he looked like the very model for a cigar-store Indian.

Craig said to Susan, "A gun has been taken. I don't know who took it. All right, Dancy, think you can fix it?"

"Oh sure, Mr. Wilson. Somebody sure made a botch of it though. Must have used a butcher knife or something like that."

Rhoda flashed out the door. Mady had a swift glimpse of her eyes as she went, and there was nothing less than terror, alive and shocking, in those wide green eyes. She ran up the stairs, stumbling a little.

She hadn't even looked at Susan. Susan, however, had her own strength and her own resources. She bent over Sancho and told him that he was a good dog and Sancho obligingly wagged his fluff of a tail. The telephone rang.

It startled them all. They had seemed to be cut off completely from the normal world, living in a world which had suddenly turned nightmarish. Craig sprang to answer it, and it was the sheriff.

"Sam!" Craig shouted. "Sam! Can you get out here? No, it's bad, Sam. Edith, Boyce's wife —" They listened. Dancy efficiently got out tools from the box he carried and began to work on the gun cabinet. Yet he, too, seemed to listen. Craig told it succinctly; he did not speculate as to why Edith had been killed; he only said that apparently she had been struck senseless, was then dragged into a car which was in a closed shed and left there with the engine running, and that he did not know who had killed her. He said that Boyce had taken Edith back to his ranch that morning.

He then listened to the sheriff, and presently said, "That's bad. Then you can't get here. What about the state police? They might be able to come in from the Fallon road. Oh! Well, look here, I may not be able to get through some long-distance calls — All right, I'll tell you. First my office in New York. Ask for Seely, tell him to get in touch with the lawyer; he'll understand. I want them to check on a man by the name of Walter Banner. I don't know his address; he says he ran a theater-ticket agency but gave it up and — Yes, he's here. Says he got lost in the blizzard. Now wait, Sam —" Indian Joe had advanced to the desk and was writing rapidly on a memo pad. Craig took it from him. "Sam, I may not be able to get through to Reno or Vegas, and anyway, it'll be police business. But I want to know when Guy Casso arrived in Las Vegas — probably he came by air — where he stayed, everything anybody can find out about his movements before he came here. Also James Marsh — try the airline passenger lists in Reno and Vegas. What's his address in New York, Mady?"

She had to tell him; she didn't want so clearly to associate herself with Jim but she remembered his address and gave it. Craig without any change in his expression or voice repeated it to the sheriff. "And find out whether he came by air to Reno or perhaps to Vegas and —" He looked at Joe's hurried notes. "He rented a car somewhere. He says Reno. The car is at Boyce's ranch — Yes, we'll try to check the license."

The sheriff apparently asked who James Marsh was, for Craig listened a moment and replied, "He's a friend of my wife's. Turned up here the day, that is, actually the second night, after Casso was found. I want to know when he left New York. I know, it'll take time. But get after it, Sam."

He looked at Indian Joe's rapidly scribbled notes. "Oh, yes. The manager of the motel thinks that Casso used the telephone, the night before he was murdered. It's a pay phone, but it might be important to know who he talked to and where — well, he did talk to somebody. How about the bridge? Are they working on it yet? Oh, Lord." Craig's shoulders drooped. He said, "Sam, can some of our boys help — Sam! Sam —" He waited, he jiggled the receiver, he put down the telephone.

Joe said, "Cut off again?"

Craig nodded. "He says Wilson Creek is flooded, took out the bridge early this morning. It's this sudden thaw. Every river and every creek in the county will be flooding. He didn't think the state police can get here."

"I don't see how they can," Joe said thoughtfully. "They'd have to cross either the big river or Wilson Creek."

Susan said suddenly, "It's a good thing Uncle Boyce's house is this side of the big river. He couldn't have got home — I'm going to take Sancho out."

"I'll go with you," Indian Joe said.

"No! It's daylight. Nobody's going to hurt me. I'm not a baby."

She flounced out into the hall. At a nod from Craig, Indian Joe stalked after her. Susan shrieked, "I said no! You — you Indian you! It wouldn't surprise me if you took that old tomahawk and —"

"Susan," said Indian Joe. It was one word only. Mady went into the hall, and apparently that one word was sufficient to quell Susan, who was sliding her arms into the coat Joe held for her in a quite docile manner. Sancho leaped around them. Mady decided to go out with them.

Mady's knees still felt oddly unsteady after the scene with Rhoda; she had all but shouted, Rhoda hadn't; Rhoda had remained a perfect lady all the way through. Rhoda was an out-and-out but skillful liar. She wondered which of them Craig believed.

Susan was skipping along ahead of Mady and talking to Joe. "— you could have hit Aunt Edith over the head, Joe," she chattered. "You never liked her. She didn't like you. You could have hit Casso over the head, too. But I don't exactly see why, unless you just didn't like him. But you are an Indian and — Why, for goodness' sake," Susan said cheerfully, "why didn't you use the old tomahawk in my father's study? That'd be more your line."

"But that," Indian Joe said reasonably, "would point to me, wouldn't it? Evidence."

Susan considered it. "I suppose so. You're too smart for that. But —" All at once the chattering, teasing note left her voice; she said seriously, "But I know you, Joe. If you thought it would help my father you'd think no more of killing Guy Casso than hitting a fly. But I really don't think you'd hurt Aunt Edith."

"Well, I didn't," said Indian Joe. "Look out for that puddle."

Mady stepped around the vast puddle of half-melted snow, too, but such is the power of suggestion that it really did strike her that Indian Joe knew his way around the house, Indian Joe could come and go as he wished and nobody would ask questions, Indian Joe could have taken the gun the previous night. And she believed Susan when she said that Indian Joe would do anything he could to help Craig.

So would Mirabel, if it came to that.

The point now, though, was the missing gun. The point now was that they were still cut off and living in their own frightening world, and no police, no sheriff, nobody at all could come to their rescue. She said, "Joe, how long will it be before the roads are passable?"

"I can't say exactly, Mrs. Wilson. It depends some on the amount of snow up the valley."

"What about the bridge over Wilson Creek?"

"That'll take some time to repair. Matter of days, I expect. There's nothing much we can do about that."

The sun blazed down upon them from a blue sky. The mountains toward the west were still white-capped but a dark mark showed the timber line. The snow was melting more quickly than it had come. The air felt as balmy as Indian summer.

Mady had snatched up a coat as she left the house, and it was so warm there in the sun that she pushed it back off her shoulders. There were slushy-looking drifts in the shadows and in protected places below the cottonwoods and in the shadows of the outbuildings, but mainly they were surrounded with puddles of water. Even those, Mady thought, must quickly disappear, soaking into the always thirsty soil.

Susan leaped ahead toward the nearest corral. The horses were out, kicking the slush and puddles and obviously enjoying the sun and freedom. Even the calm brood mares looked as if they would like to frolic after having been shut up for so long a time, and the colts were galloping and frisking around zestfully. It comforted Mady in an odd but real way when Nellie saw her, came pounding to meet her, nudged at her hand and whickered a little; she wished that she had remembered to bring an apple. Some cow ponies eyed them with interest from a further corral. Willy, the ranch dog, appeared from somewhere; he and Sancho touched noses, thought it over, touched noses again and began to chase each other happily in and out of puddles.

"Sancho will have to be dried," Mady said to Susan, who had forgotten to be an adult and was laughing and romping like a little girl.

Susan went over to Indian Joe; she even slid her hand into his. "I really don't think you killed anybody, Joe," she said. "I was just talking."

Indian Joe eyed her. "Talking can get you into trouble."

The happiness left Susan's face. "Sometimes not talking can keep you out of trouble."

"Susan, what are you keeping to yourself? You'd better tell me." Joe's voice was even but stern.

"Nothing! Don't look at me like that." She turned to Mady. "Look, Mady, how fast all the snow is going. The creeks and rivers will be flooding. Whee," she gave a whoop. "Watch me. Squaw do sun dance."

With that she flung her coat at Joe, who automatically caught it. She began a skipping little dance, lifting her head and then lowering it, lifting her arms and lowering them, and giving soft, low whoops as she did so. It was curiously rhythmic.

Indian Joe watched her. The dogs caught the contagion and ran and leaped around her. Even the colts caught the fever of youth and energy and galloped madly around their mothers, their tails flying.

When Susan was out of breath and stopped, Indian Joe said quite seriously, "You've got it almost right."

"It's exactly right," Susan said, panting. "I'll take you to visit Joe's reservation sometime, Mady. At least he used to live there and he'd take me to visit and that's where I learned."

Joe's face became completely wooden again, as he saw something behind them. Mady turned to look. Mr. Banner was picking his way toward them. He seemed to be trying to avoid puddles; he wore city oxfords and a neat overcoat that looked incongruous in this setting. He seemed very sober. "Mr. —" He hesitated. "Mr. Joe, my car is gone."

Chapter 15

Nobody knew anything about Banner's car. He had not known that it was gone, he said, until a few moments before, when he had gone to the shed, where it had stood beside Boyce's car, merely to look it over.

Joe went to the shed, stalking along, tall and lean beside the fat, waddling figure of Mr. Banner.

Susan and Mady went back into the house. Somehow the momentary zest and warmth of the sunny day had gone. They had barely reported the disappearance of Banner's car to Craig when it developed that Jim Marsh was gone, too.

Indian Joe and Mr. Banner came back to the house almost at the same moment that Boyce and a woman who proved to be Edith's maid drove up in Craig's jeep, splashing slush as the machine came to a standstill. Boyce came hurrying in. "Electricity is gone again," he said. "I have to ask for your hospitality, Craig. House is cold. This is Edith's maid. She doesn't like to stay at the foreman's cottage."

Edith's maid was eerily like Edith; she had a narrow, hatchety face and darting little eyes. She said in a rasping voice that she didn't like Mexican food and that was the only kind of food the foreman's wife cooked.

Craig told Mr. Banner politely that the telephone was not working and that he couldn't report the theft of his car.

"But who could have stolen it?" Mr. Banner cried, his brown eyes wide.

Susan supplied a possible answer, for she said, loudly, "Where's Jim Marsh?"

Boyce stared at her and then at Craig. "Isn't he here?"

Craig replied, "He was here for a short time this morning. Then he went back to your place."

"But he — I thought he was here! Why, I haven't seen him all morning. Where can he be?"

Mr. Banner said softly that he'd thank Mr. Wilson for letting the sheriff know that his car had been stolen as soon as he could use the telephone. He then made a little bow, said *À bientôt,* and smoothly disappeared out the door; and Mady knew that she had seen that exact little bow and had heard the same words, *À bientôt,* in the same voice sometime, somewhere, and still could not remember where.

But Jim Marsh had gone and nobody knew where he had gone; it was logical to surmise that he had taken Banner's car.

Craig, Indian Joe and Boyce drove back to Boyce's ranch.

They returned, but had been unable to find Jim. He was nowhere in El Rancho.

His rented car was still at Boyce's ranch. The license plates were California ones, suggesting that the car belonged to one of the big rental companies; the car had been left somewhere, Reno, according to Jim Marsh, to be picked up by another driver. The glove compartment was locked and they hadn't opened it to examine the registration of the car; they would leave that to the police, but just then it would tell them nothing.

Indian Joe said, "He had the key for the rented car. But a rented car can be traced. Might take time, but it can be done. An out-of-state car, just a tourist car, is not so easy to trace. Of course, what Marsh doesn't know is that we are practically marooned until the flood waters go down."

"But it's a big country," Mirabel said harshly. She stood listening, her strong hands folded together. "Easy to get lost. Unless, of course, he's been murdered," she said casually. "In that event, you're not likely to find him before spring — all these gullies, hidden by snow — I'm sure I hope he hasn't been murdered and I can't see why anybody would want to murder him, but —" Her keen old eyes fell upon Edith's maid, who was listening avidly, her mouth open. Mirabel roared toward the kitchen, "Manuel! Inez! Take this woman to the guest cabin Mrs. Boyce used." She turned to the maid. "What's your name?"

The maid answered, "Estelle, and I'm going to leave. I don't like this place."

"You can't leave until the roads are cleared," Mirabel said. Inez came running. Mirabel said, "Here she is. Name's Estelle. Take her over there."

Estelle and Inez disappeared.

But it developed there was a problem of logistics about Jim's possible theft of Banner's car.

Craig made it clear. "Marsh would have had to get out Banner's car — well, sometime during last night and without being heard. The shed is quite a distance from the house, and tractors have broken a trail in that direction. He'd have had to drive the car to some place where nobody would notice it. Then he'd have had to come back here and return to the guest cabin. Didn't you hear or see anything at all last night, Boyce?"

Boyce said no, he'd slept like a log. "Had a little too much to drink," he mumbled. "Can't blame me. Everything that happened —"

"Nobody blames you," Craig said patiently.

Indian Joe said, "Well, there was gas left in Banner's car, but Marsh can't get away, not really. Not now. Soon as the phone is working again, though —"

"Yes," Craig said. "We'll report the whole thing." He looked at Mady. "I really don't think anybody killed young Marsh. I think it likely that he simply wanted to get out, leave, get as far away as he could."

Mirabel rubbed her nose. "Have you found that revolver?" she asked Craig.

He shook his head. Mirabel rubbed her nose again. Joe said that he'd try the telephone. Craig and he went into the study; the telephone was silent again and presently they went out.

So Jim was gone. Mady didn't believe that he had been killed; she could conceive of no reason for anybody to murder Jim. He was, like Mr. Banner, a stranger to everyone except, of course, to her and Rhoda.

The day continued blue and warm and sunny and very, very quiet. Even the melting snow was not grimy and soot-laden as it would have been in the city; the puddles reflected only the shining blue sky. Susan, Mirabel and Mady stayed together most of the day, but they didn't talk much of Jim's disappearance. Once Susan, after a trip upstairs, came down and said that Rhoda's door was locked and she was crying.

"Didn't you ask her to open the door?" Mirabel asked.

"Yes, but she — oh, well, she said to go away and leave her alone." Susan's airiness was almost blatantly assumed.

Banner's little foreign bow, his pleasant *Á bientôt* haunted Mady. She felt that she must have seen him, perhaps in New York. Had he called in at Craig's office at some time for some reason? That seemed the likeliest answer, but it did not satisfy her; the setting somehow seemed wrong.

Jim did not return. There was no news of him. The telephone came on again about six o'clock, just as Craig returned to the house, and he leaped to answer it. It was again the sheriff and he had had a frustrating day.

Craig talked to him. Mady came boldly into the study to listen. Craig said oh, and yes, and no. He then reported Jim's disappearance and a description of the Banner car. After a lengthy conversation Craig thanked the sheriff and put down the telephone. "He's having line trouble, too," he told her. "Crews of men have been working, but there are floods everywhere. It's hard to get the wires up, let alone the poles. However, he talked to the Reno police. They're checking on the rental-car outfits. He got in one phone call to the Las Vegas police before he was cut off. He couldn't get my New York call through. He'll call every place around here he can reach and give the police a description of Marsh and of Banner's car — Las Vegas, Reno; nearer places, Fallon, Carson City, Virginia City, even the Naval Base at Hawthorne. I don't think Marsh could possibly have got that far. I don't think he could even have got across the big river or Wilson Creek. If he's holed up in the hills somewhere, he's got to come out. He's got to have food and eventually the car will run out of gas."

"Craig, I *have* seen Banner somewhere! He made an odd little bow today and he said '*À bientôt,*' like that when he left us. I know I've seen exactly that gesture, I've seen Mr. Banner —"

"Where?"

"I don't know. Possibly in your office."

Craig frowned. "People come to see me, all sorts of people with good excuses or introductions, but I'd swear I've never seen him."

"Well, then I'm wrong. It was some other place —"

Craig glanced at the door and said, "Come in, Joe."

Joe came in, closed the door and said, dourly, "I can't find that revolver anywhere. I searched George's cabin that Banner is using. I searched the bunkhouse. He's spent some time there. There are just too many places where that revolver could be hidden."

"I know," Craig said. "It's like searching for a needle in a haystack."

"Well —" Joe considered it, slid down into a chair and said, "Not quite. There are not many people who might want that revolver. Craig —" Again he forgot to use the formal address which he felt was correct. "That girl of yours knows something. And it's something that is connected with your — with the first" — he floundered a

294

little and then said — "with Mrs. Rhoda. You can see that. Every time Susan thinks somebody may accuse Mrs. Rhoda, Susan flies to her defense."

Craig sighed. "I can't get anything out of Susan that she doesn't want to tell."

"I know," Joe said with not very complimentary agreement. "Sometimes I think she's all Wilson. Just like Miss Mirabel. It wouldn't surprise me one bit if Miss Mirabel had decided to get rid of that Casso, once and for all." Craig made a startled gesture. Joe said, "Oh, she could have! She's old but she's a good rider; she's strong, and she's got a will of her own. She saw Casso here making a scene. She may have blamed him for breaking up your other marriage. Now don't get upset. I think anything Miss Mirabel does is right. I'd never tell the sheriff or the police, but she *could* have ridden over here that afternoon, easy as not, got the rail, easy as not, met Casso on the trail, took him by surprise and conked him. He wouldn't be expecting it. But —"

Joe's aquiline face seemed to grow keener; he sank down in his chair. He wore a leather jacket over his flannel shirt; his long legs stretched out in blue jeans and boots. "But how would she know that

Casso would be just there at just that time? Somebody had to know that. Casso had to be induced to come there at just that time. He had to be told to leave his car, just where he left it, and take the trail around the guest cabins that leads to the arroyo. He was a fool to do it, sure. He was a fool if he let himself be talked into coming here and carrying on like that with Mrs. Wilson. I can't see why he would do that, on his own. No motive. Also it looks as if it had to be at a time when he'd be seen. So he had to know that Miss Mirabel and Susan were coming here. If they hadn't come, you'd have shouted to Manuel, Mrs. Wilson, and Casso would be tossed out on his ear. No, it's a scheme of some kind, Craig, and the only reason I can think of for getting Casso in on it is — well, naturally, money. You've got money."

"He couldn't have — oh, blackmailed me, threatened me —"

"But suppose somebody used him. I don't know how. But suppose somebody promised to pay him. It isn't likely that Casso would even have had the money to come out here from New York. Certainly he wouldn't have come here, come to the house, then gone to the arroyo trail if he hadn't been promised money. Could they trace that phone call he made from the motel?"

"No."

"I'd like to know who he talked to and what was said. Casso couldn't have been very bright. Good looks, all that, but no sense. He could have wanted the money he thought he'd earned, so the fool followed instructions. Just, perhaps, instructions over the phone. So he went alone to the arroyo trail and whoever killed him met him there and got rid of him. Maybe."

There was a long pause. Then Craig said, "Who?"

"I don't know," Indian Joe said. "But I do believe there is some sort of scheme. Like a net, all knotted up around you —" Joe leaned forward, his elbows on his knees. "The reason I say that, Craig, is because you're the only one around here with money. I want to ask you a very personal question."

"Go ahead."

"Well, anybody can guess why Mrs. Rhoda came back here. She wants you back — and your money."

"And Susan," Craig said.

Joe didn't shrug. He said merely, "Maybe. Anybody can guess why this young Marsh turned up at almost the same time. He wanted Mrs. Wilson" — he glanced at Mady half apologetically — "to leave you and — Craig, if all that happened, what would you do about money? I mean, would you give Mrs. Wilson any money?"

"I wouldn't have taken money," Mady said.

Craig picked up the silver letter opener with the huge turquoise set in it for a handle and answered Joe. "Why, I suppose so. That is — I wouldn't have wanted my wife — well, she'd not be my wife then, but I wouldn't want her to lack money. Marsh doesn't sound like a very steady money maker."

"You'd settle some money on her, and Marsh would get the benefit of it. But —" Joe brooded, his dark eyes thoughtful but very bright. "Somehow that doesn't ring true to me. There's something more — more urgent."

Craig said, "I'll get Susan down here. We'll talk to her again."

Susan came, altogether normal and sure of herself. She perched on her father's knee and said, "Well, shoot. What do you want?"

Indian Joe said, "Nothing much. It's just

about your Aunt Edith. She couldn't have known anything about Casso's murder. So there must be some other reason for killing her like that —"

Susan cried, "Oh, but she couldn't have seen — You're tricking me!" Red flew to her cheeks and she leaped down and dashed out the door. Her red and green plaid shirt, her blue jeans twinkled out of sight.

Joe said, "Well, there! What did she think Mrs. Boyce saw? It's her mother Susan is trying to protect. Why?"

Craig waited a moment. Then he said, "I'll get Rhoda." He rose slowly, as if he dreaded his errand and what it might bring forth.

Indian Joe said softly, "Ask Mrs. Rhoda if Casso phoned her the night before he was killed."

"All right." Craig went upstairs.

Indian Joe said to Mady after a moment, very quietly, "We've got to do what we can, Mrs. Wilson. As soon as the roads clear and the police can get around, somebody is sure to accuse Craig of murder and we don't want that."

They didn't want that.

Craig came back into the room but without Rhoda. "She refused to come down," he said flatly. "She wouldn't even open the door. I asked her if she knew anything about any evidence of Casso's murder that Edith might have got hold of. She said no. I asked her if Casso had phoned to her the night she was in Las Vegas. She said no to that, too. Then she asked if Marsh had been found. She said she was going to stay there in her room. I couldn't do anything, Joe."

Indian Joe didn't speak for a moment. Then he said slowly, "I still can't believe in coincidence. Mrs. Rhoda and this Marsh and Banner — and Casso — all turning up here unexpectedly at about the same time. No, Craig, there's some link."

Jim Marsh and Banner! Mady knew then, like a flash of lightning showing the figures in a dark night, where she had seen Banner. She cried, "I know! I remember Banner! It was in a cocktail lounge. He was with — with Jim. I came in to meet Jim. It was one of those lounges that are so dark you can hardly see your way. But Banner — I think Jim introduced us. I didn't hear his name or pay any attention to him. But I remember. I'm sure. I remember that he bowed that funny little bow just as he did today and said, '*A bientôt.*' He went away and I never thought of him again." Her

heart sank as if she were in a way respon-
sible for Jim. It was what Joe, what anybody, would call a definite link between
Banner and Jim.

Indian Joe rose, his dark eyes gleaming.
"Marsh and Banner — so they knew each
other — Mrs. Rhoda and Casso — But
that's no proof of murder. Craig, I've got
to say something that you won't like."

"Go ahead."

"Well, I know Boyce as well as you do."

"Boyce couldn't — Boyce wouldn't —"

"Wait a minute, Craig. Mrs. Rhoda came
to his house to stay. Marsh turned up at
his house. Banner might have been on his
way to Boyce's when he really did get stuck
in the snow and had to stay here."

"Joe —"

"Hear me out, Craig. Boyce was under
his wife's thumb, sure. Boyce hadn't made
much of a go at ranching. His wife was
jealous of your success, anybody could see
that. Maybe Boyce felt the same way."

"But that wouldn't explain Casso. And
Boyce wouldn't have killed Edith."

Indian Joe said, doubtfully, "I expect
there were plenty of times when he'd have
liked to throttle her. Now, I'm not saying
that Boyce is in on whatever this scheme is,
but Boyce could conceivably profit by any-

301

thing that damaged you. He's your brother. He would have a certain authority and claim, next of kin, all that. Nobody in the county would suspect him of plotting against his brother. For that matter," Indian Joe said frankly, "I wouldn't really have thought that he'd have the nerve to do murder. But he's not as bright as he might be. He could have been roped into something —"

"What?" Craig said.

Indian Joe became wooden again. "That I don't know. I'm going to tackle Banner again. I'll not get anywhere. He's a slippery customer. He'll just deny everything. I wonder though — You see, if Marsh and Banner *have* cooked up something and if things were getting too dangerous for Banner, he could have got rid of Marsh very easily. We'll not be able to make a real search for either Marsh or the car until the roads and trails are better than they are now. Even then there are plenty of old dry gulches and plenty of hills. It's a big country," said Joe and went out.

Craig said, "I really don't think Marsh has been murdered, Mady."

"I can't believe that he'd enter into any sort of — Joe called it a scheme. But I did know that he wanted me to leave you and to ask you for a big settlement. He did want money."

Craig's eyes met Mady's searchingly, but she couldn't tell what he was thinking. He said, gravely, "Let's talk about money, Mady. I think you ought to know —" He checked himself. "Come on in, Susan. This concerns you, too."

Susan came in, looking very subdued. "I only shut the door after Joe."

"You were listening, Susan —"

"I don't know anything about anything!" Susan cried, then ran to her father, settled herself on his lap and put her arms around his neck. It was a little too loving to be quite natural to Susan, and her father knew it, took her arms down, laughed a little, then said seriously, "This is something else." He looked at Mady over Susan's head. "I'm selling the mines."

Mady couldn't believe it. "The mines! Wilsonite?"

"I still hold the patent for extracting it from ore. But I'm selling the mines to Flanker. He's been after them for some time. That's why he came out to meet me in San Francisco. The pilots will bring him here as soon as the landing strip is clear enough. Then we'll sign the papers."

Mady was stunned. "You love it! You

love the business, you love the excitement! Why, it's your life."

"I loved it, sure. I loved the excitement. Of course I liked all that ridiculous amount of money pouring in. But the fact is I want to live the kind of life I like best, and that's right here on the ranch. Indian Joe was right. A man ought to do what he most wants to do. It's simple. I want to live here. I'm a rancher."

Susan jumped up and clapped her hands. "Oh, cool! Then I can go to school right here in Wilson City?"

"Why, yes, if you want to."

"But now there won't be all those trillions and millions of dollars."

"You've certainly got ideas, Susan." Her father laughed naturally and fully for the first time, it seemed to Mady, since she had found Guy Casso murdered with the Golden Spike Rail.

"Whee," Susan squealed. "We'll go trout fishing in the High Sierras. We'll show Mady Virginia City and Donner Pass. That's where they ate each other," she said to Mady.

Her father intervened. "Now, Susan, you're not sure about that."

"Well," Susan admitted fairly, "I wasn't there but — Oh, and, Mady, we'll drive up to Placerville. Did you know that's the way it's pronounced? To rhyme with Glasserville. And, oh, my goodness —" Her eyes grew round with awe. "Las Vegas! All those singers and lights and — oh, and Reno and Lake Tahoe! Just wait till you see it as you drive down toward all that blue, blue, blue — Can I tell Aunt Mirabel?"

So Susan, at least, expected Mady to remain at El Rancho.

Her father replied, "Go ahead, tell her." Susan gave him a wild hug and ran for the door.

Craig watched her go, smiling. He said, as if thinking aloud, "All kinds of things I want to do. A helicopter. There's a three-year-old quarter horse, a stallion, up near Elko I'll try to buy. And I can mooch around prospecting those old silver mines. All sorts of things —"

Rhoda said from the doorway, "Mady, I want to talk to you for a minute."

Craig, dismissing Mady politely, said that he must try again to get Long Distance and talk to Seely in New York.

So she went out and faced Rhoda, who drew her into the dining room. Rhoda looked very pale; there were greenish-grayish blotches below her eyes, which were pink-rimmed. "Mady," she said in a whisper, "Susan told me — well, those riding gloves of yours. Susan found them and the dog got hold of one of them and her father took the other one and — Why had you washed them? Pigskin doesn't wash —"

Mady decided to tell the plain truth. "I washed the blood off them."

Rhoda's face couldn't have grown whiter, yet somehow it did. "Then — then you touched Guy?"

"No —"

"Then — you touched the — whatever was used to kill him with. Didn't you? What was it?"

Plain truth, Mady said to herself. "It was the rail — that part of the Golden Spike Rail —"

"Oh! And you brought it back!" Rhoda swirled away from Mady and ran up the stairs again.

Mady thought uneasily of the suddenly fixed look in Rhoda's face as she stood at the window, above the chrysanthemums and the rail. But Rhoda couldn't have killed Casso.

Manuel came through the pantry, the cocktail tray in his hands jingling with glass and silver. Mady followed him into the living room. Craig came in as she was pouring Mirabel's usual sherry. "Phone gone again," he said.

Mirabel said, "Seems very strange that that young fellow Marsh would simply leave like that. I can't understand it. He doesn't know the country; but surely he had brains enough to know that driving through a strange country after that blizzard, and with flash floods likely, could be dangerous. But if he murdered Casso and — and poor Edith, he'd try anything to escape. He arrived here after Casso's murder, but still — he might know something or — Oh, I don't know! You haven't been able to find out who took the revolver, have you, Craig?"

"No." Craig poured himself a drink.

"What does Joe think about it?"

"He's been searching for it. Hasn't found it."

Mirabel sipped, brooded and said, "Of course, it's possible that whoever took it shot Marsh. In that event, you'll find him sometime in the spring, when all the snows have gone. Him and that Banner's car. Oh, yes, it's very likely that somebody shot him." She sipped more sherry.

Chapter 16

Craig said calmly that nobody had any reason for shooting Marsh. Mirabel said, morosely, "Nobody admits to a reason for killing Casso either. They'll say you did it, Craig. Rhoda's lover. And now Marsh, your present wife's —"

Mady said, "No! I was engaged to Jim. Everyone knows that. He broke the engagement. But he wasn't — I don't even like him."

Susan came swooping in, Sancho bouncing along with her. She was dressed in a little-girl's dress she hated; it was a neat blue dress with a lace collar; she wore again white half socks and black strapped slippers. Mirabel stared. "You're never going to take the dog out in that outfit."

"Oh, no," Susan said airily. "Indian Joe said he'd take him out last thing at night. Somebody's unlocking the door!" she cried in surprise.

Somebody was unlocking and opening the door with an angry thrust. It proved to be Boyce, who divested himself of coat, overshoes and scarf and came into the living room, looking sullen. "Why do you lock up the house like that?" he grumbled. "First time in my life I couldn't just walk in."

Craig gave him a swift look, went to the cocktail table, poured a drink for Boyce and said, almost casually, over his shoulder, "But you have a key to the house, Boyce. You've always had."

Boyce was still cross. "Sure. Here on my key ring."

Mady thought, Of course Boyce would have a key. He could come and go as he wished in the house.

Mirabel looked at the golden sherry in her glass and said as casually as Craig had spoken, "I suppose Rhoda has a key. We really ought to gather up the keys or have new locks put in."

Susan answered, "No, Mother doesn't have a key. She told me so."

"How did you happen to ask her about it, Susan?" her father said.

But Susan bent over the dog and took an enormous paw in her hand. "Oh, I only wondered if anybody could have — well, got hold of Mother's key and come into the house last night and got into the gun cabinet. Of course, it does seem very odd that Indian Joe wouldn't have heard it. Maybe he didn't want to hear. Maybe he broke into the cabinet —"

"He has a key," Craig said, "and he'd have no reason to break into the cabinet —"

"Is he going to stay in the house again tonight?" Susan asked, getting another of the dog's paws in her hands. That was too entangling for Sancho, who struggled to release himself. Susan let him go and gave him a pat.

Craig said, "Why, yes. He'll be here."

"I heard Aunt Mirabel say that Jim Marsh was murdered, too, and he'd be found maybe sometime in the spring somewhere. Do you think so, Father?"

"I don't know."

Susan thought that over; Boyce swallowed half his drink. Mirabel brooded and watched Susan. Finally she said, "You're a little girl, Susan. We do treat you as if you were grown-up, don't we?"

Susan scrambled up. "I'm hungry. Mother says she's not coming down to dinner."

Rhoda's place had been set at the table; in an odd way she might as well have been there. Craig sent Inez upstairs with a tray, but Inez came down almost immediately.

"She doesn't want dinner. She wouldn't unlock the door."

"Oh," Craig said, "well, thank you, Inez."

It was not a quiet dinner, however, for Susan was bursting with the news that Craig was to sell the mines and return to life on the ranch. Mirabel's old eyes began to shine happily. Boyce listened and mumbled a little to himself. Mirabel offered some advice. "Better buy a generator while you're making improvements," she said happily, eagerly. "Then it won't matter if the electricity goes out."

Craig said that it was a good idea. Boyce mumbled again, something to the effect that of course he couldn't afford a generator or indeed any improvements. They had coffee again in the living room, and while they were there Indian Joe came. He took Sancho out for his night run. Susan waited until they returned and then reluctantly went to bed. "It's very dull around here," she said.

This shook Mirabel as nothing else, even murder, appeared to have done. She turned slightly purple and said, "Good heavens!"

Mady felt as if she could not possibly sleep, so she went to the kitchen to heat some milk and there found Manuel pouring coffee into a thermos. "It's for Indian Joe," he told her. "I made it very strong tonight. Left some for him last night and he didn't even wake up when the gun cabinet was broken into."

Mady said, "Oh —"

Manuel shot her a dark glance. "Of course I knew about it. Saw it when I went to Mr. Wilson's study to clear out the fireplace. I was going to tell him as soon as he got back to the house. But then he found it himself. So did you and Miss Mirabel." He gave the top of the thermos a strong twist. "There now. If Joe can sleep with that coffee inside him, he can sleep through the last Trump. Talk about Indians being so wide awake all the time, hearing every leaf fall! Huh," said Manuel with scorn and untied his white apron. He did get out milk and a saucepan for her and told her not to let the milk boil over, before he disappeared toward his own room. It was rather disconcerting to hear a bolt drawn across the door of his room. Manuel was taking no chances.

Rhoda had locked herself in her room, too.

Mady took the glass of milk and started upstairs. Indian Joe and Craig were again

312

in the study, Craig talking, apparently over the telephone, to the sheriff. She heard him say "— but it'll be days before they can get that bridge repaired. No report of the Banner car? No, we've heard nothing here —"

Mady thought of Mirabel's saying that in the spring Jim would be found somewhere. She wouldn't have had anything like that happen to anybody she had ever known. Yet somehow Jim seemed very far away, scarcely to be remembered.

She was very tired; they were all physically exhausted, with taut and overstrained nerves. She undressed and went into Craig's room and sat there, hoping he would come soon, sipping her milk and making a resolve. She would try to arrive at an understanding with Craig that very night.

She could go on no longer with that intangible, yet seemingly impassable barrier between them. She would make every attempt to break it down. She would take her courage in heart and hand. She would tell Craig that she wouldn't leave him and she'd tell him why, but if he then admitted that he'd made a mistake in marrying her, that he regretted their marriage, that he really wanted Rhoda back — why, then she'd have to accept it.

She thought it all over; Craig never objected to plain speaking or truth telling. He'd hear it now. The resolve alone gave her courage.

She had finished the milk when she heard the front door open and a murmur of voices. She thought she heard Boyce speaking, but his words were jumbled up. It sounded as if he said, "— but she won't give them to me. She won't come here. She insists on seeing you —"

She? Mady thought. The front door closed heavily again. The hot milk and probably the decision she had made to have the truth from Craig no matter what it might cost her, both combined to give her a sleepy sense of having already crossed bridges. She dropped her dressing gown over the foot of the bed and slid into it to wait for Craig. She thought, dreamily now, of how strange it was that she could have been so happy during their long trip together after their marriage and hadn't for a moment even suspected why she was happy. She thought that Craig had seemed happy, too. She wondered drowsily if other people reach peaks of happiness without knowing it. It had been a good marriage; even when they both believed that it was a merely friendly and companionable marriage, it had been a good one. She now knew that for her at least it had been happy and she hadn't even known it.

She drifted off to sleep and Craig had not returned. She had left the bedside lamp turned on. She woke to an odd sense of motion, somewhere near her, and thought first, dreamily, that it was Craig and that he had turned off the lamp so as not to wake her. She said, "Craig —"

Jim answered out of the darkness beside her. "Get up! Put something on. You're coming with me. Hurry —" She must have started to scream, for his hand clapped down over her mouth. "Be quiet! I'm going to get you away from here. I've got Banner's car waiting. You can't stay here! Come with me — hurry —"

She couldn't get away from his hand; it was clutched over her mouth with unbelievable strength; she twisted and fought and then stopped, for something cold was pressed against her temple.

"I've got a gun," Jim whispered. "Of course I — I wouldn't hurt you! But you must come with me." His hand was like steel; he pressed the gun harder against her, so she lay still. "It's loaded," he whispered.

Mady thought, So it was Jim who took the revolver.

She thought, Where is Indian Joe? Why doesn't he come?

She thought, This cannot be happening.

And then she thought, Craig! Has Jim killed Craig?

A flood of light came from the hall, outlining Jim's figure in black against it. Rhoda swept into the room, hugging a green dressing gown around her. She closed the door and whispered sharply in the sudden darkness, "You can't! I'll not let you. They're not taking you away for your own safety, Mady. They'll never let you come back —"

The pressure of the gun against Mady's head seemed to waver, then it pressed harder.

Jim whispered, "Hurry. Pay no attention to Rhoda —"

"Mady," Rhoda whispered, "He'll kill you. They killed Guy." She caught her breath with a gasp, and for a second or two the room was only very still and very black, yet Mady thought she heard a faint movement of some kind, somewhere. Rhoda began again, whispering, "I know now. It's Craig's money. That's why Jim got engaged to you, Mady. It was because you worked for Craig, you were close to Craig. He thought that there might be some way he could get at Craig's money through you. But then he met me. He thought I might be an easier mark. He didn't know how but — but then I provided what they thought would be a means of getting money. But I never knew that Guy had to be murdered. Not till today, not till —"

Jim's voice, low and ugly, cut into Rhoda's frantic whispering. "All right, you know so much. Yes, that was why Guy was killed. He had to be killed. You didn't see that. Banner saw it as soon as I gave him your letter. Banner planned it all. Now you've got to go on with it."

Mady thought again she heard a faint sound on the other side of the room, near the dressing-room door, like a stealthy footfall.

Rhoda caught her breath loudly; again she whispered, "I'll scream. I'll wake Indian Joe —"

"You can't wake him if you put those pills in his coffee as you were told to do." There was something like a giggle in Jim's whisper. "You're in this too, Rhoda, remember. You're an accessory. You wrote those letters. You were so sure you could get Craig back again. I'll see to Mady. You go on with your part."

Rhoda broke in, "You meant to kill Guy from the beginning. But I never knew — Have you got the gun?"

Jim's whisper was almost boastful. "In my hand. I had to kill Edith. She found the letters. She tried to deny it, but I knew. And I'll kill Mady if we can't get rid of her any other way —"

There was a rush of sound as the dressing-room door swung open. No light came through, but something was flung across the room, for a lamp fell over on the floor with a splintering crash. Almost at once a strong odor of lilacs came wafting through the darkness. Mady recognized it as her own perfume; somebody had thrown a bottle across the room.

It was a diversionary tactic. Jim jerked the gun from her head and began to fire into the blackness across the room. Mady could barely see a lithe figure leaping into the darkness. She could hear the sounds of a struggle. It didn't last long. There was a kind of hard thud. Then Indian Joe said, "Turn on the light, Mrs. Wilson."

Mady moved as if strung on wires; she jerked over on her side and turned on the bedside lamp. The room sprang into being. Jim was sprawled on the floor. Indian Joe had the gun in his hand. He gave her an odd look, almost a smile. Then he turned to Rhoda. "So you put more sleeping pills in my coffee tonight. I nearly caught you at it last night. Tonight I decided to watch you — Mrs. Casso."

Mrs. Casso, Mady thought. Why, of course. It explained some things; Rhoda couldn't have married Craig if Casso had been her husband. Yet she could certainly have found some grounds on which to divorce him. Yes, the marriage explained some things, but not all!

Rhoda cried, "I never knew. I never realized that they had based their whole scheme upon Guy's murder and my dreadful letters. They told me that Guy could come here and make that scene with Mady and it would be arranged so Craig would hear of it and he would begin to doubt Mady and — You see, I knew that I had to separate Craig and Mady somehow and — They called it alienation. It was necessary —"

Mirabel roared from the hall, "What's going on? Those shots!"

Susan shrieked from further down the hall. "There's a car at the door! It looks like Banner's car — Who was shooting? What is it?"

Indian Joe shouted back, "It's all right. Nobody's hurt —"

But in an instant Jim Marsh recovered his senses, rolled like an animal toward the hall door, and in a flash was up and on his feet, running, stumbling down the stairs. Joe ran after him, leaped down the stairs, and was a second too late. The front door flung back with a bang that seemed to Mady as loud as another shot. Mady had a glimpse of Rhoda's red hair and green dressing gown flying down the stairs.

She got herself out of bed; she wrapped her red dressing gown around her as Susan and Mirabel continued, like an antiphonal chorus. Mirabel: "Who is it? Who was shooting? Who ran down the stairs?" Susan: "A man is running out to Banner's car. He's getting in. Why, I think it's Jim Marsh. They're leaving — they're leaving — as fast as they can go. There's Indian Joe running after them. Why, he's shooting —"

There were shots, muffled now, only a few, then Joe banged the front door and said sourly into the stunned silence in the house, "First time I ever let a rattlesnake get away from me."

Mady was on the stairs, following Rhoda. Mirabel was there, too. Susan came running. Indian Joe said, "I'll try to get the sheriff."

"Joe!" Mady cried. Her voice was like a scream. "Joe, where's Craig? Where's Craig?"

Craig answered. He and Boyce came plunging into the house. Craig's eyes blazed to Mady and then to Susan; he ran to them and scooped them both, somehow, hard into his arms. "We heard the shooting! We saw Marsh running for Banner's car! The engine was going. They were off before we could stop them —"

Indian Joe, in the study, was speaking into the telephone, "— same car we described to you. Just left the place — Yes, two of them, in cahoots. Murdered Casso — Yes, and Mrs. Boyce — Yes —"

As if his voice were a magnet, everyone moved into the study, but Craig still held Susan close in one arm and Mady in the other. Strangely, at that hurried moment, Mady knew that all her resolve had been unnecessary. Craig had not believed Rhoda. He had believed Mady. When there had been danger, Craig had come first to her and to Susan. And even in that hurried moment she was caught up, shielded, made warm and strong by that same knowledge.

Rhoda slumped down in a chair and put both her hands over her face.

Joe said, "Right. We'll explain," and put down the telephone.

Mirabel boomed, "Well, the police can't get them tonight, Joe! But they can't get away either. They don't know that."

Indian Joe said, "Banner and Marsh knew that Casso was your husband, didn't they, Mrs. Casso?"

Rhoda nodded without looking up.

Craig was not surprised. Boyce mumbled, "We found them. That is, the maid, Estelle, found them. She was making up her bed and she found them in a pillowcase where Edith must have hidden them. The maid wouldn't give them to anybody but Craig. She wouldn't come here. So I had to come and get Craig and —"

Rhoda dropped her hands. "So you found the letters!"

Craig drew three pieces of paper from his pocket. They were peculiarly shiny and all the same size.

Rhoda cried, "That's not my writing paper!"

Joe's eyes were very intent. "Those are copies."

Craig nodded. "I expect Banner has the originals."

Joe said, "Yes — yes, he'd have made sure that when they were in a position to blackmail Mrs. Rhoda, Banner would get his full share."

Rhoda put her lovely face in her hands again. She said tonelessly, "Read the letters, Craig. But I never meant murder."

Susan walked quietly over to stand beside Craig and look at the letters in his hand.

"I'm sorry, Rhoda," Craig said and started to read: " 'Guy, you must not insist upon seeing me. I'm tired of it and you. If you don't stay away from me I'll go to the police —' "

"There's a blur here," Craig said.

Rhoda said from behind her hands, "I decided it wasn't strong enough. So I — I went to get another drink and I — I guess I exploded. I added to the letter. Read the rest of it."

Craig read on. It was indeed explosive, and after Casso's murder it would have been dreadfully incriminating. " 'I told you to leave me alone. You keep after me for money. Craig will never give me another penny if he knows the facts. I hate you, and I will kill you, if you don't do as I say. If you come near me again —' "

Craig paused and said, "The words trail

323

off into scribbles here."

Rhoda said, "My head was swimming. I went to lie down. The maid roused me when Jim came, but it took a little while for me to pull myself together."

Susan cried shrilly, "But she didn't mean it. I saw that letter. I read it. Mother wasn't — well that day. She didn't know that I had come to see her. I went away and — and I saw Jim arriving —"

Rhoda said, "Oh, yes. He got the letter then. And my marriage certificate, too. The maid didn't tell me that Susan had been there. Later, when I remembered the letter, I thought I must have thrown it away. But —" She dropped her hands and stared at Susan. "Why, that — Jim was afraid you would tell it! He couldn't risk Craig or anyone knowing that he had the letter. So he — Oh, no! No!"

She put her face in her hands again. Mady's memory flicked back to a few words between Jim and Susan. Susan had told Jim that she hadn't seen him since one day in the spring when she was leaving her mother's apartment and Jim was arriving. So Jim had believed, correctly as it happened, that Susan had read the letter he himself found. Jim had been frightened; he had scribbled the note which he signed with Mady's name, perhaps in the hope of adding another cause which might lead to alienating Craig and Mady. It was a casual, swift and terrible decision which might have succeeded.

Rhoda said, "I really believed Susan was cross at Mady for some reason and thought up the trick herself, just to pay off Mady. I'm sorry, Susan."

Susan cried, "My mother wouldn't have killed Guy. When he was killed, of course I remembered her letter and sometimes I was afraid she had killed him, but — but most of the time I knew she hadn't. She didn't mean a word of that letter —"

Indian Joe said, "There is another letter —"

"Oh, yes," Rhoda said. "Banner told Jim to tell me to write it. Jim took it to Guy. I gave him Guy's address. They lied to Guy, too."

Craig read the second letter. It was in a much more placating, even a friendly, vein. " 'Dear Guy,' " Craig read, " 'I started to write to you recently. I was very angry then but didn't send the letter and I'm glad now. We've been separated for some time but I feel that you will be of help to me. I hope to make things up with Craig. If I succeed I can pay you handsomely and will. But first we must continue to keep our marriage a secret. Craig must never know of it. Trust the friend who will give you this. Do as he says. Later we can arrange a very quiet divorce so I can marry Craig, but Craig must never know of our marriage.' " Craig folded up the letter.

Rhoda said, "Jim took it to Guy, and of course Guy could see that Craig had to — as Banner said — be alienated from Mady. I didn't know, I couldn't — I wouldn't believe that one of them killed Guy. But then Edith — I couldn't let it go on after that. I suppose she prowled around and got those copies from wherever Jim kept them, and somehow Jim guessed she had them, she —" Rhoda leaned back in the chair. "You heard him, Joe. You heard him upstairs just now —"

Indian Joe said after a moment, "Do you want me to say what I think happened?"

Rhoda's lips moved as if to say yes.

Indian Joe said gravely, "I believe that the first letter was the start, the beginning of their plan. Banner planned it. But both Marsh and Banner must be the kind of unscrupulous men — rare and dreadful — who spend half their lives looking for some get-rich-quick scheme. Yes — that first letter provided it, but there were some necessary requirements. Casso had to be murdered. Craig's present marriage had to be ended. Mrs. Rhoda had to induce Craig to remarry her. Once those things were accomplished, they had a hold over Mrs. Rhoda. They could have blackmailed her for the rest of her life. Yes — they told her to bring them that rail." Rhoda nodded. Joe went on, "It added to the threat of the letters; they could always say, if she rebelled, But you were an accessory. And, of course, the rail linked Casso's murder with El Rancho. It also, they thought, would serve to protect them — only somebody who knew the house and the rail could have taken it. That part of their plan misfired, thanks to your wife, Craig."

Rhoda said, "I didn't know certainly about the rail until I asked Mady today."

Joe said slowly, "Their whole plan was to reinstate Mrs. Rhoda as your wife, Craig. But unless Casso was murdered, Mrs. Rhoda's letters had no force, no value to them. Yes, murder was essential. An ugly, devious plan — a long-range plan."

Mady said clearly, "But when Rhoda understood it, she tried to stop it. She saved my life. She and Indian Joe —"

Indian Joe said, "I damn near let it go too long."

"But you didn't —" Mady began, and Rhoda said, miserably, "Jim told me that a murder investigation is never over until the murderer has been found and convicted. So he said — for all the rest of my life I had to do what he or Banner told me to do."

Indian Joe said inexorably, yet with a kind of compassion, too, "You *did* everything they told you to do. You gave Marsh the house key —" Rhoda nodded. "You did that so he could get into the gun cabinet while I was full of sleeping pills. You knew he had taken a gun —" Rhoda nodded again. "And he made some excuse, so you gave him the rail."

"Oh, yes," Rhoda said behind her hands. "I had told Jim things about El Rancho; he asked so many questions. I had told him about the rail and — oh, yes, of course, the trails, the arroyo trail. And the times when nobody was around the house. And — yes, I came here that afternoon. I had seen Mady ride away, so I knew the coast was clear. I got the rail. Nobody saw me. I drove into Wilson City and gave it to Jim. He was waiting at the motel where Guy Casso had been staying. Jim wouldn't explain. He said he didn't know why but Banner wanted it. And then I went to the

Ladies' Toggery."

Joe said, "You had phoned Craig in San Francisco. You had pleaded with him to return. And Marsh had written a letter to Mrs. Wilson. I suppose Banner had arranged somehow for Marsh's letter to be postmarked the day of Casso's murder. They had everything planned. Then Mrs. Edith found those copies — She could not be allowed to tell anyone. She had hidden them in the cabin. She was killed. But Marsh had to have the letters. He must have searched the cabins —"

"Yes," Rhoda said, "I think he did this morning. I met him there. But he told me *he* still had them. That's when he told me the letters could be used against me. Oh, I've been such a fool and so frightened and so —"

"She saved my life," Mady said again.

Rhoda said in a whisper, "I began to face the things I had done. But not murder."

"You were a tool," Indian Joe said. "You and Casso and Marsh were all tools of Banner's. Banner was wily and determined. The minute Marsh saw that first letter and your marriage certificate, he must have felt that in some way they could be valuable. So he took the letter and certificate to Banner. Banner mulled it over and made their plan. It was a long shot, but it was the nearest he or Marsh had ever come to a way to get hold of money. So they decided to try it. Jim was sure that he could get the present Mrs. Wilson back again. And Mrs. Rhoda —"

Craig said, "Rhoda, you kept your marriage to Casso a secret because of that condition for your alimony. I was to continue it only until you remarried. So you couldn't let me know of your marriage to Casso. But if you had told me, I'd have kept on giving you money."

Rhoda said, "I couldn't have been sure of that! I had to have that alimony, Craig. And I knew that if you ever knew that I'd married Guy and still kept on taking alimony, you would never trust me again. I know that much about you, Craig, you would never forgive me for lying and — But of course, if we could have separated you and Mady, if you knew nothing of my marriage to Guy, I could have gotten a very quiet divorce which you would never have heard of — Oh, it was a chance."

Joe said, "You must have believed that you had a good chance to remarry Craig."

Rhoda drew herself up; for an instant she was so beautiful that her beauty alone seemed to reply. But then she said, "And

Susan. Susan was my strong card to play. And Susan told me once that Craig still loved me. Not Mady. Yes, I thought I had a good chance."

"Father," Susan said. "Father, listen. I did tell her that. One day she was worried and upset and said she should never have left you and I — I felt sorry and wanted to make her feel better so I — well, I lied, but it wasn't exactly a lie. That is — well, I didn't think it would hurt anybody. It was just after you and Mady were married and I — at first I didn't like that. I felt sort of left out. And so was Mother, and I — well, that's what I did. I told her you still loved her."

Rhoda said, "I believed her. At least, I wanted to believe her. So when Banner worked out this scheme I felt — not entirely confident of remarrying Craig but — yes, I thought I had a good chance."

Mirabel reached out a long arm and drew Susan to her. After a moment Joe said, "Yes. That scene Casso made on his first visit to El Rancho was one of Banner's ideas. It was supposed to help alienate Craig from the present Mrs. Wilson. But also it got Guy here. He had to be murdered sometime —" He turned to Craig. "Remember that phone call the manager of the motel said he thought Casso had made, the night before he was killed? Seems likely that Casso was backing out —"

Rhoda said, "Yes, he was. Jim told me that, too. He said that Guy phoned to Banner in Las Vegas. He talked only to Banner, not to me or to Jim. But he told Banner that he hadn't realized what a strong position he was in. He told Banner that if he wasn't paid cash, then and there — he said ten thousand to start with — unless Banner gave him that, he would go to Craig and tell him the whole thing. Our marriage — and Banner's scheme and everything."

"So they decided that Guy would have to be killed right away," Indian Joe said thoughtfully. "Mrs. Rhoda had her plan. Casso had his plan. Banner and Marsh had Banner's plan. The three different plans coincided only for a part of the way. Is that right?" He spoke to Rhoda.

She nodded again. "Guy didn't know they had my first letter."

"He didn't know that he was to be a victim, certainly," Joe said. "Mrs. Rhoda didn't know of the real underlying scheme. Banner and Marsh would have had no hold over Mrs. Rhoda unless Casso was killed. That alone could give force or value to their possession of those letters. All four of you met then in Las Vegas."

Again Rhoda nodded, and Joe went on. "Now then, the logistics. Casso rented a car and came to Wilson City. Stayed over the night when he first came to El Rancho, phoned his ultimatum and threats to Banner. Banner made swift preparations for Casso's essential and necessary murder. He told Casso to meet him on the arroyo trail. He told Marsh to order Mrs. Rhoda to bring the rail to him; Marsh didn't tell her why. Then Banner came to Wilson City, bringing Marsh with him." He addressed Rhoda. "You gave the rail to Marsh. You didn't question Banner's reason for demanding it. Then you went to the Ladies' Toggery. Banner and Marsh came here. Easy enough; it was a deserted time of day. There was the screen of cottonwoods, guest cabins, plenty of ways to get onto the ranch and that trail without being seen. Marsh killed Casso, then left the rail there, and Banner drove Marsh back to Vegas. The next night in the storm Marsh drove here and said he had come from Reno. We could have traced his car if — But it would have taken time. Banner came too. He —" There was a faint trace

333

of grim humor in Joe's voice. "He had to protect his investment. Was that it? He meant to come here, that's certain. He couldn't trust Marsh or you, Mrs. Rhoda, to carry out the orders he had given you. The blizzard gave him an excuse to stop, but he'd have made up any excuse. Probably he was prowling around when you went out in the storm —"

Indian Joe turned to Mady. "And you took him by surprise and he simply pushed you away. We may never know about that, but it doesn't matter now. The fact is he felt that he had to be here, on the spot, ready to help. Ready to — Why, yes, he drove his car out last night and hid it somewhere so Marsh could find it. They thought it would be harder to trace them in his car than a rented car. Marsh has been waiting most of the day to get Mrs. Wilson —"

Rhoda lifted her head. "At first he couldn't believe that Mady didn't want him. But then at last he did believe her. But he still thought that if Mady were — disposed of," said Rhoda drearily, "I could get Craig to marry me again. There was Susan, you see. An argument."

Susan made the slightest move, close to Mirabel; the old woman's strong arm gathered her in.

Boyce said thickly, "Did you suspect Marsh, Joe, all this time?"

Joe gave Boyce a long look. "I got to the place where I suspected you, Boyce —"

"Me!"

"— and Miss Mirabel and — But I knew that Craig had to be the target for whatever was going on, because Craig has money. Nobody else. Then I began to see why Mrs. Rhoda had phoned Craig and got him to come back that afternoon. It was because Craig was valuable to somebody; they had to make sure that he had an alibi for the time of Casso's murder. They couldn't trust to chance. Yet the time of the murder was uncertain enough so they could make Mrs. Rhoda believe that she could be accused — if, that is, later they had to enforce their demands upon her. For the present, they induced her to trust them implicitly. But the letter — the one Marsh wrote and was postmarked the exact day of Casso's murder — that was to be an alibi for Marsh. Craig and Mrs. Rhoda and Marsh — Banner couldn't do without any of them. Banner himself was the only one who had no alibi at all; he thought he didn't need an alibi."

Indian Joe looked at Craig. He wasn't a

wooden Indian now but coldly relentless. "Banner's plan didn't end with your remarriage to Mrs. Rhoda. How long do you think you'd have lived if you remarried her? She'd have had a claim on your money then, communal rights. But as your widow she'd have had —"

"No!" Rhoda cried. "I wouldn't have let them murder Craig."

Joe said, "Banner is an evil, devious man. A man who could convince Mrs. Rhoda — Casso himself — even Marsh. An evil man sitting like a spider in his web. A man who made patient, long-range plans. He had three tools to use. Marsh isn't very bright. Neither, I suspect, was Casso. Mrs. Rhoda —"

Rhoda rose and without a word went out of the room. Susan started after her, paused, and came back slowly to her father, who said, "Give things time, Susan. Time —"

Mirabel said firmly, "Susan is a Wilson. She'll be all right."

Rhoda's light footsteps went on up the stairs. Joe said, "I wish we could keep her out of any trial. She did save Mrs. Wilson's life. She didn't mean Banner's plan to turn into murder."

Craig said slowly, "How can we prove

that Marsh killed Edith and killed Casso?"

Indian Joe said, "Here's the gun. Finger-prints on it." He had taken the gun from his belt. "I heard him threaten Mrs. Wilson. I heard him threaten Mrs. Rhoda. I heard him admit murder. Mrs. Wilson heard him. Mrs. Rhoda heard him — Oh, there'll be proof. If it comes to a trial," he said, and stopped abruptly. He seemed almost to see something none of them could see. "The blizzard played into their hands, yet I'm not so sure."

That night Craig and Mady talked; there was not much that needed to be said. Craig said once, though, that he had believed Mady, not Rhoda — yet he had also half-believed that Mady was still in love with Jim Marsh. "I thought so once," Mady said. "I only thought so —" Craig went on, "So I had to offer to let you go. When we were married we had trust and companionship and — but then, for me it was different."

"Yes," Mady said, "yes. Craig, you came, though, as soon as Rhoda phoned you —"

"Huh," Craig said startled. "Why, of course! I wanted to find out what she was up to and get her to leave!"

"Oh," Mady said. "Oh."

There was no trial. If there had been,

Rhoda at the least would have been a material witness; more likely, an accessory, if not before the fact, certainly after it. Yet she had deceived herself. (She won't look at things she doesn't want to look at, Mirabel had said.) But the next day, when the flood waters were beginning to recede, Banner's car was found in the big river; there had been a flash flood. Banner was trapped in the car. There were some soggy papers in one pocket — Rhoda's letters and her marriage certificate. Jim Marsh was found downstream, in low-hanging willows.

There were conferences with the state police and with the sheriff; statements were taken. Reports began to pour in from Las Vegas and New York, but they added little to what was already known, except for the admission of a woman who had worked for Banner who said that she had mailed the letter to Mady on November third; this argued premeditation.

In the end, however, Rhoda, who had stayed on at Boyce's ranch until the investigation ended, was allowed to leave, and no charges were made against her. Indian Joe took her in one of the ranch cars to Reno, where she boarded a plane. He came back late, tired and cross.

"Red Hair speak with forked tongue," he said. "She says she wants Susan, and in the same breath says Susan would be bored living with her. All she could talk about was the Argentine. She has shed the whole thing, sure of herself, happy as can be. That," he said somberly, "was their weakness, her weakness and Marsh's. They were both too sure of themselves. Red Hair was sure she would get you back, Craig. Marsh was sure he could induce your wife to leave you. Banner knew their weakness and played upon it." He eyed Craig. "You gave Red Hair too much wampum. I saw it when she opened her handbag and gave me money to buy her tickets."

Susan had gone to bed. Mady, Mirabel and Craig were in Craig's study. Perhaps by chance Indian Joe's gaze went to the tomahawk over the mantel and grew obsidian black. After a moment, though, he sighed wistfully. "Red Hair would make a fine scalp. Sometimes spirits of forefathers know best. But —" he shrugged — "perhaps better this way."

We hope you have enjoyed this Large Print book. Other Thorndike Press or Chivers Press Large Print books are available at your library or directly from the publishers.

For more information about current and upcoming titles, please call or write, without obligation, to:

Thorndike Press
P.O. Box 159
Thorndike, Maine 04986 USA
Tel. (800) 257-5157

OR

Chivers Press Limited
Windsor Bridge Road
Bath BA2 3AX
England
Tel. (0225) 335336

All our Large Print titles are designed for easy reading, and all our books are made to last.